'I do not believe it would be a good thing for you to dance with Lord Coleridge too often,' Mrs Henderson said, coming up to her.

'He is a perfect gentleman, Helene, and well liked—but you must not set your heart on him. He mixes in circles that we shall scarcely enter, my dear.'

'I am very certain he would not do for me, Mama,' Helene replied primly, though a little voice at the back of her mind told her that she was not telling the whole truth.

She did like Lord Coleridge, more than she was prepared to admit, but of course it would not do at all. He was a member of the aristocracy—and she had vowed long ago that she would never give her heart to anyone who might break it as her mama's had been broken.

Author Note

This is the second in my *A Season in Town* mini-series. Amelia Royston has invited Helene to stay with her for the season. Helene knows that she must marry well, and she is very attracted to Lord Coleridge, but she does not think he could possibly be interested in a girl like her. However, it seems that someone is bent on causing him harm, perhaps taking his life, and Helene is instrumental in preventing one such attack. Can she and Max discover who is behind these attempts, and can they find happiness together?

Amelia is feeling a little low, because it seems that Gerard has forgotten her and the love they once shared. She will have to settle for living alone and inviting her friends to stay, because she could not contemplate marrying anyone else.

Book Three is Amelia and Gerard's tale. I hope you will enjoy these stories, and I thank all my readers for their continued support. Please keep writing to me at linda@lindasole.co.uk

AN INNOCENT
DEBUTANTE IN
HANOVER SQUARE

Anne Herries

First published in Great Britain 2009
Harlequin Mills & Boon Limited,
Eton House, 18-24 Paradise Road, Richmond, Surrey TW9 1SR

© Anne Herries 2009

ISBN: 978 0 263 86799 2

Set in Times Roman 10½ on 12¾ pt
04-0909-83381

Harlequin Mills & Boon policy is to use papers that are natural, renewable and recyclable products and made from wood grown in sustainable forests. The logging and manufacturing process conform to the legal environmental regulations of the country of origin.

Printed and bound in Spain
by Litografia Rosés, S.A., Barcelona

AN INNOCENT DEBUTANTE IN HANOVER SQUARE

Anne Herries lives in Cambridgeshire, where she is fond of watching wildlife and spoils the birds and squirrels that are frequent visitors to her garden. Anne loves to write about the beauty of nature, and sometimes puts a little into her books—although they are mostly about love and romance. She writes for her own enjoyment, and to give pleasure to her readers. She is a winner of the Romantic Novelists' Association Romance Prize.

Recent novels by the same author:

MARRYING CAPTAIN JACK
THE UNKNOWN HEIR
THE HOMELESS HEIRESS
THE RAKE'S REBELLIOUS LADY
A COUNTRY MISS IN HANOVER SQUARE*

A Season in Town trilogy

And in the Regency series
The Steepwood Scandal:

LORD RAVENSDEN'S MARRIAGE
COUNTERFEIT EARL

And in *The Hellfire Mysteries*:

AN IMPROPER COMPANION
A WEALTHY WIDOW
A WORTHY GENTLEMAN

Chapter One

'Oh, no, you don't!' Max Coleridge said as the urchin attempted to pluck a kerchief from the pocket of his companion. His hand shot out, grasping the dirty boy around his wrist with a grip of iron. 'That is thieving, my lad, and it will land you in prison. You will end with your neck stretched at the nubbing cheat if you continue this way.'

'Let me go, guv,' the boy whined. 'I ain't done nuffin' bad, honest I ain't—but I ain't had nuffin' ter eat fer a week!'

'Indeed?' Max's right eyebrow arched. 'Should I believe you, I wonder? And what should I do with you supposing that I do?'

'Let the ruffian go and be done with it,' Sir Roger Cole advised. 'I dare say he deserves to be handed over to the beadle, but it requires far too much effort.'

'Your trouble, my friend, is that you are too lazy,' Max replied with a smile that robbed his words of any offence. 'No, I shall not let the boy go—he would simply rob someone else and eventually he will die in prison or at the rope's end.' His grasp tightened about the lad's arm. 'Tell me your name, lad. I shall take you home and tell your father to keep you off the streets.'

'Me name's Arthur,' the boy muttered sullenly. 'I ain't got no home nor no farvver or muvver neivver. Ain't got no one. Let me go like the gent said, sir. I won't trouble you no more.'

'No family at all?' Arthur shook his head and Max sighed. 'Unfortunately, if I let you go, you would trouble my conscience far more than you imagine. I shall take you with me. You are going to school, Arthur—whether you like it or not.'

'School? Wot's that?' Arthur asked and wiped his running nose on his sleeve. He eyed the large man suspiciously. 'You ain't one o' them queer nabs, are yer?'

'I am certainly not,' Max denied with a wry smile. 'If you are hungry, you will like school—you will be fed three times a day, if you behave yourself.'

'Food fer nuffin'?' Arthur stared at him suspiciously. 'Wot's the catch, guv?' As to be a catch. No one does nuffin' fer nuffin'…'

'No, I dare say they do not where you come from,' Max said. 'In return, you will have to give up a life of crime—and grime—and learn a trade…'

'I ain't goin' up no chimneys!'

'Good grief, I should hope not,' Max said. 'You might like to be a carpenter or a groom, perhaps—or even a politician?'

'You shouldn't put ideas into the boy's head, Coleridge,' Sir Roger said. 'A politician, indeed!'

'He could not do much worse than those we have in power at the moment,' Max replied wryly. 'But I would advise an honest trade—perhaps a baker?'

'I like cake,' Arthur said, his eyes suddenly bright. 'I pinched some orf a baker's stall once on the market.'

'There you are, then,' Max said, hiding his smile. 'The future looms brighter already, Arthur—a baker you shall be.'

'You are mad, quite mad,' Sir Roger said and grinned. 'It is hardly surprising that you are not married, my dear fellow. I do not know whether any sensible woman would have you.'

'I dare say she wouldn't if she knew my habit of picking up boys from the streets,' Max replied and smiled at his friend. 'Excuse me, I have a rather dirty ruffian to scrub before I present him to someone who will teach him a few manners…' He neatly avoided a kick from the struggling urchin. 'I should give up if I were you, Arthur. I could always change my mind and hand you over to the constable, and then you might never eat cake again.'

Helene eyed the chimney-sweep wrathfully, one hand on the shoulder of the small boy at her side. Her eyes just now were the colour of wet slate, her normally generous mouth pulled tight in an expression of disgust.

'You will go and you will leave Ned with me,' she said, her voice strong and fearless despite the knots tying themselves in her stomach as she faced the great brute of a man she had caught beating his climbing boy. 'You are lucky that I do not call the magistrate and have you arrested for cruelty. This child is too ill to do his work.'

'Lazy ingrate that's what he be,' the sweep muttered. His hands were ingrained with soot, his face streaked with it. He had a fearful scar on one cheek and he squinted with his left eye. He was scowling so fiercely that Helene's courage might have deserted her had she not seen the scars on a previous climbing-boy's back. Jeb had died of his injuries. She was determined that it would not happen to Ned. 'I bought the brat from the workhouse. He belongs to me—and that's the law. You can't take him from me, miss.'

'What did you pay for him?' Helene was haughty as she faced her much larger opponent across the kitchen of her uncle's home. She knew that the sweep could fell her with a blow of his huge fist, but she refused to feel afraid. 'Tell me and you shall be paid.'

'I paid ten gold guineas for him,' the sweep growled.

Helene knew that he was lying. No one paid so much for a boy from the workhouse. However, she understood that she must pay the price if she wished to take the child from him.

'Very well, you shall be paid,' she promised. 'You may go. I will send the money to your wife tomorrow.'

The sweep scowled at her, anger flashing in his eyes. 'If you don't send the money—all of it!—I shall come and take him back,' he muttered and went off, stomping out of the kitchen in a temper.

'You've landed yourself in a pickle again, miss.' Bessie stared at her. 'Where will you find ten guineas to pay him? And what are we to do with the lad now we have him?'

Helene felt the lad tremble beneath her hand. 'Don't send me back to Mr Beazor, miss,' he said, sniffed and wiped the back of his hand across his nose and then on his disreputable breeches, smearing more soot on his face in the process. 'He'll kill me sure as hell is full of the devil.'

'You watch your language,' Bessie warned him sharply. 'Speak respectful to Miss Henderson. She just saved you from a terrible beating.'

'Please do not scold him, Bessie,' Helene said and smiled at the maid she thought of as her best friend. Bessie was her mama's only servant and had helped Helene out of scrapes many times when she was a girl. 'I think he needs a bath and something to eat.'

'He could certainly do with a bath,' Bessie agreed. 'He doesn't smell too sweet.'

'What's a bath?' Ned eyed them suspiciously. 'Does it hurt?'

'Lord bless him!' Bessie laughed. 'We're going to put you in a tub of hot water and wash all the soot and grime off you, lad.'

'Nah…don't fancy that…' Ned backed away from them nervously.

'I promise you it won't hurt,' Helene told him. 'Afterwards, I shall put some ointment on your back and then you can eat your meal.'

'What's to eat?' Ned looked round hopefully, a sign of interest in his eyes now.

'You shall have a hot meat pie and some cake,' Bessie said, seeing the gleam and smiling inwardly. 'But you've got to be clean. I can't have dirty boys in my kitchen.'

'Are you certain it don't hurt?' Ned's nose twitched as the smell of pies baking reached his nostrils.

'I promise,' Helene said and turned as one of the other servants entered the kitchen. 'Jethro, will you fetch the tub from the scullery, please? We are going to give this lad a bath.'

Jethro nodded. 'I saw Beazor looking like thunder.

He's a bad man, miss. He's already done for two work-house lads. He's been warned that if it happens again he won't get another.'

'Is that all they can think of to threaten him with?' Helene's eyes flashed. 'In my opinion, a beating is the least he deserves. He has killed boys and no one does anything to stop him.'

'Yes, miss, a few of us were thinking the same,' Jethro said, his expression grim. 'I'll fetch the tub and give you a hand with him, Bessie. Your uncle was looking for you, Miss Henderson.'

'Yes, I know he wished to speak with me,' Helene said. 'I shall have to ask him what we should do with Ned.'

'You can leave him to me, miss,' Jethro said. 'I need a lad to help out in the yard. He'll do with me. No need to bother Mr Barnes.'

'No, I would rather not…' Helene thanked him, told Ned to be good and hurried away to keep her appointment with her uncle. Edgar Barnes was a fair-minded man. He had taken his sister and her child in when Helene's father died from a fever after a fall from his horse. However, he was not a wealthy man. He had promised to do something for her, and she knew that he had summoned her to his library to talk about her dowry that morning. She had been offered a Season in town by a good friend of her mother's. Her uncle had already given her fifty pounds towards her spending money in town, but the dowry would need to be a more substantial sum if she were to stand a chance of making a good match. Especially in view of what some might see as her unfortunate background.

Helene could ill afford to give Beazor the ten guineas

she had promised him, but she must do it. Her mother had spoken of Miss Royston being very generous, but Helene was not perfectly sure what that meant, though she knew they were to be guests at Miss Amelia Royston's town house. Neither her uncle nor her mother could have afforded to give her a London Season and she felt very grateful to the lady she remembered only vaguely. It was very kind of Miss Royston to send such an invitation.

Helene hesitated outside her uncle's door, then took a deep breath, knocked and opened the door. He was writing at his desk, but looked up as she entered and smiled.

'Ah, Helene, my dear. I am pleased to see you. Come in, niece, and sit down. I want to talk to you about your visit to town.'

'Yes, Uncle. I am sorry I am a little late, sir.'

'No matter...' He waved his hand in a dismissive manner. 'I am sure you understand your great good fortune and the opportunity this visit affords you?'

'Yes, Uncle. I am very grateful to Miss Royston for inviting us.'

'You must make the most of it,' Uncle Edgar told her, his fingers touching as he placed his hands in the steeple position and looked serious. 'I have two sons to see through college and I must do something to secure the future of my younger boy. Matthew wants a set of colours and that is an expense I can scarcely bear. I had thought I might give you fifty pounds a year, but some of my investments have failed miserably and I am no longer able to make the commitment.'

'I am sorry for your loss, sir,' Helene told him, her heart sinking. Without a dowry she would stand little chance of making an advantageous match. The fact of her maternal grandfather having been in trade was a disadvantage in itself, though Helene herself was proud of being Matthew Barnes's granddaughter. He had fought his way up from lowly beginnings to become a man of some fortune, which accorded well with her notions of equality. Unfortunately, a quarrel between Helene's mama and her father had meant that Mrs Henderson had been left a mere competence. Helene had nothing at all, for she had not been born when Matthew Barnes died.

'Then I have no dowry at all?'

'I can give you a hundred pounds extra now and that is all,' Uncle Edgar said with a sigh of regret. 'I am sorry, Helene. It is fortunate that your mother has a good friend in Miss Royston.'

'Yes, the visit will be pleasant, though I think I may not be able to oblige Mama by making a good marriage…'

'Miss Royston understands the situation and she is giving you five thousand pounds as a dowry.' Helene gasped at the news and her uncle smiled. 'Yes, it is a very large sum, Helene. It should help you to make a good match. All the more reason why you should make sure you please your benefactress. You must strive to be on your best behaviour and to make the most of your chances. You must not be too particular, Helene. Do not expect a great match, my dear. He should be a decent man, of course—and you must not go against the wishes of Miss Royston. However, I know you to be a sensible girl…most of the time. But I shall say nothing of your little lapses, which I know come from your heart. You care about others and that is not a bad thing, but sometimes you are led into the wrong paths by impulse.'

Helene wondered if he had heard anything of the scene in his kitchen earlier, but she did not ask. Her uncle would not want to be involved in the quarrel, for he always took the line of least resistance if he could, and he would probably say that Ned should be returned to his master. He certainly would not approve of paying ten guineas to the sweep!

'I do try to be sensible, Uncle,' Helene told him. 'It is just that I cannot stand cruelty in any form.'

'I do not like it myself, but sometimes one has to look the other way, Helene.'

'Yes, Uncle. I shall try to remember.'

Helene's thoughts were very different to her words. She and Bessie had done what they could to save the climbing boy who had been beaten so badly that he died. The sight of his emaciated body, the bruises and the way he had just turned his face to the wall and died had lived in her mind, because she had known that his spirit was broken, too. If she'd had a little money of her own, she would have set up a school for poor boys and alleviated the worst of their suffering. However, even then she could help only a few, and she had often thought the answer lay with men like her uncle. Edgar Barnes was not wealthy, but he had standing in the community. He and others far more powerful should put a stop to the barbaric laws that allowed children to be bought for a few shillings, half-starved and forced to work for their bread.

However, she knew better than to voice her opinion on the matter. Most gentlemen believed ladies should be seen and admired, treated with utmost gentleness, but their opinions seldom counted for anything other than in the matter of the household they ran. Such attitudes might have made Helene angry had she not understood it was simply the way of things. Because she might otherwise have said too much, Helene had fallen into the habit of saying little in the company of her uncle's friends. They were all older men, gallant, charming and entrenched in their traditions. To challenge their long-held beliefs would have been rude. As a result she was deemed to be a quiet girl, pretty enough but perhaps a little shy?

As Helene left her uncle's study, her thoughts returned to the problem of the sweep. She decided that she would consult Jethro in the matter of payment. She would give him the money and trust him to pay what was necessary. Anything he saved could be spent on some decent clothes for Ned. She could hardly expect him to support the boy entirely from his own pocket.

As she went upstairs to her bedchamber, Helene mentally reviewed the gowns she was taking with her to London. She had four new evening dresses, one morning gown and one for the afternoon; all the others had been worn several times before she went into mourning for her father. Would they be enough to see her through the Season? If her uncle gave her the hundred pounds he had promised, perhaps she might purchase a few extra gowns, for she was certain they would be needed if they were invited to some modest affairs. It was hardly likely that she would attend the most prestigious balls taking place in the houses of the aristocracy—although her father had been a gentleman, he had never possessed a vast fortune or a title.

Helene decided that she would wait until she got to

London before purchasing more gowns. It would not be long now and she might not actually need them. The money would be better saved for more important things…

Helene stood just behind her mother, as their hostess received them. The house was a three-storey building in an elegant square in the heart of London, beautifully furnished and quite large.

'Marie—how lovely to see you. You are looking very well,' Miss Royston greeted them as they were shown into the comfortable parlour, which they had been told was used for private afternoons. 'And this is Helene, I believe? You have grown, my love. I knew that you would be a young lady by now, but I did not think you would be so very pretty!'

Helene's cheeks turned to a delicate rose. She felt a little uncomfortable as she bobbed a respectful curtsy. 'You are so very kind, Miss Royston,' she said. 'Indeed, Mama tells me you have been extraordinarily generous. I do not know how to thank you, ma'am.'

'Please call me Amelia when we are private together,' Amelia said. 'I need no thanks, Helene. I shall enjoy having friends to stay—and as for the other—' Helene lowered her gaze, feeling slightly embarrassed '—please do not feel under any obligation, my dear. I was very fortunate in being left a great deal of money by my aunt, far more than I could ever need, in fact. Helping my friends is a great pleasure to me. I do not wish you to feel you owe me something, for I have known what it is like to be beholden to others.'

'Mama told me that you were not happy in your brother's house,' Helene said and raised her eyes to meet

Amelia's. 'Uncle Edgar has been kind to us, but I must admit it is not like living in your own home.'

'No, it cannot be,' Amelia replied. 'I have asked my dressmaker to call in the morning, Helene. We all need new gowns and it will be amusing to choose them here. We can look at patterns and materials together… but I am forgetting my manners. This lady is Emily Barton. She is my friend and my companion. I am not sure what I should do without her—she completely spoils me!'

Helene turned her gaze on the lady standing silently by the fireplace. She had dark blonde hair and the saddest eyes that Helene ever remembered seeing.

'Miss Barton,' Helene said and dipped a curtsy, 'I am pleased to meet you.'

'I am pleased to meet you,' Emily replied. 'Shall we sit together on the sofa?'

Helene went to sit by Emily. Amelia Royston turned her attention to Mrs Henderson, drawing her to a comfortable chair near the fire and offering refreshment.

'Would you care for tea—or something a little stronger? A glass of wine, perhaps, to keep out the chill of the day. It has turned a little cold for the time of year, do you not think so?'

'How kind,' Mrs Henderson said and sat down near the fire. 'I should not mind a glass of wine, Amelia. The roads were terribly rutted in places and we were rattled so in my brother's carriage. I thought we should break a pole or lose a wheel, but we arrived safely. Edgar talks of buying a new carriage but his sons are at college and he cannot afford such luxuries for the moment.'

'When you go home, you shall be taken in my carriage,'

Amelia told her. 'Had I known, I would have sent it to collect you, Marie. Forgive me for not thinking of it.'

'Oh, no—you have already done so much.'

'Really, it is very little to me,' Amelia assured her with a gentle smile. 'I am glad to entertain my friends, you know. I am not lonely now that I have Emily, but we both like to have friends to stay.'

'In the matter of Helene's clothes…I have some money,' Mrs Henderson began, a slight flush in her cheeks, but Amelia shook her head.

'We do not need to speak of it. My seamstress will send her bills to me and we shall talk about this at the end of the Season. If we are fortunate and Helene secures a good husband, neither of you will have to worry about money again.'

'Yes…' Mrs Henderson looked doubtful. 'You look…beautiful, Amelia. Scarcely older than when I last saw you.'

'Oh, I hardly think that,' Amelia said on a laugh. 'I am approaching my twenty-seventh birthday, Marie.'

'No one would know if you did not tell them.' Mrs Henderson arched her brows. 'Have you never thought of marriage yourself?'

'I thought of it some years ago, but my brother did not approve…' Amelia frowned. For a moment her expression was sad, pained, but then she raised her head in a determined fashion. 'I fear I am past the age for marrying now, Marie. You were no more than nineteen when you married, I believe?'

'Hardly that,' Mrs Henderson said and sighed. 'It was an imprudent match, for my William did not have sufficient fortune and it caused a breach with my father.

In his anger he struck my name from his will. Papa did not hold with the aristocracy—he thought them proud and arrogant. I believe he would have reinstated me later, but he died suddenly, just before Helene was born, and I was left with a fraction of what might have been mine. I do not regret my marriage, for my husband was a good man and I loved him, but I have regretted the lack of fortune for my daughter's sake. I had hoped her uncle might do something for her, but he finds himself in some financial difficulty, I believe.'

'It is the way of things—and sons can be expensive,' Amelia said. 'My brother has two sons and he often complains to me of their extravagance. John has taken a pair of colours, but the younger son prefers to live in London. Your brother was widowed just before you lost your husband. Is it your intention to return and keep house for him—even if Helene should marry well?'

'Oh…I am not certain,' Mrs Henderson replied. 'Edgar has a very good housekeeper and I am not necessary to him, though he would not turn me away.' She could not prevent a sigh escaping. 'He was very good to take us in but…you understand, of course.'

'Ah, yes, I do. I was forced to reside with my brother and his wife until I went to live with my aunt,' Amelia said and gave her a look of sympathy. 'You are not alone in your predicament, Marie, for many women find themselves reduced to living on a competence when their husbands die. It cannot have been comfortable for you, my dear. Well, we must wait and see what kind of an impression Helene makes—if she is to be accepted, she needs to be well dressed.'

Helene blushed as the two ladies looked at her. It was

obvious that she was expected to make a good match. She was determined to do her best, for her uncle's warning had played on her mind. She did not think he would be too pleased if she returned at the end of the Season with no prospect of a good marriage before her. However, she knew that her mama had not been well treated by her father's family, who had frowned on the marriage and cut her most cruelly because of her background. Knowing her mama's story had helped Helene to become quite radical in her thinking. She was not sure that she approved of the aristocracy and their privileged way of living. In that she probably took after her maternal grandfather. Mrs Henderson said that she had his temperament and was equally as stubborn.

It would not do for Helene to be married to one of the idle rich! She must hope that she could find a sensible man who had compassion for those less fortunate than himself. Helene knew that her mama had great hopes for her and she was afraid that she might be disappointed if her daughter's choice turned out to be less important and wealthy than she hoped.

Helene found Emily Barton easy to talk to, because she seemed genuinely interested in hearing about Helene's life. She was attractive and Helene thought she could have been lovely had she dressed her hair less severely. Her voice was soft, musical and her laugh was infectious. However, she revealed almost nothing of herself, allowing Helene to talk without interruption.

Helene did not know how it was, but she found herself confiding in her new friend about the climbing boy she had rescued from his cruel master.

'He was beating poor Ned,' she said. 'I made him stop and sent him away. He said I must pay ten guineas, but in the end Jethro made him take two. I think he would not have been pleased, but he made his mark to show that the boy was no longer his property. I think Jethro may have threatened him, though of course he said nothing of it to me.'

'How brave you were to stand up to him,' Emily said, her blue-green eyes seemingly intent on Helene's face. 'It must have been frightening, for he might have attacked you.'

'He might,' Helene admitted with a little shudder. 'To be honest, I did not consider the possibility. I just ordered him to desist and—fortunately, he did.'

'Yes, I see…' Emily smiled. 'It is a sad thing when a child can be bought and sold for a few guineas is it not?'

'Yes, it is,' Helene said and her eyes caught with an inner fire that was not often present when in polite company. 'If I were wealthy, I should open a school for orphan boys and feed them on good wholesome food so that they grow strong and healthy. It breaks my heart to see children with rickets or sores on their faces, because they do not get the proper diet. So many of them die before they reach maturity.'

Emily nodded. 'I can see that you have put a deal of thought into the matter. The situation is even worse in town than in the country, you know. There are areas where the filth runs in the gutters and the inhabitants are for ever ill with some dread fever. Some of them spend their lives drinking gin to deaden the pain of hunger and hopelessness.'

Helene's eyes brimmed with tears. 'I have heard of

these places and wish with all my heart that I could do something for them…'

'Amelia does,' Emily told her and smiled. 'This winter she set up a school and a home for orphans—not just boys, girls as well. I have not been to visit yet, though I intend to quite soon.' She arched her brows at Helene. 'Perhaps you would care to accompany me? Amelia visited yesterday. She said it was heartbreaking to see the new cases, but that the ones who had been with the school for some months were a joy to behold, for they had grown strong and were gaining an education for themselves.'

'Oh, yes, I should like it above all things—may we go tomorrow?' Helene's face lit with eagerness. 'It is just the sort of thing I should do if I were rich!'

Emily smiled and shook her head. 'Amelia has many things planned for you, Miss Henderson. You must be properly dressed, you know. In a week or so, when things have quietened a little, we may choose our opportunity to slip away one morning.'

Helene wanted to protest—of what importance were fancy clothes when there was so much poverty in the world? However, she held back the words. There would be chances enough for her to discover more of what interested her. She must not forget her duty to Mama or her sense of obligation to Miss Royston. It was obvious from what Emily had told her that her hostess was a generous woman, not only to herself but to deserving cases, and therefore deserved the utmost respect and consideration.

'How long have you lived with Miss Royston?' she inquired.

'Oh, a little over nine months,' Emily replied. 'She is the kindest employer I could wish for and the best of friends.'

'I see…' Helene frowned. 'Is she the first lady you have worked for—or is it impolite of me to ask?'

'Not at all,' Emily said and her eyes clouded with sadness. 'I looked after my mother for some years after my father's death. Papa was…an intolerant man and he made Mama's life uneasy. She became an invalid some years earlier. When she died, I found myself with little money, for my father's estate went to his nephew. I…was forced to find work, but I was very fortunate— I have little to do but enjoy myself here. Amelia makes few requests of me. All she really needs is someone to keep her company.'

'Yes, I see.' Helene nodded. Emily's warm affection for her employer was further evidence of Miss Royston's goodness. Helene's sense of obligation deepened. She must take care to please Amelia in any little way she could, because it would be rude to do anything else, and she had been properly brought up. 'You must tell me if there is anything I can do to make myself useful to you or Miss Royston.'

'I am sure Amelia only wishes to see you happy. She has the kindest heart, though she can be stubborn when she chooses,' Emily said and shook her head as Helene raised her brows in enquiry. 'Now, if you are ready, perhaps I may show you to your room?'

'Thank you so much,' Helene said and stood up. She nodded to her mother and Amelia as they went out into the hall. She was a little in awe of Miss Royston, because of her goodness and generosity, and she was glad of Emily's presence. 'I should very much like it if we could be friends?' she said with a shy glance at the older woman. 'If you would like it, too?'

'Certainly I should,' Emily assured her with a smile. 'I can see that you are a lady who thinks of others and that is something I admire…' For a moment that flash of sadness was in Emily's eyes again and Helene wondered what secret sorrow she held inside. However, she would not presume to ask, for she believed that people told you things when they had learned to trust you, and Emily did not yet know her. 'Now, we must talk of other things.'

'What kind of things?' Helene asked.

'Amelia has asked me to show you the house, and to tell you how we go on here. You are to have your own maid while you stay here, Helene. I know your mama has brought her own maid, but you will have one all to yourself. Tilly is a skilled needlewoman and she can dress your hair as well as look after your clothes. She has already unpacked your trunks and will have pressed a gown for you for this evening. Amelia has no guests for this evening. She thought we should all get to know each other, and we shall do that better by ourselves.'

'Yes, that is a good idea,' Helene agreed. 'I think we shall be friends, Emily—but I must admit I feel a little in awe of Miss Royston.'

'You must not,' Emily told her. 'She would not wish it. You are not the first young lady she has helped. Last season she brought Miss Susannah Hampton to town. Susannah is now Lady Pendleton. We visited Pendleton at Christmas and she seemed very happy. I do not think you will meet her in town, for she is in a delicate situation—she is to have her husband's child this summer, I understand.'

'Oh…she must be pleased,' Helene said, her cheeks warm. 'How fortunate for her.'

'Susannah is very happy,' Emily told her. 'She fell in love with Lord Pendleton and he with her. It was a love match—and they might never have met had it not been for Amelia.'

'That is indeed fortunate. I am not sure that I shall ever truly fall in love, but I must marry if a respectable gentleman should offer for me. It is my duty to Mama.'

'Well, perhaps,' Emily said and something odd flickered in her eyes. 'I think you are very pretty, Helene. I am sure you will have a great many offers. You will not be forced to take the first man who asks for you.'

Helene looked at her curiously. She would have liked to ask Emily what she thought of marriage, but she did not yet know her well enough. Besides, she suspected that Emily had no money of her own. Helene knew that without the dowry Miss Royston had given her, she would have been unlikely to find a husband. Perhaps that was why Emily looked so sad. Helene hoped that one day Emily might like her enough to confide in her, but for the moment she would not ask.

The next morning was entirely taken up with the visit from the seamstress and her young assistant. At first Helene felt a little nervous about giving her opinions, for she was very conscious of the fact that this must be costing a great deal. However, when she discovered that Emily was also being fitted for a new wardrobe, she lost most of her inhibitions. She found it easy to confer with Emily, to discuss styles, colours and quality, and also quantity—though she found it a little shocking when she discovered just how many new gowns were considered necessary.

'Shall I really need so many?' she asked, for she could not help thinking that some of the money could be put to better use. 'I already have four evening dresses I brought with me.'

'They are very pretty and quite suitable for when we dine at home,' Emily told her and smiled as she saw Helene's doubtful look. 'I felt as you do when I first came to live with Amelia—but she has so many friends. We are invited everywhere, you know. You cannot be for ever wearing the same gown, Helene. You would not wish to appear dowdy? No, of course not. Now do look at this green silk. It would be perfect for your colouring—do you not think so, Madame Dubois?'

'*Oui,* of a certainty,' the Frenchwoman exclaimed. 'It will look well for an afternoon gown, but the young lady should wear white for evenings. White and simple will be perfect for one so young and beautiful.'

Helene held the shimmering white material to herself, glancing in the mirror. She felt that white was a little insipid for her, but hardly liked to protest. However, Emily shook her head.

'I cannot agree, *madame,*' she said. 'I believe Helene would look better in colours—that pale blue and the yellow…and perhaps that very pale pink with a deeper cerise trim.'

The seamstress pulled a face. 'Very pretty, but the petite is so young…'

'I think I agree with Emily,' Amelia said as Emily

draped the yellow and blue materials against Helene. 'White is necessary if you are presented, Helene, my dear, but I am not sure that your mama wishes for a court presentation.'

'I think that might be better left for the future,' Mrs Henderson said and looked thoughtful. 'I was never presented at court even after my marriage. I doubt that Helene will be, either.'

'Oh, no, Mama, I am sure it is not necessary,' Helene assured her. Since she had no intention of marrying into the aristocracy, it would be a waste of money to invest in such elaborate gowns.

'Well, we shall see what happens,' Amelia said. 'We can always order a court gown if it seems likely that someone will offer to present you, Helene.'

'I am sure they will not,' Helene said. 'I am quite content with the gowns I already have, thank you.'

'How many have you ordered?' Amelia inquired of the seamstress and shook her head as she was told. 'That is not enough. I think you should have an evening gown made of this straw satin as well—and I think a ballgown in this beautiful peach silk, Helene. Hold it against you and look in the mirror. It is perfect for you, my dear.'

Not content with that, Amelia ordered two further morning gowns, two afternoon gowns and a riding habit in dark blue velvet. Helene felt overwhelmed—she had never owned so many gowns. She was relieved to see that Emily was also pressed to order more gowns.

'Well, I think that will do for now,' Amelia said. 'When can you deliver the first gowns, Madame Dubois? The very first should be the peach gown for Miss Henderson, please. Emily and I may wait a few days.'

The seamstress promised to have several gowns delivered by the end of the week, and the peach gown in two days.

'That is perfect,' Amelia said after she had gone. 'We have been invited to a prestigious dance that evening. Helene will need her new gown. We shall have to shop for some spangles tomorrow. A pretty stole and some dancing shoes to complement your gown, my dear. You might like to take Helene shopping, Emily? You know all the best shops and can show her what is usually worn at these affairs.'

'Yes, of course,' Emily said. 'Would you care to accompany us, Mrs Henderson?'

'As it happens, I have agreed to accompany Amelia somewhere,' Mrs Henderson said. 'You two go and enjoy yourselves.'

'I had planned to visit the lending library this afternoon,' Emily said and looked at Helene. 'Would you like to come?'

'Yes, thank you,' Helene agreed. 'Unless Amelia needs me for anything?'

'No, I do not think so,' Amelia said. 'I am at home this afternoon. You must not stay out too long, for I am sure we shall have several callers and they will want to meet Helene.'

'It will take no more than an hour,' Emily assured her. 'A walk to the library and back will be quite uneventful. We shall be back in plenty of time for tea.'

'Then do go, my love,' Amelia said. 'It will be pleasant for Helene to see something of the town, and you may meet with some friends.'

'You may bring a book for me, Helene,' her mama

told her. 'It is so nice to have the opportunity of borrowing new books. Edgar had very little of interest in his library at home.'

'Emily—look!' Helene grabbed hold of her arm as they were returning from the library. 'Do you see that man over there? He is beating that poor donkey with a stick. Oh, how wicked! It is obvious the creature is exhausted and can go no further…'

Helene had been holding Emily's arm, but she broke away from her and ran across the road to where a man dressed in filthy rags was trying to force a donkey to continue pulling the heavy wagon. The wagon was piled high with all kinds of rags, discarded furniture and metal pots. The donkey was scarcely more than skin and bone and exhausted. Its owner had lifted his arm to beat the unfortunate beast once more when a whirling fury grabbed hold of him, holding on to his arm and preventing him from carrying out his intention.

'You wicked, wicked man!' Helene cried. 'Can't you see the poor creature is exhausted? If you force it to go on, you will kill it…'

The man tried to throw her off, but Helene held on, struggling to catch hold of the stick and wrench it from his grasp. She was determined not to let go even though he was much stronger than she and obviously possessed of a nasty temper.

'Damn you, wench,' the man snarled. 'Leave me be or it will be the worse for you!' He managed to pull his arm free of her grasp and raised it again, intending, it seemed, to beat her instead of the donkey.

'No, you don't, sirrah!' a man's deep voice cried and

the bully's arm was caught, this time in a grip of steel. The vagabond growled and tried to free himself, but ended with his arm up against his back, his chest pressed against the side of the wagon. 'If you do not want your arm broken, stop struggling.'

'Let me be,' the vagabond whined. 'She attacked me, sir. I were only defending meself.'

'Be quiet, rogue, or I'll break your neck,' the man commanded. His eyes moved to Helene. 'Would you like to tell me what happened here, miss?'

'He was beating that poor creature,' Helene said. 'You can see for yourself that it is half-starved—and that load is far too heavy. The poor beast is too exhausted to pull the cart another inch.'

'Did you attack him?' The man arched his brows.

'I tried to stop him beating the donkey.' Helene lifted her head proudly, refusing to be ashamed of her action.

'I see…' Max released the vagabond, turned him round and glared down at him. The vagabond opened his mouth, then shut it again. The newcomer was a gentleman and a rather large one, his expression threatening. 'What have you to say for yourself, rogue?'

'The stupid beast is useless. It is lazy and a worthless bag of bones. I have to beat it or it will not move.'

'It might work better if you fed it occasionally,' Lord Maximus Coleridge said wryly. 'Here, take this in exchange for the animal and be off with you before I call the watch!' He thrust a handful of gold coins at his victim. The vagabond stared at the money in astonishment, bit one of the coins to make sure it really was gold and then took off as fast as he could before the *mad* gentleman could change his mind.

'That was too much. One of those coins must have been sufficient,' Helene protested as the large gentleman began to undo the donkey's harness, freeing it from its burden. She patted the donkey's nose. 'The poor thing. It must have had a terrible life.'

'Yes, I dare say,' Max said and frowned. He arched his eyebrows in enquiry. 'What do you propose we should do with it now?'

'Oh…' Helene stared at him. 'I am not sure, sir. The poor creature needs a good home and something to eat. It looks quite starved.'

'I wonder if it would not be kinder to put a ball through its head and end its misery.'

'No! You must not,' Helene cried and then blushed as his dark grey eyes centred on her face. She thought him an extremely attractive man, large and powerful, and, it seemed, exactly the kind of man one could rely on in an emergency. 'I mean…could you not have it taken to a stable? At least give this unfortunate beast a chance to recover…please?'

'Helene…' Emily had waited for her chance to cross the road. 'Are you all right, my dear? I would have come sooner, but there was a press of carriages.'

'Because we are blocking the road,' Max said wryly. 'Good afternoon, Miss Barton. I did not know that you were in town. I trust you are well—and Miss Royston?'

'Lord Coleridge,' Emily said and dipped in a slight curtsy. 'We are both well. May I introduce Miss Henderson? Helene—Lord Coleridge. Helene and her mama are staying with us this Season, sir.'

'My compliments to Miss Royston. I shall call,' Max Coleridge said and turned his gaze back to

Helene. 'So, Miss Henderson—what do you suggest?' He saw the pleading in her eyes. 'I hope you are not suggesting that this flea-ridden beast should rub shoulders with my cattle...'

'Could you not find a small corner for him in your stables, sir?'

'Oh, no.' Max shook his head. He turned his head and signalled to someone. A youth of perhaps fourteen years came running. 'Jemmy, this lady wants us to take care of this donkey—what do you suggest we do with him?'

'Sell 'im to the knacker's yard, sir?' the youth said and grinned.

'Much as I think you may be right, I find myself unable to agree,' Max replied, a twinkle in his eye. 'I think you should take charge of him, Jemmy. I dare say we could find a corner for him somewhere.'

'That bag of bones? You're bamming me, milord,' Jemmy said, staring at him in horror. 'We'll be the laughing stock of the *ton,* sir.'

'I dare say,' Max replied. 'However, I do not intend to drive the wretched beast. Once it has recovered—if it recovers—we may find a better home. I shall make inquiries.'

'You want me to get that thing 'ome?' Jemmy was clearly horrified. 'I dunno as it will move, sir.'

'Do your best, Jemmy. I fear we are holding up the traffic.' Max gave Helene a direct look. 'I believe we should move out of the road—do you not think so?'

'But the donkey...' Helene moved on to the path, joining Emily and Lord Coleridge. Jemmy was trying to get the donkey to move without success. 'I think you need a bribe.' She saw a barrow boy selling vegetables and darted back across the road to buy a carrot from him. It was rather wrinkled and past its best, but she thought the donkey would be hungry enough to be tempted. She paused for a moment and then dodged between a cart and a man leading a horse, narrowly avoiding being run over by a coal cart. 'Try tempting him forward with this.' She handed her prize to the lad.

'Give it 'ere, miss. I'll have a go.' Jemmy held the carrot under the donkey's nose. It snickered and then made a loud noise, trying to grab the food and succeeding. 'Blimey! He snatched it...' Jemmy's mouth fell open.

He looked so astonished that Lord Coleridge gave a shout of laughter. He tossed the lad a gold coin. 'I think you need to buy a large supply of treats,' he said. 'Be more careful next time.'

Jemmy caught the coin and started over the road. The donkey made an ear-shattering noise and trotted over the road after him. Discovering that there were many more carrots on the stall, it snatched another, and when the barrow boy yelled in anger, took off down the road at a run, Jemmy in hot pursuit.

'Not quite as exhausted as we thought,' Max said, highly amused. Helene stared at him indignantly as he laughed. He sobered as he caught the look in her eye. 'Forgive me, Miss Henderson, but you have to admit that it was funny.'

'Yes, it was,' she said and the laughter suddenly bubbled up inside her. 'Oh, dear, it seems I have cost you a great deal of money and a lot of trouble for nothing.'

'Oh, no,' Max told her. 'To see that donkey with Jemmy in pursuit was worth far more than a few guineas, Miss Henderson. I do not know how he will live it down. I can only hope that my eloquence will be enough to retain his services—he may feel that he can no longer work for such a ramshackle fellow as myself.' He glanced over his shoulder. 'My groom awaits me patiently. Ladies—may I take you up in my curricle?'

'Thank you, but we shall walk for the house is not far away,' Helene said before Emily could reply. 'It was kind of you to help us, sir—but we shall take up no more of your time.'

Max lifted his hat, his eyes bright with amusement. 'I shall see you another day, Miss Henderson. If you manage to avoid being run over by carts or attacked by rogues, of course. Good afternoon.'

Helene watched him walk away. She turned to Emily, looking thoughtful. 'He was very kind. I am not sure what would have happened if he had not come along just then. However, he seems to be one of those gentlemen who takes nothing seriously.'

'I am sure you misjudge him. Lord Coleridge is fond of a jest, but quite a gentleman. You might have been in some danger,' Emily told her. 'That rogue would have hit you if he could. It was a little reckless of you, Helene.'

'Yes, I know. My uncle has warned me of my impulsive nature—but I cannot abide cruelty, Emily.'

'No, I see that you cannot,' Emily said and gave her a look of approval. 'Well, you were impulsive, Helene— but no harm came of it.'

'No…' Helene said, but she was thoughtful. She had rather liked the large gentleman, despite his tendency to levity—but whatever must he think of her?

Chapter Two

Amelia glanced through the pile of cards on the silver salver in the hall when they all returned from an outing the following afternoon. She looked pleased as she mentioned one or two names, and then frowned as she came to the last one. Her housekeeper was hovering near by and she beckoned to her.

'When did Lord Coleridge call, Mrs Becks?'

'Just after you all went out, Miss Royston.'

'Was he alone?'

'Yes, miss. I believe so. Is something wrong?'

'Oh…no,' Amelia said, but she still looked slightly bothered about something as she took off her hat and handed it to Mrs Becks. 'I was just a little surprised that he should call. He is Lord Pendleton's friend rather than mine.'

'Do you not approve of Lord Coleridge?' Helene asked as she followed Amelia into the small parlour, which they used when not entertaining. 'He seemed very pleasant when he…when we met yesterday.'

'You met yesterday?' Amelia glanced at her, surprised. 'You did not mention it, Helene. Are you acquainted with Lord Coleridge?'

'Oh, no,' Helene said and blushed. 'I suppose I ought to have told you about the incident, but there were visitors when Emily and I returned—' She broke off and blushed, for during the night she had lain awake, remembering her impulsive behaviour, and shuddering at the thought of what might have happened if Lord Coleridge had not come to her rescue. 'I hope you will not censure me…' She repeated what had occurred and was rendered a little anxious when Amelia frowned. 'I know it was impulsive, and perhaps I ought not to have done it, but I cannot abide cruelty.'

'No, nor can I,' Amelia said and looked serious. 'I would not recommend such behaviour, Helene, for if Lord Coleridge had not happened to be passing you might have been in some trouble. Also, your behaviour might be censured by some in society, though not by me. I can understand your feelings, my dear, though I would urge caution for your own sake.'

'I am sorry if I have displeased you.' Helene looked at her anxiously. 'You will not mention it to Mama, please?'

'No, of course not. And you have not displeased me,' Amelia told her. 'At least it explains why Lord Coleridge called this afternoon. No doubt he wanted to inquire after you, to make sure you had suffered no harm.'

'That was kind of him, was it not?'

'Yes, though I should be a little careful of becoming too friendly with that gentleman.' Amelia shook her head, an odd expression in her eyes. 'No, forget I said that, Helene. He is perfectly respectable…and it was a long time ago. I should not have said anything.'

Helene would have asked her to explain further, but her mother, who had gone straight upstairs earlier, now entered the room and looked at her. 'Have you decided which dress you will wear this evening, my dearest? It is a soirée, so you will need one of your new gowns that we brought with us. I thought the pale green satin might look well—especially with the gloves and slippers you bought this morning.'

'Yes, Mama,' Helene said. 'I think the green is perhaps the nicest of the gowns we brought with us.'

'It will be very suitable for this evening,' Amelia said. 'Lady Marsh's affair is quite small, but she is a particular friend and knows all the best people. We are fortunate to be invited to one of her musical evenings. You will meet some new acquaintances, which will make things easier for you tomorrow at the dance. You do not want to be sitting with your mama when the dancing begins, for everyone hates to be a wallflower.'

Helene smiled and thanked her. Amelia had warned her of becoming too friendly with Lord Coleridge, though she had immediately retracted her words. What had been in her mind? Despite her retraction, and her assurance that Lord Coleridge was perfectly respectable, Helene suspected that she either did not like or did not approve of Lord Coleridge. Why? What had he done that had made her feel it would be better if Helene did not form a friendship with him?

As Helene went up to change for the evening she was still pondering the question. She had liked Lord Coleridge. He had come to her rescue and dealt swiftly and firmly with what might have been an awkward situation, but, more than that, she had responded to his sense

of humour and the twinkle in his eyes. However, on reflection, she recalled that he was a member of the aristocracy and perhaps it would be best to put the small
incident from her mind. It would not suit her to marry
a gentleman who had no idea of the value of money and
wasted his blunt when it might be put to good use. Her
mother had been slighted and ill used by Papa's family
and Helene did not wish for something similar to
happen to her. She would do much better with a gentleman of moderate fortune who thought as she did
about the important things of life.

She was a thoughtful girl and was sensible of the fact
that she owed her chance to enter society entirely to
Miss Royston. Without Amelia's generosity, she would
never have been given a Season in London. Rather than
offend her hostess, she would try to avoid Lord
Coleridge's company as much as possible, though of
course she would speak to him when they met. He had
done her a service and mere politeness demanded that
she thank him at least once more. However, it was more
than likely that she would not often meet him. He was
a titled gentleman and she did not suppose that he would
be in the least interested in a country nobody. Nor
indeed was she interested in anything more than a
nodding acquaintance with a man like him!

'Max!' a voice hailed him loudly from across the
road as he was about to enter his sporting club. Max
turned and looked round; he grinned as he saw the
younger man approaching on foot. 'I am glad to have
caught you. I am just this day come to town. Harry sent
me to look at some decent cattle he heard of and I think

they are just what I need. I wondered if you would give me the benefit of your advice in the morning?'

'Toby Sinclair…' Max clapped him on the shoulder. 'The newest member of the Four-in-Hand. So Harry put you on the right track, did he? Your uncle is one of the best judges of horseflesh I know. I doubt you need my advice.'

'I should like it none the less,' Toby said. 'I have no engagements in town as yet.'

'Ah…' Max nodded, looked thoughtful, then, 'I am promised to Lady Marsh this evening. I think you know my great-aunt Edith? I am certain she would welcome you.'

'Thank you,' Toby said, his eyes lighting up. 'I could have spent the evening at a gaming hell, but I've just accepted an offer from Harry to join him in a business venture and I am trying not too waste too much blunt at the tables.'

'Sensible,' Max said and frowned. 'I happened to see Northaven this morning. I was surprised to see him back in town after what happened at Pendleton last year. He would have done better to take himself off abroad as Harry bid him.'

'I dare say his pride would not let him.'

'I dare say you are right.'

'I have wondered if it was Northaven who attempted to kidnap Amelia Royston in Pendleton woods last summer,' Toby said. 'If, indeed, it was an attempt to snatch her and not merely a botched robbery?'

'Ravenshead has his own ideas on the subject,' Max said and looked thoughtful. 'Miss Royston is in town, you know. She has some friends staying—Mrs Henderson and her daughter Helene.'

'Really? I must call tomorrow,' Toby said. He looked round as they entered the sporting club together. 'Are you going to box or fence today?'

'I thought to see who was here,' Max said. 'Do you fancy yourself with the foils, Sinclair?'

'Well, I'm not sure I'm up to your mark, Coleridge,' Toby said and grinned. 'But I'm game if you are?'

'Delighted,' Max said and clapped him on the back. 'Tell you the truth, I've been missing Harry and Gerard. Harry invited me down to Pendleton, and I may go in a few weeks, but I have not heard a word from Ravenshead since he went to France. I am not certain he intends to return.'

'Oh, I think he may,' Toby said. 'Susannah told me that he had written to Harry. He has been delayed, but he has engaged an English nanny for his daughter and I think he will open the house at Ravenshead in another month or so.'

'Ah, that is good news. I dare say he may visit with Harry and Susannah for a while, and I shall certainly go down at the end of the Season.' Unless he found a lady to propose to in the meantime, Max thought. He said nothing of his plans to take a wife, which had been forming slowly for a while.

He did not know why he had not married sooner—he wished to have children, and not simply because he needed an heir for his estate. Max had been an only child after his younger brother died in childhood. He had joined the army more out of a desire for companionship than a wish to be a soldier and had formed some strong friendships. However, Harry Pendleton's marriage to a spirited young girl, and Gerard's absence in France, had made him aware that his life was empty.

If he could find a girl who would put up with him—one he could feel comfortable with on a daily basis—he might decide to settle down quite soon. Max was not sure whether or not he needed to love the girl. Perhaps that was not necessary for a marriage of convenience. Affection and compatibility was possibly more important? He did not think that he could put up with a simpering miss who was interested only in her new gown or some fresh trinket, though he could afford to indulge his wife with all the trinkets she required. A little smile touched his mouth as he recalled the girl and the donkey. Now Helene certainly had spirit and her indignant look had made him smile…

Helene glanced at herself in the cheval mirror. Her gown was not as stylish as some Amelia wore, but, caught high under the bust with a band of embroidery, it became her well. She had added a new spangled stole and some long white gloves and white slippers. Her dark brown hair was dressed simply in a knot at the back of her head, fastened with pearl pins, and she wore a string of pearls about her throat. They had belonged to her father's grandmother, so she had been told, and were the only jewellery she possessed, apart from a matching pair of earbobs.

A knock at the door announced a visitor. Helene had dismissed her maid once she was ready, and called out that whoever it was might enter. She smiled as the door opened and Emily entered. She was wearing a dark blue gown, very simple in design, but of quality silk and cut most elegantly.

'You look lovely,' Helene exclaimed. 'I like you in blue, Emily. I do not know why you do not wear it more often.'

'Amelia has been trying to wean me from grey for a long time,' Emily said. 'I am particularly fond of blue, but I used to think it was not a suitable colour for a companion.'

'Amelia does not think of you in that way,' Helene assured her. Her face was thoughtful as she studied the other woman. Emily looked much younger now that she had abandoned her habitual grey. 'I believe she values you as a friend.'

'Yes, she has told me so many times,' Emily agreed. For a moment she looked sad, but it passed and she was smiling again. 'You are beautiful, Helene. That dress becomes you.'

'Thank you.' Helene glanced at her reflection once more. 'It is not as stylish as your gown, or those we have ordered, I dare say—but I do not think I shall disgrace Amelia this evening.'

'I am very certain you will not,' Emily said and laughed softly. 'You look everything you ought, Helene. I was sent to see if you were ready—shall we go down?'

'Yes, of course,' Helene said. 'I am a little nervous about this evening. It is my first outing into London society and I am not sure what to expect.'

'That is why Amelia chose carefully for you,' Emily said. 'I am sure everyone will approve of you, Helene, for your manners are good and you think before you speak—and I think you will like Lady Marsh, who is your hostess this evening, for she is very kind. She is Lord Coleridge's great-aunt on his father's side. She has been kind to me even though I am just a companion.'

'You are a lady, anyone can see that,' Helene said.

'Being a companion does not make you any the less respectable, Emily.'

Emily laughed. 'That is not always the opinion of everyone, Helene—but I am very fortunate to have Amelia as my employer. She is respected everywhere. Because of her kindness I have been accepted by most— and you will be, too, Helene.'

'Thank you, I feel a little better now. Shall we go?'

Helene's nerves returned when they alighted from the carriage and walked along the carpet that had been laid on the ground outside the large house to protect the ladies from getting their gowns soiled. Lanterns were being held for them by linkboys, and the carriage had been obliged to queue when they first arrived—and this was supposed to be a modest affair! Helene was glad of Emily's company as they walked into the house together. They were greeted first by their hostess. Lady Marsh was a small plump lady of perhaps sixty years, dressed in a purple gown and a gold turban, and she kept them talking for a moment before allowing them to pass on to the reception rooms.

The first elegant salon was half-empty, a mere half a dozen couples standing around, talking and greeting each other. Amelia smiled and greeted two ladies, who lifted their hands in welcome as they entered. She introduced Mrs Henderson and Helene.

'Lady Renton, Lady Jamieson,' she said, 'may I make you known to some good friends who have come to stay with me for a while—Mrs Henderson, and Miss Helene Henderson…and, of course, you know my dearest Emily.'

Helene felt herself being scrutinised. She dipped a respectful curtsy, wondering if she were being approved. Lady Renton seemed a little aloof in her manner, as if reserving judgement, though Lady Jamieson was friendly enough. Helene was relieved as they passed on to the next group of two ladies and a gentleman.

'Miss Royston, I am pleased to see you here,' the gentleman said and then looked at Helene, one eyebrow raised in expectation.

'Mr Bradwell,' Amelia said. 'Mrs Bradwell, Miss Bradwell…may I present my friends—Mrs Henderson and Miss Helene Henderson… Mr Nicholas Bradwell and his mama and sister.'

'Charming, quite charming,' Nicholas Bradwell said and inclined his head. 'I am happy to make your acquaintance, ma'am—Miss Henderson.' His eyes had fixed on Helene's face. 'Tell me, do you enjoy music, Miss Henderson?'

'Yes, sir, I like it very well.'

'And do you play an instrument yourself perhaps?'

'Yes, sir. I play the pianoforte, though I cannot profess to be accomplished.'

'Helene, you are too modest,' Mrs Henderson said and gave her a reproving look. 'My daughter plays very well, sir. I have heard her spoken of as talented, but she does not like to say so herself.'

'A truly modest young lady.' Nicholas Bradwell looked at her and nodded. He was a gentleman of perhaps forty years or so. Of medium height and slim build, he was dressed fashionably, his hair cut short and brushed back from his forehead, the wings sprinkled with grey.

'Perhaps you would let me take you in, Miss Henderson? I shall make you known to your fellow guests.'

Helene glanced at her mother, who nodded her consent. Feeling her stomach tighten with nerves, Helene laid her hand on his arm and allowed him to draw her into the next reception room. Here it was more crowded, and most of the chairs and sofas were occupied. Helene saw that it was here that the musical entertainment would be given a little later.

'Shall we reserve that sofa?' Nicholas Bradwell asked, gesturing towards one that was still unoccupied. 'I shall sit with you and give up my seat when your mama comes.'

'If you wish, sir,' Helene said and glanced round, feeling uncomfortable. He had promised to introduce her, but now seemed bent on reserving her company to himself. She did not mind it for he was not unattractive and she felt at home with him. He reminded her of her uncle's friends, gentlemen who had treated her kindly in the past. 'Though if older ladies are standing, I should perhaps give up my seat.'

'I dare say some of the gentlemen will repair to the card room when the music begins,' Nicholas Bradwell told her with a smile. 'I myself came for the music. We have a fine tenor to entertain us this evening. He is Italian, you know, and I think his voice one of the best I have heard. However, many of the younger gentlemen will no doubt find their way to the tables before long. Some of them have no ear.'

'Oh…' Helene was not sure what to say. Her cheeks had heated slightly because she had noticed two gentlemen enter the salon together—and one of them was Lord Coleridge. 'I thought everyone would wish to hear

Signor Manzini…' She drew her breath in as she saw that Lord Coleridge was walking towards them. She looked down at her lap, her hands clasped as he bowed before them.

'Miss Henderson, I am delighted to see you this evening. Bradwell—good to see you here, sir. I heard that you had been unwell.'

Helene sensed the tension in the gentleman beside her. She had a feeling that he resented the interruption and risked a glance at him. A tiny pulse was beating at his temple.

'It was a mere chill,' Nicholas Bradwell replied. 'I may call on you in a day or so to settle the little matter between us.'

'Whenever you wish, there is no need for haste, sir,' Max said and smiled at Helene. 'I hope you suffered no ill effects of your experience the other day, Miss Henderson. I have to tell you that Jemmy is doing very well with his charge, though we have not as yet found Jezra a new home.'

'Jezra?' Helene's gaze flew to his face. She saw the laughter lurking in his eyes. 'You have given that poor creature a name? Do you expect him to recover? I know that you were uncertain of it.'

'I believe Jezra is tougher than we all imagined,' Max told her. 'He is gaining weight and I am reliably informed that with the proper treatment his appearance will improve—though whether my credit will survive his arrival I do not know.'

'Yes, I did hear that you had a donkey in your stable,' Nicholas Bradwell said, a smirk on his lips. 'Not quite in your style, Coleridge?'

'Oh, the creature grows on one, you know,' Max replied carelessly. 'I dare say it might do to pull the children of my head groom in a cart, in the country, you know—once it has recovered its strength, of course.'

'A children's pet,' Helene nodded, her expression thoughtful. 'It is the very thing, sir. You are good to consider it.'

'It was a matter of finding somewhere for Jezra to go before he quite destroys my reputation,' Max replied in a casual manner. 'Jemmy told me that he considered leaving me for Lord Carrington's employ, but he considers that I am fractionally the better whip and has decided to give me another chance. So I must count myself fortunate…'

'That tiger of yours is a deal too free in his manners,' Nicholas Bradwell said sourly. 'If a stable lad spoke to me in that way, I should instantly dismiss him.'

'Should you, Bradwell?' Max arched his brow. He was very much the aristocrat in that moment, almost arrogant, his expression unreadable. 'I must advise him not to offer his services to you should he decide that I am beneath his touch, which he may yet do. I confess that I should be devastated should he take himself off.'

'You are a wit, sir.' Bradwell glared at him. 'Forgive me if I do not see merit in such levity.' He glanced at Helene, his mouth pulled into a grim smile. 'You must excuse me for a moment, Miss Henderson. I have seen someone I must speak to.'

'Oh, dear…' Max glanced after him, a glimmer of satisfaction in his eyes. 'I fear I have upset that gentleman. I am sorry to have lost you your admirer, Miss Henderson.'

'Do not be ridiculous, sir! I have only just met Mr Bradwell. I assure you that he is not my admirer.'

'But he will undoubtedly become so,' Max said and nodded. 'I believe you have made a conquest—the first of many, no doubt.'

'I doubt it very much, sir.' Helene shook her head at him. 'Please, make me no empty compliments, for I do not care for them. I know you were funning just now, but pray tell me why you called that creature Jezra?'

'Jemmy said he should be called Jezebel, for his temperament is uncertain to say the least—sly and devilish, my groom described him as. I explained that Jezebel was a female, and so we settled on Jezra. I hope the name meets with your approval?'

'My approval is not necessary, but I find it apt,' Helene said. His humour was infectious, though she did wish that he might be serious for a moment. 'Shall you truly send Jezra to the country? I thought you might give the beast to someone.'

'I could not be certain the poor beast would not be beaten and starved again,' Max told her. His eyes seemed to be warm and approving as they surveyed her. 'Having given Jezra a taste of what life can be like when there is a warm stable and food, I do not think it fair to abandon him. Besides, I think that would have earned me your disapproval, Miss Henderson.'

'I should have been sad had the creature gone to a cruel master, for I cannot abide cruelty,' Helene told him. 'But I have no right to approve or disapprove of what you do, sir.'

'Do you not?' Max looked thoughtful. 'Be that as it may, I would rather have your good opinion—' He broke off as her mother came up to them. 'I am remiss. I have not introduced Toby to you, Miss Henderson—Toby Sinclair, Miss Helene Henderson.' He smiled at the older lady as the two exchanged greetings. 'Ma'am, we met earlier when we arrived. Pray take your seat. Toby and I are on our way to the card room. Please excuse us.'

Mrs Henderson sat down as he walked away. She frowned at her daughter. 'I suppose Mr Bradwell introduced you. Lord Coleridge is a pleasant enough gentleman, but above our touch, Helene. I heard that he may be looking for a wife, but I dare say he will look higher. Someone said that he has been paying attention to Miss Fitzherbert. She is an heiress of some note, though not present this evening. I would not advise you to think of that gentleman as a husband, Helene. Remember my experiences. I should not wish you to be slighted by his family as I was by your papa's.'

'Mama! I was not setting my cap at him,' Helene said and blushed. 'We were merely talking. Besides, you know that I would never forget the way you were treated.'

'You seemed almost on intimate terms with him,' her mother remarked. 'I have seldom seen you look so animated in company, Helene. I dare say he would be a good catch if you could get him, but I think we must set our sights lower, my love. Mr Bradwell is of far less consequence, but I believe him to be quite warm—not an old name and fortune like Coleridge, of course. Mr Bradwell was once married, I am told, but his wife unfortunately died of a fever without giving him an heir. I feel certain that he must be looking to settle his nursery, for he is past forty. He would be a good match for you, my love.'

'Mama, please do not,' Helene begged, her cheeks hot with embarrassment. 'Supposing someone were to hear? I am very certain Mr Bradwell has no such notion, at least as far as I am concerned.'

'Well, he seemed taken,' her mother said. 'Not that there is any hurry, for this is your first evening affair… and now we should be silent for the music is about to begin.'

Helene was tempted to remind her that she had done most of the talking, but she was too well bred to argue in public. Nor would she have said much had they been at home. It was clear to Helene that her mama was anxious for her to make a good match, and she felt that she must do her very best to oblige her. She did not dislike Mr Bradwell, though she had thought that his good manners had deserted him when he was addressing Lord Coleridge. Indeed, that gentleman had made him seem almost dull and boorish in comparison.

Helene held her sigh inside. She knew which gentleman she preferred, but it was clear her mother did not wish her to encourage Lord Coleridge. Nor ought she to think of it herself. Helene did not wish for the life of a society lady. Marriage was a necessity for a girl in her circumstances, but she hoped to share her life with a gentleman who had the good of others at heart. Perhaps a member of the clergy might suit her as well as any.

She hoped that she would in the next few weeks meet someone she could like well enough to marry who also met with her mama's approval.

'You will make a fine swordsman if you continue this way,' Max said and saluted Toby with his foil. 'Harry and I both learned as young men, but fighting on a battlefield is a different affair to fencing for sport.'

'Yes, it must be,' Toby agreed as they replaced their swords in the stand and walked to the changing room together. 'I should have liked to join Wellington when Boney escaped from Elba. I was still at Oxford, of course, but that was not the reason I did not offer my services. Mama begged me not to go, because of my father's health. She said that if anything happened to me it would be the end of him. I felt obliged to do as she asked.' He looked rueful and Max smiled. 'I have always felt that I ought not to have listened to her.'

'Sometimes it takes more strength of mind to give up the chance of adventure than to take it, Toby. Do not feel that you missed out. War is something best avoided if you can. If it had not been for Harry and Gerard, I should have died in Spain. Harry carried me for more than an hour on his back. We were all of us lucky to get out…' Max frowned. 'I joined Wellington in Brussels as his aide in the last action, but saw little of the fighting. I got shot at a few times while delivering Old Hooky's messages, but I seem to have the luck of the devil.'

'That's as well,' Toby said looking at him thoughtfully. 'You have never married, Coleridge. What would have happened to the title and your estate had you been killed?'

'I have a cousin. Robert Heronsdale.' A tiny pulse flickered at Max's temple. 'My father's sister's son. I suppose Robert would inherit through his mother if I were to die without issue, but I do not think it too late to render that unnecessary.'

'Has he ever been to town?' Toby asked. 'I do not recall the name.'

'No…' A strange expression flickered in Max's eyes. 'I invited him to stay with me on my return from Brussels, but he was unwell. I have been told that he suffers bouts of periodical sickness.'

'Unfortunate for the poor fellow,' Toby said and nodded. 'Mama worried that I might have inherited Father's weakness of the chest, but thus far I am hale and hearty.'

'Nothing to fear as far as you are concerned,' Max said and the strange look disappeared as he grinned. 'If you were my heir, I should not be concerned for the future, Toby. As it is, I believe I must seriously consider marriage.'

'As to that, there was some talk of your showing Miss Fitzherbert particular attention. I heard yesterday that she had accepted the Duke of Melbourn.'

'I did consider it when we met at a house party at Christmas,' Max replied. 'However, after further consideration I decided we should not suit. Poor Jane did not find my sense of humour amusing. Indeed, she did not always realise when I was funning. I fear that I do have a rather irreverent humour and she is not alone in disapproving of levity. Nor would she approve of certain other activities of mine, I fear.'

'Mr Bradwell was not amused by your humour last night,' Toby said and arched his right eyebrow. 'However, Miss Henderson seemed to approve of your actions over the donkey. I should have liked to see her when she pounced on that rogue, Max. From what you told me, she was very brave.'

'Yes, very,' Max confirmed. 'I should not have told you had you not been so taken with that wretched donkey, Toby. You must not tell anyone else of her part in the affair. I would not wish to damage her reputation. She seems to be taking well at the moment.'

'You need not have cautioned me,' Toby said. 'She sounds a good sort of person, Coleridge.' He threw Max a mocking look. 'Perhaps you should fix your interest with her before Bradwell does?'

'Damned young pup!' Max said and gave him a stare of mock severity. 'I shall admit to you privately that I like her. However, these things should not be rushed.'

'I'll wager that Bradwell will ask her before the week's out and be turned down,' Toby said and grinned wickedly. 'A hundred guineas she sends him away with a flea in his ear!'

'It is most improper of you to take that young lady's name in vain,' Max said, but his eyes gleamed. 'I'll take you—but if word of this wager gets out I shall skin you alive!'

'It is just between us,' Toby said. 'We must watch for the signs, Coleridge. They are both certain to be at the Marquis of Hindlesham's ball this evening.'

'Amelia was right about that colour,' Mrs Henderson said as Helene came downstairs wearing her new gown that evening. 'You look beautiful, my love.' Helene's hair had been dressed in a knot at the top of her head, and then allowed to fall to her shoulder in one elegant ringlet. Her hair was a dark, shining brown, her slightly olive-toned skin brought to life by the warmth of the deep peach silk. She was wearing a pendant of diamonds and pearls loaned to her by Amelia, and a matching pair of earrings. 'I think you need a bracelet, my love. Wear this, Helene. Your papa gave it to me as my wedding gift.' She handed Helene a small velvet pouch. Inside was a narrow bracelet of diamonds set in gold.

'Mama, your bracelet,' Helene said and hesitated. 'Are you sure you wish to lend it to me? It is so precious to you—and I should be distressed if I lost it. Did you not say that the catch was loose?'

'I have had the catch seen to,' Mrs Henderson said. 'Had your papa been a richer man, you might have had jewels of your own, Helene. I am sorry that I could not give them to you, but you may borrow my bracelet while we are in town.'

'Oh, thank you, Mama,' Helene said. 'Will you fasten it for me, please? I shall take very good care of it, I promise.'

Helene admired the bracelet on her wrist. The stones looked well against the pristine white of her long evening gloves, but she was still a little apprehensive of wearing it, because she knew that her mama treasured the lovely thing. She had been forced to sell some of her jewellery since Papa died, but the bracelet was too precious to part with unless the necessity became too pressing. Helene tested the clasp by giving it a gentle tug. It held and she felt relieved, because it seemed that the fastening was now secure.

Amelia and Emily joined them at that moment. Emily admired the bracelet, complimenting Helene on her appearance.

'That colour looks wonderful on you,' she said. 'So much better than the white Madame Dubois would have had you wear.'

'I suppose she was thinking that white is generally favoured by young ladies,' Mrs Henderson said.

'However, I think Amelia was quite right to advise against it. I believe the carriage awaits—shall we go?'

In the carriage, Helene was careful not to sit on Amelia's gown. It was quite a squash with four of them, but, by being considerate of each other, they managed to arrive with no damage to their gowns. A red carpet had been laid for the ladies to walk on, and there were linkboys everywhere with their torches and lanterns. Footmen were waiting to conduct the guests inside, and the ladies were greeted by smiling maids who took their evening cloaks. Directed by one of the footmen, they walked up a magnificent staircase to meet the Marquis and Marquise of Hindlesham.

The marquis was a large, portly man dressed in a dark puce coat, his wife a tiny woman, exquisitely lovely in a gown of sparkling silver. She must have been at least twenty years his junior and was now recovered from the birth of her first son. The grand ball was being given in celebration of her success in producing the heir; the magnificent diamonds around her throat were evidence of her husband's delight at her cleverness.

Amelia congratulated both the marquis and his wife and received a kiss on the cheek from the young mother, who was not much above Helene's own age. Helene curtsied and thanked her hostess for the invitation.

'You are very welcome, Miss Henderson,' the marquise replied and smiled. 'Amelia Royston is a friend—any guests she cares to bring are always welcome to me. Perhaps we may talk later.'

Helene inclined her head and moved on, because there was a line of guests waiting to greet and be greeted by their hosts. She had thought there were a lot of guests at the soirée the previous evening, but this was clearly a much grander occasion. There were two large reception rooms, which were overflowing with guests. Footmen circled with trays of champagne and many people were content to linger here. However, Amelia was moving steadily through the crush, Emily, Mrs Henderson and Helene following in her wake. Beyond the two crowded reception rooms was a large, long room, which was where the ball was to be held. Helene could hear music playing and already a few couples had taken to the floor.

She looked about her, entranced by the theme. Yards and yards of some pale pink gauzy material had been draped over the stage where the musicians were grouped. Banks of pink roses and carnations were at the foot of the stage, and arranged tastefully in alcoves to either side.

'Where on earth did they find so many roses?' Helene asked of no one in particular and heard a throaty chuckle just behind her. Turning, she found herself staring up at Lord Coleridge. 'My lord…' She dipped a curtsy. 'I was just admiring the flowers. There are such a profusion and it is a little early in the year, would you not agree?'

'I believe they are all forced in a hothouse,' Max told her, a gleam in his eyes. 'Have you remarked that they have little scent? For myself I prefer a natural rose…one that is allowed to blossom in its own good time. Ours at Coleridge House begin to flower from May onwards in the most sheltered spots, and there is one white bush that always gives us a rose at Christmas. When I was a child my father always plucked it for my mother on Christmas Day.'

'How lovely,' Helene said. She felt a flutter in her stomach as she gazed up into his dark, slate-grey eyes. There was something so very attractive about him! 'Tell me, do your roses smell wonderful?'

'Yes, particularly a dark red one that was my mother's favourite—and an old pink damask rose that no one knows anything about.'

'Someone must know something of it, surely?'

'No, it is true that no one can name it, and no one remembers it being planted. My mother was a great gardener until her health went and she died suddenly when I was young, but even she could not remember having it planted. My head gardener thinks it must have grown from a seedling—but we have no record of it. I have made inquiries, but even the experts cannot put a name to it.'

'How fascinating. If it is truly a new variety you must name it,' Helene said. 'I love gardens and gardening. I had my own at home, but my uncle's gardener does not wish for help.' She looked at him steadily. 'I am sorry that your mama died when you were young. I know what it is to lose a parent too soon.'

'Yes, your mama is a widow, I believe. We have something in common, Miss Henderson. In Mama's case, it was very sad because in his grief my father neglected her garden—and a garden gives much pleasure,' Max told her. 'I am sorry your uncle's gardener does not wish for your help, but I am sure you will have your own garden again one day.'

'Yes, perhaps I shall.'

'May I ask if you will dance this with me?' Max asked as they saw couples beginning to take the floor for a country dance. 'I hope you like to dance, Miss Henderson?'

'Yes—at least, I have not had much opportunity, though I have been given lessons.'

'I am sure you will enjoy the pastime now that you have the opportunity,' Max said and offered her his hand. 'Shall we, Miss Henderson?'

Helene gave him her hand, smiling up at him. The answering smile in his eyes made her feel instantly at home with him, and she found the steps came easily to her. He was a large man, but she was acutely aware how well he danced, seeming to have a light step and an elegant bearing that some of the other gentlemen did not quite possess.

It was for Helene an enchanted moment—it seemed only a moment before he was returning her to her friends.

'That was most enjoyable, Miss Henderson,' Max told her as he bowed. 'May I ask you to reserve the dance before supper, please?'

'Yes, certainly,' Helene said. Her heart did an odd little flip as he wrote his name, nodded his head and walked away. Her mama was looking at her, but before she could make a remark, another gentleman approached and asked her to dance. Since she had already met Mr Peters in Amelia's company, Helene was in the happy position of being able to accept. He wrote his name in one further space at the end of their dance.

'Miss Henderson, I hope you have reserved a dance for me?'

Helene turned her head as she heard a familiar voice. 'Good evening, Mr Bradwell. I have not reserved anything, for I did not know if you were here,' Helene said. 'But there are still several spaces.' She offered him her card and he wrote in two of them.

After that, several young men she had not previously met approached Helene and it was not long before every space on her card was filled. Helene found herself swept from one dance to the next, scarcely finding the time to draw breath. When the supper dance became due, her cheeks were flushed and her eyes shone with pleasure. She had not expected to be this popular at her first dance and felt pleasantly surprised.

'You are enjoying yourself this evening?' Max asked as he arrived to claim her for the supper dance. 'I believe this is a waltz, Miss Henderson. You do not object?'

'Not at all,' Helene said. 'Mama has given me permission to waltz and I have done so twice this evening.'

'I like it very well,' he said, placing his gloved hand at the small of her back. 'But I know some ladies find it very shocking to be held so. It was held to be fast when it was first introduced and I believe some still feel it so.'

His eyes held a gleam of humour as he gazed down at her. Helene wondered if he was trying to provoke her.

'Yes, I believe it was frowned upon at first,' she said. 'I understand that one cannot dance a waltz at Almack's unless one of the hostesses gives permission. Not that it can signify. I do not suppose that I shall be given vouchers.'

'Not be given vouchers?' Max looked at her quizzingly. 'Why should you not receive vouchers? You seem a respectable young lady to me.'

'Oh…I hope I am respectable,' Helene said and gurgled with laughter. 'But we are not important. Papa had no title and hardly any fortune. He was a gentleman, but if it were not for Miss Royston I dare say I should not have been invited here this evening. I am not certain I shall be approved by society, sir.'

'Nonsense! You have been seen, Miss Henderson. News of your beauty and good nature will spread. In the next few days you will be invited everywhere—and I am certain you will receive vouchers for Almack's. You have not lacked for partners this evening, I think?'

'No, not at all…' She wondered if she might have more to thank him for than she knew. Had he perhaps sent his friends to ask her to dance? 'But Almack's is rather different, I believe?'

'I assure you that you will receive your invitation, Miss Henderson. It is unthinkable that you should not.'

'Perhaps…' Helene held back a sigh. 'Mama is so grateful for this chance for me.'

'It would be a pity if someone of your nature were not to grace the drawing rooms of society more often,' Max said. 'However, I am certain that I am right. By tomorrow everyone will be wanting to know you.'

'You are kind,' Helene said and smiled up at him. 'I hope you are right—for Mama's sake as much as my own.'

He nodded and looked thoughtful, but said no more. Helene was glad that there was no need to talk, because she wanted to enjoy the wonderful sensation of being in his arms. She had thought him a good dancer earlier, but waltzing with him was divine. She wished that she might stay like this for the rest of the evening, but that would be most improper. Their dance ended all too soon.

Helene hoped that he might ask her to take supper with him, but he merely bowed to her and her mother, said that he would call soon and then walked away.

Watching him, Helene saw him speaking to some ladies that she did not know.

'I do not believe it would be a good thing for you to dance with Lord Coleridge too often,' Mrs Henderson said, coming up to her. 'He is a perfect gentleman, Helene, and well liked—but you must not set your heart on him. He mixes in circles that we shall scarcely enter, my dear.'

'I am very certain he would not do for me, Mama,' Helene replied primly, though a little voice at the back of her mind told her that she was not telling the whole truth. She did like Lord Coleridge more than she was prepared to admit, but of course it would not do at all.

As they moved towards the supper room, Emily and Amelia joined them; a sumptuous buffet had been laid out on long tables and waiters were circulating with trays of champagne. Laid out for their delectation were platters of cold meats, chicken, beef, ham, tiny pies and pastries containing both sweet and savoury fillings and a huge variety of relishes, cold peas and soft sweet plums in a syrup.

Helene took a small glass of syllabub and a spoon and followed Amelia and Emily to a table by the window. She glanced back at the buffet table, discovering that an attractive lady, to whom Helene had as yet not been introduced, had detained her mother. Mrs Henderson seemed to be nodding and smiling a great deal, and when she returned to the table she had a slightly dazed expression on her face.

'Well…' she said as she put a small plate on the table. 'You could have knocked me down with a feather. I have just been talking to Lady Jersey. She asked me to bring Helene to a picnic in Richmond she is planning for next Thursday—and she has promised to send us vouchers for Almack's for the whole of the Season. I was most surprised, for I did not expect it.'

'I am so glad,' Amelia said and smiled at Helene. 'I knew all my friends would invite us to their affairs, but vouchers for Almack's are not within my gift. I thought it might happen, but that was very swift, Marie. The picnic is an honour, because Sally Jersey does not invite every young lady she meets to her more intimate affairs.'

'Are you sure she promised us vouchers for Almack's, Mama?' Helene said. She bit her lip, because the lady her mama had spoken to at the buffet was one of those she had seen Lord Coleridge conversing with before they entered the supper room. She was almost certain that he had urged the lady to invite them to her picnic and to send them vouchers.

'Yes, quite certain,' Mrs Henderson said. 'She told me that she wished to meet you, Helene—and I am to take you to her after supper. She said that she hoped we would call and take tea with her when she is at home to visitors.

'I was quite overcome—I was certainly not expecting anything of the kind,' Mrs Henderson said. 'Is Lady Jersey a particular friend of yours, Amelia? She said that a particular friend had spoken to her about Helene.'

'I know Sally Jersey quite well,' Amelia replied. 'I am not certain she would call me a particular friend. I wonder…' She shook her head as Mrs Henderson looked at her. 'It was just a thought. I shall say nothing for the moment. It is not impossible that you were asked because you are staying with me. I have many good friends in society.'

'Yes, indeed you do,' Mrs Henderson agreed. 'Well,

Helene, we have been fortunate, my dear. If Lady Jersey should take a fancy to you, you will be welcomed everywhere.'

Helene did not answer. She felt uncomfortable, certain that she knew exactly who had brought about this tiny miracle. However, she did not think that it would be a good idea to mention her suspicion to her mama.

Chapter Three

Helene yawned and stretched as she woke to see the sun pouring in through the window. They had been out late again the previous evening, but she had asked her maid to wake her so that she would be dressed and ready to join the party driving to Richmond that morning. She threw back the covers and jumped out, feeling a thrill of pleasure. When they met at the Marquis of Hindlesham's ball, Lady Jersey had told her that she would send an escort for Helene and her mother, to bring them to the picnic.

Helene had not inquired further, but she had an odd, excited sensation in the pit of her stomach as she dressed. Two carriages were being sent to fetch them, because Amelia and Emily had also been invited.

Helene took her time choosing her gown for the day. In the end she decided on a striped green linen. It had a modest neckline with a white, scalloped lace collar, a wide band of white was caught up under her bust and a flounce at the bottom, the skirt slim but with sufficient play to allow her to climb into and out of carriages. She chose a pair of black leather half-boots, because there was bound to be a certain amount of walking and, since it had rained the day before, there might be wet grass and even mud in the park. Her white shoes would be ruined, but these sturdy boots would allow her to enjoy herself without worrying.

Helene was wearing a white stole and a bonnet that tied under her chin with green ribbons when she met the others downstairs. She saw that they had all chosen sensible footwear and smiled, because she was pleased to have made the right choice. When a knock sounded at the door and two gentlemen were admitted, Helene's heart leaped in her breast. She had guessed right, because Lord Coleridge and Mr Sinclair walked in, greeting the ladies with broad smiles.

'Lady Jersey has sent us to convey you to the picnic,' Max said. 'I am driving my curricle, but Mr Sinclair has his carriage and a splendid team of four.'

'Miss Royston, Mrs Henderson, would you do me the honour of driving with me?' Toby said. 'I see that Miss Henderson is wearing a bonnet that ties under the chin and will do well enough in an open vehicle. Miss Royston, that fetching hat will blow away for there is a slight breeze today. You will do better inside. Miss Barton, will you join us—and I believe you might prefer it, ma'am?' Toby smiled at Mrs Henderson.

'Yes, I believe I should.' Mrs Henderson glanced at her daughter. 'Helene, will you be all right in the curricle?'

'Yes, of course, Mama,' Helene said. She glanced at Emily. 'Your bonnet will not blow away—would you care to ride with Lord Coleridge?'

'Perhaps when we return,' Emily said. 'You go, Helene. I shall do very well in the carriage.'

'As you wish,' Helene said and looked at Lord Coleridge as he stood aside for her to go out of the front door.
'I prefer riding in an open carriage, sir. It is such a lovely
day, even if there is a breeze.'

'Oh, I think it slight,' Max said innocently and
avoided her honest gaze. 'But Toby wants to show off
his skill with his team. He has not long been a member
of the Four-in-Hand—did you remark his waistcoat?
He is wearing it in your honour today.' His mouth
quirked with irreverent humour. 'I must admit I have
one rather like it at home, but I do not wear it today.'

'It is a rather fine waistcoat,' Helene said, a little
amused; in truth, it had looked a little odd. 'I have
heard it said that you are also a member of that club—
you did not choose to drive your four today?'

'I thought a curricle would be nicer. Pray tell me you
are pleased with the idea, Miss Henderson—you would
not prefer that I had brought Jezra?'

'Sir! You are bamming me,' Helene said and shook
her head at him. 'You are a wicked tease. Are you never
serious? I do not think you would drive that wretched
creature in town.'

'I fear my credit would not survive it,' Max said
mournfully. 'I must tell you that Jezra has to date kicked
each and every member of my stable at least once. The
healthier the wretched creature becomes, the more
stubborn it grows. I have decided that it must be sent to
the country before my grooms desert me.'

'I am sure they would not dream of it,' Helene said
and laughed, for he was amusing. She glanced at
Jemmy, who was with the horses, steadying them. 'You
are a wicked jokester, sir. Has the donkey really been
such a trial to you?'

'He be the devil in disguise, miss,' Jemmy piped up from the back of the carriage, but subsided at a look from his master.

'I am in the fortunate position that I am the only one not to be kicked, perhaps because I take care to stand well back,' Max told her. 'I have heard of an orphanage just outside London. They are in need of a pet for the children, and the donkey would be well cared for. I can vouch for it that they are good people. Jezra may be asked to draw a small cart occasionally, but nothing too heavy. Would such a scheme win your approval?'

'An orphanage—oh, that is just the thing,' Helene said, her eyes bright as she turned to look at him. He gave her his hand, helping her into the curricle, and then swung up beside her. 'How did you come to hear of it? I know Amelia is connected with a home of some kind in London. I am hoping to visit one day. Perhaps I could visit the one you know of at some time in the future? Do you think it would be permitted?'

Jemmy made a sound, as though he intended to say something, but thought better of it. He jumped up at the back of the vehicle.

'Would you wish to?' Max asked as he gave his horses the order to walk on. 'The children are from the poorest of families. They are healthy enough these days, but boisterous. Like Jezra, the better they feel, the worse they behave. They would surround you and beg you to play with them, I fear.'

'I should like that, sir. I believe it becomes everyone who may do so to take an interest in others less fortunate than themselves. There are many ills in this world, not least the unfairness of inequality and poverty. It cannot be right that there should be such a divide between the richest and the poor,' Helene said heatedly and then blushed. 'But perhaps it would be a trouble to you to take me there? I should not have asked. I dare say you are a busy man.'

'It would be no trouble at all. I visit most weeks when I am in town,' Max told her. 'Do you think Mrs Henderson would permit it? Visiting an orphanage is not precisely the reason she brought you to town, I think.'

'No, perhaps not,' Helene said and her cheeks heated. He must think her pretentious to speak out on such a subject when she was here for the purpose of enjoying herself and in the hope of contracting a good marriage. 'I know we have engagements most days for the next week or so, but perhaps at a later date…'

'Yes, I think one day we might arrange it,' Max replied. 'When we know each other a little better, perhaps.'

Helene glanced down at her gloves. She was a little conscious that she had been too familiar and lapsed into silence. Obviously, he took some interest in the orphanage and might think it presumptuous of her to lecture him on the evils of society. It was some minutes before he spoke again, changing the subject.

'Have you visited Almack's yet, Miss Henderson?'

'Our first vouchers are for this Wednesday evening,' Helene replied, relieved that he had rescued her, for she had not known how to begin a conversation.

'Shall you go?'

'Yes, I am certain we shall,' Helene replied and looked down at her hands. 'I dare say you find the entertainment a little insipid. I have heard some gentlemen say it does not amuse them.'

'Indeed, some of my friends visit only when their sisters beg it of them,' Max said. 'I have seldom visited in the past, but Sally Jersey has been urging me to do so for an age. I believe I may oblige her this Season.'

'Oh…' Helene could not bring herself to glance at him. 'It will be pleasant if we should meet there, sir.'

She could not help but think that his words had a deeper meaning. Was he suggesting that he would visit Almack's this Season because she would be there? If so, it would be a special compliment. The thought made her feel warm inside.

No, she must not let herself be carried away! Mama had warned her that he would look much higher for his bride. To allow herself to dream of a future when he might begin to care for her would be foolish. Besides, the gap between them was too wide. Lord Coleridge was rich, titled and accustomed to spending his time amusing himself in society. She had always pictured herself as the wife of a deserving man, perhaps even a missionary who would carry her off to far lands where she would administer to the sick and dying.

The drive to Richmond was so pleasant! Helene thought that this picnic must be one of the most enjoyable events she had attended since she had come to town. The company was select, and she was made to feel very much a part of things. For a while Lady Jersey kept her at her side, talking to her and asking a great deal of questions about her life and her opinions on almost everything. However, after everyone had eaten, the company began to stroll about the park, though some of the older ladies made themselves comfortable in the shade of the trees.

'Would you like to walk, Miss Barton—Miss Henderson?' Toby asked. 'Or do you prefer to rest in the shade?'

'I should like to walk,' Emily said and Helene got to her feet at once. 'We shall join you, sir.'

'Thank you, sir. It is such a lovely day.'

Toby offered his arm to Emily. Lord Coleridge had come to join them. He offered his arm to Helene. Another lady, Miss Trevor, and her brother joined them and the six set off to walk about the park.

'This is a beautiful place,' Helene said, feeling that she needed to say something. 'I like to walk by the river—do you admire water, sir?'

'At home I have a lake, but no river, I am afraid,' Max replied. 'I am at this moment in the process of adding a little waterfall. I think there is nothing so pleasant on a warm day as the sound of water tumbling over rocks. Since we do not have a natural feature, I have decided to install one.'

'Oh, how lovely,' Helene cried. She was about to say that she would love to see it, but held the words back. They were much too forward and would sound as if she was angling for an invitation to his estate, which would be terrible. It was bad enough that she had asked him to take her to the orphanage earlier. 'I have never been to the sea—have you?'

'Yes, many times, and over it when I was with Wellington in Spain and France. My estate is not far from the sea, it is situated in Norfolk, but a few miles from the coast.'

'Oh, yes, of course. You must be fond of the sea,' Helene said. 'I think someone told me you were given a medal for your service in the last war?'

'A mere bauble,' Max said modestly. 'I rode dispatch missions, nothing more. I have also been to Brighton. You must know that the Regent has a house there and is in the process of refurbishing it. I believe it is something exotic and strange—or will be by the time he has finished it.'

'Oh, yes, someone was saying that it is a little odd,' Helene replied. 'Does it resemble an Eastern pavilion or some such thing?'

'Some such thing would probably describe it best,' Max said and chuckled. 'Perhaps your mama will take you to Brighton for some sea air when the Season is done. Many people will go down in June or July, you know.'

'I do not think it,' Helene said and turned away, for she could not confess that they could not afford such trips. Her eyes were for some reason drawn to a stand of trees. Something had caught her notice, a splash of colour amongst the trees. She did not know why it had taken her attention, but she continued to look at the trees and then she saw the man plainly. He was wearing a dark blue coat, a black hat pulled low over his face, hiding it. Something about him caused Helene to feel a sliver of ice at the nape of her neck. She watched as he brought his arm up, a gasp of surprise on her lips as she saw that he was holding a pistol, the sunlight glinting on the long barrel. It took her a few seconds longer to realise that the pistol and the man's intense gaze was pointed in their direction—not at her, but the man by her side. 'Sir!' she cried and gave Max an almighty push, sending him staggering sidewards. So startled was he that for a moment he fell to one knee, and the crack of a pistol was an instant later, the ball passing so close that Helene felt the whistle of it as it passed between them. 'Over there…' She pointed in the direction of the trees. The man in the blue coat had turned and was running away. 'I saw him. He was going to shoot you.'

'Good grief! She is right, Max,' Toby came to him hurriedly. 'I'm not carrying a weapon or I would go after him. Damn it! I never thought I should need it today, though my groom has one.' He glanced towards the carriages, but they were too far away. No one had even heard the shot. 'It would be no good—he'll be long gone before we could fetch it and follow.'

'No, let the fellow go,' Max said in a harsh voice. 'Thankfully, he missed. We could not risk a shooting match, there are ladies present.' He gave Toby a look deep with meaning. 'It would be too much of a risk.'

'Who would want to kill you?' Helene looked at him. Her heart was beating rather quickly and for a moment she had felt sick. 'Forgive me for pushing you, but it was the only thing I could think of.'

'You may have saved my life,' Max said. 'It was quick thinking, Miss Henderson, and brave. You might have been hit yourself.' He looked angry, his eyes glinting dangerously.

'I did not think it,' Helene said. 'The pistol was clearly aimed at you—and I do not think I am important enough for anyone to wish to kill me. You were most certainly his target.'

'I am sorry that it should have happened while you were present.'

'You must set up an inquiry,' Toby said. 'If someone is trying to kill you…' He frowned as something occurred to him. 'You don't think…that business last year with Northaven?'

'I have no idea,' Max said, as puzzled as he by the incident. 'I was not much concerned in that, you know. Besides, the ladies are anxious. We must return to the others and talk of this privately.'

'Yes, of course. My apologies, ladies,' Toby said. 'Max is right. Miss Henderson—you were very brave. Many young ladies would have screamed and fainted if such a thing had happened in their presence.'

'As I almost did,' Emily said and went to Helene. 'You did just as you ought, but I think we should return to the others—and it may be best to say nothing.' She looked at the other lady and gentleman, who had been a little behind and had just come up to them. 'Nothing happened here—are we agreed?'

'Yes, certainly. We do not wish to cause concern,' Miss Trevor said and her brother agreed. 'But should you not call a constable, Lord Coleridge? If a dangerous man is at large, something must be done. He might have killed you.'

'Rest assured that I shall put the matter into the appropriate hands,' Max said at once. 'I apologise for the interruption to your pleasure, ladies, but I think we must return to the carriages.'

There was a murmur of agreement from the others. They turned their steps towards where the remainder of the company was beginning to stir and look for their carriages.

'I am sorry that such a thing shoul happen on a pleasure outing,' Max said to Helene. 'I must thank you sincerely for what you did just now. That ball came too close for comfort. Had you not acted so swiftly, I might have suffered some harm.'

'It was instinctive,' Helene said. 'I assure you that I do not regard it.'

Max looked at her, a thoughtful expression in his eyes. However, he said nothing more to her. When they reached the rest of the party, he spoke to Toby in a low voice. Toby nodded, and the context of their conversation became clear when Toby suggested that all four ladies might like to go with him.

'Lord Coleridge has noticed that one of his horses has a shoe working loose,' he said. 'There is room in my carriage for all of you. Max begs your pardon, but he must take his horses to the blacksmith in the village, and asks you to excuse him.'

'Of course,' Amelia said. 'Come along, Helene, there is plenty of room—and Toby is an excellent whip.'

Helene glanced at Lord Coleridge, who was speaking to his tiger. He turned his head as if sensing her gaze and inclined his head. She nodded and then climbed into the carriage. Clearly, he did not feel the incident was closed. She thought that perhaps he was concerned that he might be attacked again, and was making certain that she was safely inside Toby's carriage.

Helene had been quiet as they were driven home. Amelia and Mrs Henderson had seemed to have enjoyed the day and talked a great deal about Lady Jersey and how delightful she was as a companion. Emily had also been quiet for much of the time, her thoughtful gaze on Helene.

Helene went straight upstairs to her room when they reached the house. Emily followed and knocked at the door a moment later. Helene opened it and invited her to enter.

'You were very quiet on the way home, dearest,' Emily said. 'Are you all right? It was such a shocking thing to happen. You were very brave and acted promptly at the time. Has it upset you now that you have had time to think of what might have happened?'

'I am not distressed for myself,' Helene assured her. 'I am concerned only for Lord Coleridge. I saw that man and the way he concentrated his aim—I am certain that it was his intention to kill Lord Coleridge. He made light of it for our sakes, but he must know that his life was in danger—mustn't he?'

'I am sure he is perfectly sensible of it,' Emily said. 'He wanted you to ride with us, because he feared another attempt might be made on the journey home, and he was concerned for your sake. I think he will take all possible precautions in future.'

'Yes…' Helene frowned. 'But what can he do really? If someone is determined to kill him, they will try over and over.' The thought that something might happen when no one was by to warn Lord Coleridge was intolerable. She felt so upset that it forced her to sit down before her legs gave way.

'Do not distress yourself, Helene,' Emily said. 'You can do nothing more. Indeed, you did more than could have been expected. You must try to put this unfortunate incident from your mind, dearest. After all, it does not truly concern you.'

'No…' Helene turned away, because she was not sure that she could control her emotions and she did not wish to burst into tears. Emily was right to remind her that Lord Coleridge was nothing to her—but the thought of his being killed by a wicked murderer was almost more than she could bear. However, she must endeavour to put it from her mind. She must not dwell on the incident, for it was not her concern. Lord Coleridge was not a fool and he would do all he could to protect himself. 'You are very right, Emily. It is not my affair.' She must not let anyone guess how much the incident had disturbed her, least of all Lord Coleridge himself.

'Who do you imagine it was?' Toby asked when they were in Max's library later that evening drinking a glass of wine. 'Do you have enemies—anyone you know of?' He frowned. 'You don't suppose it could be Northaven, do you? He hates you and Gerard almost as much as he hates Harry.'

'I know that the Marquis of Northaven carries little love for any of us,' Max said and frowned. 'However, I believe he is in the country at the moment. A friend of mine told me that Northaven has hopes of being left something by an elderly aunt. She summoned him a day or so ago and he left town immediately. I doubt he would return and lose his chance of a small fortune for the opportunity to take a pot shot at me. He has had plenty of chances in the past—why decide to murder me now?'

'If it is not him, it must be someone who bears you a grudge. Have you won too much at the card tables recently?'

'I have lost small sums on each of the last four occasions I played,' Max replied. 'Bradwell lost five thousand to me at the tables a month ago, but he settled yesterday. I think he was annoyed over the loss, but I believe him to be warm enough to stand it. He may dislike me, but I acquit him of wanting me dead. Indeed, most of the people I play with are my friends and gentlemen of honour. If they had a quarrel with me, they would be open with it. What happened today was the act of a coward…he might have killed Miss Henderson had his aim gone astray.'

'You are right. She was very cool,' Toby said admiringly. 'I have sometimes thought her quiet. She does not always say much in company—though she talked more today.'

'I find her an interesting companion,' Max said. 'You are right in saying she is sometimes quiet in company— but she speaks intelligently when you take the time to ask her opinion on any subject.'

Toby looked thoughtful. 'Have you no idea who might want you dead?'

'No…' Max got up and wandered to the window, looking out into the courtyard at the back of his town house. Some birds had come to drink at the fountain and were squabbling amongst themselves. 'At least…I may have an idea, though I cannot truly credit that he would wish me dead. If I had been killed today, he would have inherited almost everything, for I made a will in his favour when I was in the army.'

'Are you speaking of your cousin?' Toby was incredulous. He stared as Max turned and he saw the troubled look on his face. 'Heronsdale—the fellow who is unwell at times? Surely it cannot have been he? The rogue who shot at you made off so fast that he cannot have been an invalid.'

'No, it seems unlikely,' Max said. 'It would grieve me

if Robert were behind this…though it need not have been him, of course. He could have paid someone to be rid of me.'

'Surely not—your own cousin?' Toby looked shocked. 'I suppose…is he short of funds, do you suppose?'

'My aunt has been living in the dower house since her husband died. Heronsdale was deeply in debt and his estate had to be sold. I allowed them to live on my estate. I could hardly do anything else for she had little enough and Robert was…too poorly to earn a living.'

'I should have thought they would be grateful,' Toby said and frowned.

'Aunt Harriet is always grateful,' Max said. He frowned—he sometimes found her gratitude almost too much to bear. She was inclined to be too interested in his affairs. 'I have not seen Robert for two years. He has been confined to his room, too ill to allow visitors each time I am there.'

'Sounds as if he is trying to avoid you.' Toby looked thoughtful. 'It leaves a nasty taste in the mouth, Coleridge—but the finger of suspicion would seem to point at him.'

'Yes, I suppose it looks that way,' Max replied. 'It may have been a disappointment to my cousin when I returned from the war, hale and likely to live for another forty years.'

'At least that long,' Toby said. 'It beats me why he should expect or hope for what is yours. He can only inherit through his mother. I am not even sure if he is entitled to the title…'

'It would require some documentation, I dare say, though I do not think there is anything to stop the title passing to issue from the female line. Robert would have most of what is mine if I were to die before I have a son—unless I change my will. I am loath to do it without proof of his ill intent.'

'Perhaps you should think about marriage very seriously, Max.'

'I have considered taking a wife,' Max replied. 'I do not want to rush into marriage, because that could mean a lifetime of unhappiness for us both if I chose unwisely. However, I have it in mind—but for now I am uncertain if such a step would be wise. If it was Robert or his agent in the park, and he did intend to murder me for the estate—would he stop there?'

'You mean it might put the lady you marry in danger—and your child when you have one.'

'It is possible,' Max said and frowned. 'Another thing, can we be sure that I was the intended victim this afternoon? If I was, which I believe—is it too risky for me to entertain the idea of marriage?'

'Whoever he may be, you cannot allow this rogue to order your life, Max,' Toby said. 'You would be constantly looking over your shoulder. Could you not pay your cousin a surprise visit? See if you can shock him into confessing?'

'I may have to do just that,' Max agreed. 'However, if I went down immediately, I think it might alert whoever shot at me that I have my suspicions. Besides, I have business in town. I think for the moment I shall carry on as if nothing had happened, though I shall take certain measures…'

'Yes, I see what you mean,' Toby said and nodded. 'If you need anything, you know you have only to ask. I should be happy to be of service.'

'For the moment, I would ask only that you are alert for anything that strikes you as unusual,' Max said and smiled oddly. 'I had a letter from Gerard this morning. He intends to be in London quite soon. I would not take Harry from his wife at this time, but it will be good to have both you and Gerard close by if I should need you.'

Helene looked about her eagerly as they entered the hallowed halls of Almack's, that most prestigious of clubs, the following evening. Lord Coleridge had hinted that he would be here and she was eager to see him. Thoughts of him and the rogue who had tried to shoot him had occupied her mind since the picnic. She hoped to have a chance to talk to him that evening, to ask if he had discovered anything. However, after some twenty minutes, she knew that he was not present, and she could not help feeling a deep disappointment. It was almost as if he had broken a promise to be there, for he had certainly made a point of asking if she intended to visit Almack's. Perhaps she was letting herself expect too much, as her mama had warned.

'Miss Henderson.' A gentleman's voice made Helene turn. Mr Bradwell was bowing to her. 'Lady Harris has been good enough to say that she will recommend me to you.'

'You may waltz with Mr Bradwell,' Lady Harris said, smiling on her as she gave gracious permission. 'Sally told me that you are a very well-behaved young gel.' She inclined her head and walked away, leaving Helene with no option but to accept.

'How kind of you, sir,' Helene said and offered him her hand. 'I am much obliged.'

'I am honoured, Miss Henderson,' he replied and took her hand, leading her to the dance floor.

Mr Bradwell was a good dancer. Helene could not complain of anything as he swept her into the dance, whirling her back and forth in time to the music. However, being held in his arms did not make her feel as she had when dancing with Lord Coleridge. She barely held back a sigh as she felt her keen disappointment at his absence. She had been so sure he meant to come!

When the dance was over, Mr Bradwell returned her to her mother's side. Helene saw that Amelia was talking to Toby Sinclair and walked to join them.

'Miss Henderson,' Toby said and smiled at her. 'You look beautiful as always. Will you give me the pleasure of this dance?'

'Thank you, sir,' Helene said and gave him her hand. 'I was wondering…Lord Coleridge did not accompany you?'

'No…' Toby frowned. 'I think he had a pressing engagement elsewhere, someone he needed to see. He may come later.'

'Oh…' Helene did her best to hide her disappointment. 'He is well, I trust—nothing untoward has happened?'

'No, nothing at all,' Toby assured her, but looked slightly uncomfortable as if he would have wished to say more. 'I dare say he will be sorry to have missed you this evening, though of course he may yet turn up.'

'Yes—' Helene smiled '—perhaps an affair of this kind is not much in his line.'

'I dare say,' Toby agreed. 'I only popped in to see how you went on, Miss Henderson. I shall not stay long.'

'Oh, but you must dance with Emily,' Helene said, because she knew that Emily rather liked him. 'Surely you will?'

'Miss Barton…' Toby glanced across the room and nodded. 'Yes, certainly I shall ask her, though she does not always dance.'

'I think she might if you asked,' Helene said as the music ended. 'Come with me and ask her now.'

Toby glanced at her. 'What are you up to, Miss Henderson?'

'Nothing at all,' she said artlessly. 'It is merely that Emily has not yet danced this evening.'

Toby made no reply. However, he asked Emily for the next dance and was accepted. Helene's card was not yet full and she wandered over to the open window, standing by it to catch a little air. She had not been there more than a moment when Nicholas Bradwell came up to her.

'You are not dancing, Miss Henderson?'

'I just felt a little warm,' Helene told him. 'It is cooler here by the window.'

'It is a beautiful night. Perhaps you would care for a stroll outside?'

'I believe not,' Helene said with a smile to soften her refusal. 'I think Mama needs me.'

'Forgive me, I did not mean to be too forward. You would be quite safe with me, Miss Henderson. I admire you. Everyone speaks of your quiet manners and your dignity. I believe you must be the kind of young lady that would make any gentleman a worthy wife.'

'Please, do not say such things,' Helene said swiftly. 'It is much too soon. We hardly know each other. Excuse me, I must return to my mother.'

She left him quickly, her cheeks on fire. She was certain that he had been on the verge of proposing to her. Had she given him any encouragement, he must have done so after such a statement! Her heart was racing and she felt her stomach clench. To come so close to an embarrassing proposal on such slight acquaintance was a shock for her. She had hardly known how to cope with it and was afraid she might have offended him. It was much too soon to be thinking of marrying anyone!

Helene was relieved when her next partner claimed her. She made an effort to forget the embarrassing incident, deciding that she would stay close to her mother or Emily for the remainder of the evening.

The hour was late and Helene's mother was saying that they should leave soon when Lord Coleridge walked into the room. Helene's heart leapt in her breast, for he smiled and walked to meet her immediately.

'I believe there is one more waltz,' he said as he bowed his head to her. 'May I hope that you will forgive me for my tardy arrival and grant me the favour?'

'It should be Mr Sinclair's,' Helene said hesitantly.

'Toby will not mind,' Max said and held out his hand. Helene gave him hers, her pulses racing as they joined the last few couples on the floor. She trembled as he drew her close, his gloved hand at the small of her back. 'You look lovely, as always, Miss Henderson.'

'Thank you,' Helene said and smiled shyly up at him. Could he hear the frantic beating of her heart? Had he any idea how much pleasure it gave her to dance with him like this? Oh, it was so foolish of her to feel so happy just because he had come after all! 'I thought you were not coming this evening.'

'I had as good as given my word,' Max said. 'I was detained on a matter of importance, which I regret, for I fully intended to dance with you more than once this evening.'

'I should have enjoyed that.' Helene's cheeks were a little pink and she could not bring herself to look up at him. Her heart was beating so fast that she thought he must be able to hear it.

'I was wondering if you would like to take a drive out with me the day after tomorrow,' Max said. 'Since it is a fair distance, I thought perhaps Miss Barton might accompany us. I have business at the children's home I told you of, Miss Henderson. I thought perhaps it would please you to see Jezra settled in his new home?'

'Yes, I should enjoy such an outing on several accounts.' Helene laughed softly. 'I am sure Emily will agree. We have an evening engagement that day, but nothing for the morning.'

'Then I shall call for you both at nine-thirty in the morning—unless that is too early?'

'No, not at all. I rise early and Emily has the same habit. We are often on our way to the lending library or the shops by that time.'

'I shall look forward to it,' Max said, giving her a look of approval. 'I have engagements most of tomorrow, but I believe we may meet at Mrs Andersen's card party in the evening?'

'Yes, I am sure we had a card for that, though we may also have one for something else,' Helene said. 'I shall hope to see you, sir—if not, we shall have our drive to look forward to.'

'Yes, we shall,' Max said. He gazed down into her eyes as the music came to an end. 'I am afraid that is the end of our dance—and of the evening. I must say good night, Miss Henderson.'

'Yes…good night, Lord Coleridge,' Helene said. 'Thank you for coming this evening.'

'The pleasure was all mine,' Max told her. He lifted her hand to his lips, kissing the back briefly. 'Now I must return you to your mama, for I see that she is anxious to leave.'

Helene looked at her mother. Mrs Henderson's expression was hard to read, for she was frowning. Surely she could not be displeased because Helene had danced the last waltz with Lord Coleridge?

Max bowed his head to Helene's mama. 'Forgive me for keeping your daughter, ma'am. I was detained and was unable to come earlier, but I could not resist one dance with her.'

'Amelia has the headache,' Mrs Henderson said in a sharp tone. 'She and Emily left some minutes ago. I told her we would take a hackney and that she was not to send the coachman back for us.'

'It will be my pleasure to take you home,' Max offered at once. 'My groom is waiting downstairs. By the time you have your cloaks, my carriage will be at your disposal.'

'You should not trouble yourself, my lord,' Mrs Henderson said, but he shook his head.

'I assure you, it is no trouble at all. It will give me the pleasure of your company for a little longer.'

'You are very kind, sir,' Mrs Henderson said, but her manner was stiff and Helene sensed that she was displeased.

She looked at her mama as they went to fetch their cloaks. 'Is something the matter, Mama? You do not dislike Lord Coleridge?'

'I am sure he is quite respectable and there is nothing to dislike in his manner or his person,' Mrs Henderson replied. 'But I think you should be careful, my love. I do not wish to see you hurt.'

'Why?' Helene asked, her throat tight with suppressed emotion. 'Has he done something that makes you disapprove of him.'

'Of course not.' Mrs Henderson frowned at her. 'You cannot have forgotten what happened to me, Helene? I know that you have been well received in society, but marriage to an aristocrat is another matter. You cannot imagine that Lord Coleridge's family would accept you?'

'I am not ashamed of Grandfather,' Helene said, a militant sparkle in her eyes. 'You have told me that he was a decent man and I will not allow the fact that he owned a tannery to be a disadvantage. An honest hardworking man is the equal of any in the land.'

'You may think so, Helene. There are others in society who would not feel the same. I have not made a secret of my parentage. My mother was the daughter of a younger son and brought up as a lady, but my father had no education to speak of and was looked down on by Mama's family. You know that your papa's family shunned me. When he died I was left to struggle alone. Had my brother not taken us in, we might have ended in the workhouse.'

'Papa's family were unkind and ungenerous,' Helene told her. 'If I ever had the chance I should like to tell Papa's father what I think of him—but you should not concern yourself, Mama. I dare say Lord Coleridge will not even think of asking me to marry him. If he did, I should naturally tell him the truth.'

'Oh, Helene, be careful,' her mother warned. 'I shall not forbid you to think of him. If he should ask, you must of course tell him the truth—but be prepared for his disapproval. He comes from a proud family and may well feel that he could not marry a girl of your background.'

Helene said no more on the subject.

Later, as she lay drifting into sleep, it occurred to her that her background might be a disadvantage if she wished to marry a man of Lord Coleridge's standing. She had always thought that she did not wish for such a marriage; the image she'd carried of a worthy man who would be grateful to have her at his side as his helpmeet was still strong, but of late she had begun to think too much of a handsome gentleman with laughing eyes.

Helene did not think that she would wish to spend all her life going from one entertainment to another. She loved to dance and was enjoying her visit to London very much, but life should be about more than enjoying oneself surely?

It was all very perplexing, for she owed it to her mother to marry well. Mama was unhappy living in her brother's home. If Helene were fortunate enough to secure a man of some means, he would naturally provide for Mama. Yet the idea of marrying Mr Bradwell or some of her other acquaintance was not a pleasing one. Only one man made her heart leap when they met.

She tossed restlessly on her pillow. It was all so foolish! She was almost sure that Lord Coleridge was not in the least interested in making her an offer, so why should she lose sleep over the idea?

Chapter Four

'I was sorry you felt unwell last evening,' Helene said the next morning. She had visited Amelia in her bed-chamber, finding her sitting up in bed wearing a very pretty lace peignoir. 'Are you feeling better this morning?'

'Yes, much better,' Amelia told her. 'I do not know why I should have had a headache last evening. I do not often suffer from them.' A little sigh escaped her. 'I shall get up later. I thought we might go visiting this afternoon. We should pay a few calls—if you have nothing better to do?'

'I have promised to fetch a book from the library for Mama this morning,' Helene replied. 'I should be happy to run any errands you have, Amelia—and I should like to go visiting with you this afternoon. Emily and I have been invited to drive out with Lord Coleridge tomorrow. Did you know that he is one of the patrons of a children's home? At least, he has not actually said so, but I think he must be for he takes a great interest in the children.'

'Yes, I did know. He set it up himself, but I know he does not speak of his good works in company,' Amelia said and smiled. 'We have sat together on various com-mittees on occasion and I know he takes an interest in the plight of unfortunate children.'

'Emily told me about the home you funded,' Helene said. 'I should like to visit that one day, if I may?'

'Of course, if you wish it—though this was supposed to be a pleasure visit, Helene. Are you sure that you wish to concern yourself with such things? Some of the children are quite well now that they have enough to eat—but some of them will never recover from their unfortunate beginnings. It can be heartrend-ing to see them, especially those crippled by poor diet and disease.'

'That is sad and all the more reason to help if one can. I should always be willing to help in any way you think I might, Amelia.'

'Well, there is nothing for the moment, though I am planning a charity ball at the end of the Season. Perhaps you would like to help Emily write out the invitations? I have a shocking hand. Emily does it well, but there will be a great many to do, for we must invite everyone. There is no charge, of course, but many of the guests will make generous donations to the cause. I find that even those who do not concern themselves with these things are willing to give a few guineas if one asks.'

'Yes, of course I shall help,' Helene agreed at once, though she had hoped she might be given something more taxing. 'Is there anything I may do for you today?'

'Nothing, thank you,' Amelia told her. 'I shall see you at nuncheon, dearest.'

Helene nodded and went downstairs. Emily was waiting for her and they went out together, pleased to find that it was yet another warm day. They were very comfortable in each other's company and talked all the way to the library, laughing and enjoying the outing. It was when they stopped to look in the window of a fashionable milliner that Helene became aware that someone was standing a few feet away, staring at them. She turned her head to look at the gentleman. He was dressed in a style that had been fashionable some years previously, though his clothes were of the best quality. He was a man of perhaps seventy years. When he doffed his hat to her, Helene saw that his hair was snowy white.

As he turned and walked across the road to where a rather old-fashioned carriage was waiting, Helene touched Emily's arm. 'Do you know that gentleman? He was staring at us just now.'

Emily turned her head to look. She frowned and then shook her head. 'No, I do not think so. I believe I have seen that crest before… I think he must be the Duke of Annesdale, but I cannot be certain. I wonder why he was looking at us?'

'It was a little odd. He doffed his hat to me when he realised that I had noticed him. I am sure I have never seen him in company.'

'If it was Annesdale, it is unlikely you would have seen him in company. I believe he belongs to the court set, and was once an adviser to his Majesty—but he seldom comes to London these days. He is said to be a recluse, especially since his eldest son died without child. He has no heir…' Emily frowned as she looked at a bonnet in the milliner's window. 'Do you see the way that bonnet is trimmed, Helene? I think I may buy some ribbons for my straw and trim it in just that way.'

Helene looked at the bonnet. 'Yes, it is very pretty. I like the pink ribbons, but you could use almost any colour.'

'I was thinking of blue, to match my best pelisse,' Emily said. 'If you do not mind, I should like to call at the haberdasher on the way home.'

'Of course not,' Helene agreed immediately. 'I think I may buy some green ribbons. It is so easy to change the style of a bonnet with a new ribbon.'

They walked on in perfect harmony, the slight incident forgotten. However, when she was changing for the afternoon, Helene thought about the gentleman she had seen watching them earlier. Was he really the Duke of Annesdale—and why had he been so interested in two young ladies looking at bonnets?

The afternoon was spent calling on ladies of their acquaintance. Some were at home and they went in to take refreshment and gossip about inconsequential things. They did not spend more than twenty minutes anywhere, and at two houses they merely left their cards. It was past five when they returned home to find a small pile of visiting cards on the salver in the hall.

Amelia flicked through them. 'This note is for you, Helene. Marie, my dear—there is a letter for you. Nothing for you, Emily. The rest are simply calling cards. Mr Sinclair called and says he hopes to see us this evening.'

'I was not expecting anything,' Emily said, and for a moment her eyes were bleak, but in another moment she was smiling. 'If you will excuse me, I shall go up now for I have a bonnet I wish to trim—unless you need me, Amelia?'

'No, there is nothing I need for the moment,' Amelia

told her. 'I have drunk far too much tea, so I think I shall go to my room and rest for a while before I change.'

'I shall do the same,' Mrs Henderson said.

'May I come with you?' Helene said to Emily. 'I should like to see how you intend to trim your bonnet.'

'Of course,' Emily said. 'But do you not wish to read your note?'

'It is from Miss Marshall,' Helene said. 'She said that she would be inviting me to a picnic soon. I dare say it may be that.'

'Then it will keep until later,' Emily said. 'Why do you not fetch your own bonnet and we may see what we can contrive between us?'

It was more than two hours later, as Helene was dressing for the evening that someone knocked at her bedroom door. It opened almost at once and Mrs Henderson came in. She was looking anxious, a little flustered, as she told the maid to leave them and return in ten minutes.

'Is something wrong, Mama?' Helene looked at her. 'Your letter was not bad news?'

'My letter…' Mrs Henderson frowned. 'It was of no account. Someone I have not seen for many years asked if I would be at home tomorrow. He wishes to call on me. I was wondering—did you tell me that you and Emily would be out most of tomorrow?'

'Yes, Mama. Lord Coleridge is taking us to visit his orphanage.'

'Ah, yes, I thought it was something of the sort.' An expression of relief entered her eyes. 'What was your own letter, Helene? Anything I should know about?'

'It was from Miss Marshall. She has invited me to a picnic next week.'

'Her brother is Captain Paul Marshall, is he not?' Mrs Henderson's expression was thoughtful. 'I thought him a rather pleasant young man when we met the other evening. The family is not wealthy, but I believe he has expectations from his grandfather. It would not be a grand match, but all the better for that I think.'

'Mama! It is an invitation to a picnic. Nothing more.'

'I was making an observation,' Mrs Henderson said. 'There is time enough yet for you to meet someone you like, Helene. However, I beg you not to waste your opportunities. Once this visit is over you will have precious little—unless one of your uncle's friends should offer for you. Edgar told me that Colonel Blake rather liked you but I wanted something better than a man twice your age with a brood of children.'

'I would not marry the colonel if he asked.'

'No, I did not think you would—but you must marry someone.' Her mama sighed. 'I do not wish to seem hasty, Helene, but you know our position. I cannot afford to support a home of our own and I am not sure how long we can impose on Edgar's good nature. He made it plain to me before we left his house that he expected you to be settled before we returned.'

'I do know that I have a duty to marry respectably, Mama,' Helene said softly. 'I hope that the right person will offer for me, but as yet no one has made me an offer. We have been in town not quite two weeks, Mama.'

'I know. As I said, I do not wish to push you into anything—but think carefully if you should receive an offer. I speak only for your good, my love. I do not wish you to be in my position.'

'I promise you that if I receive an offer I feel to be acceptable, I shall not refuse it, Mama,' Helene said, her cheeks hot. 'Who is the gentleman who wishes to call on you?'

'His name is not important, for I do not wish to receive him,' Mrs Henderson replied. 'Well, I have kept you long enough. I have decided that I shall rest this evening and read the book you fetched for me. You will be well enough with Amelia and Emily.'

'Are you unwell, Mama?'

'I am quite well, my love. I simply feel that I would prefer to stay at home this evening. You may ring for your maid. I shall leave you to finish dressing.'

Helene frowned as her mother went out, closing the door behind her. She was certain that something had upset her. She seemed on edge, uneasy—and she was clearly anxious for Helene to find a suitable husband. Was it only because she did not wish to return to her brother's house or was there something she wasn't telling Helene?

She had a feeling that her mother had lied to her about the letter she'd received that day. She did not know why she should lie, but something made her a little uneasy as she went down to join the others that evening. What was Mama hiding from her—and why?

Helene was pleased to see that Lord Coleridge was present when they arrived at the card party. They were a little late—they had also attended a soirée first and therefore arrived just as supper was being served. It was quite usual for guests to arrive later in the evening, because there were so many events in the social calendar that it was sometimes only possible to spend a part of the evening with one set of friends before moving on to another.

'I had begun to think that you were not coming,' Max said as he joined Helene at the buffet table. 'I should have been sorry to miss you, though since I was promised to Lady Sarah Annersley and Mr Hardwick for the first part of the evening, I could not have spent much time with you. Do you intend to stay long enough for a hand of cards? If so, you may make up a four with Sinclair and Miss Trevor and myself later.'

'I believe Amelia intends to stay until eleven, so if that is time enough…'

'Ample. We are not serious gamblers. We play for pin money and amusement only.'

'Then I shall be delighted to join you, sir.'

'Do you think you could bear to call me Coleridge? At least in private.'

'Yes, if you wish it,' Helene said and blushed. 'My name is Helene, as you well know.'

'Very well, Helene.' Max grinned at her. 'When we are alone like this I shall call you by your name. You have not changed your mind about tomorrow?'

'No, indeed!' Helene said. 'I am looking forward to it very much. I think it will be most instructive, for I take a great interest in these things.'

'It will be a pleasant drive, I believe, for I think the weather is set fair for the time being.'

Helene found herself a part of a group of Lord Coleridge's friends as she ate a delicious supper. Soon afterwards, they moved back to the card room and she was soon engrossed in a light-hearted game of whisk. With Toby Sinclair as her partner, Helene pitted her wits against Max and Miss Trevor. Lord Coleridge took the first hand, but Helene trumped the second and third. The fourth was hard fought, but eventually went to Toby.

They all laughed and declared that they would call it quits for the evening. 'I have seldom enjoyed a game more,' Miss Trevor said as they rose from the table. 'It is almost a pity to leave, but I have a busy day tomorrow.'

'Yes,' Helene agreed. 'So do Emily and I, so it is time we went home.'

She said good night to Toby and then turned to Lord Coleridge, offering her hand. 'I look forward to seeing you tomorrow, sir.'

'Sweet dreams,' he replied and surprised her by lifting her hand to kiss it. 'I shall be prompt in the morning.'

Helene smiled and withdrew her hand, her pulses racing wildly. It was not the first time he had kissed her hand, but something had been different this time—or perhaps she had imagined it.

Helene slept well that night, but her maid had instructions to wake her early and she was dressed in a green carriage gown by the appointed time. Emily came downstairs a few seconds after Helene. She was wearing a dark blue pelisse over a pale grey gown, her bonnet trimmed in the new way with matching blue ribbons. Helene thought that she had seldom seen her look more attractive. They hardly had time to exchange a greeting before the doorknocker sounded and it was opened to admit both Lord Coleridge and Toby Sinclair.

'Nothing would do but that Toby should come, too,'

Max told them, mischief lurking in his eyes. 'He has his curricle. I hope that you will agree to drive with him, Miss Barton?'

'Yes, of course,' Emily agreed easily, a faint colour in her cheeks. 'It is such a beautiful day that we shall do much better with an open carriage.'

'We thought so,' Max agreed. His gaze turned on Helene. 'Miss Henderson—shall we?'

'Yes, thank you,' Helene replied, her heart fluttering as she saw his intent look. She followed him outside to where the horses and carriages were waiting, held by their grooms. Max offered his hand, helping Helene into the curricle. He climbed in beside her and Jemmy scrambled up at the back as Max gave the order to move off.

Helene looked about her as they drove through the town, leaving the better houses behind as they passed through meaner streets. Here the gutters were choked with filth and the stench was often unpleasant. It was early yet and the streets were still fairly empty. A milkmaid carried her yoke, crying out her wares. Servants came out of the houses with jugs or cans to buy from her. A fish coster was pushing his barrow over cobblestones, the rattle of wheels adding to the general noise of the city as it began to wake, but as yet there were few ladies or gentlemen taking the air.

After a while they began to leave the noise and bustle of the town behind. Grimy streets and mean houses were replaced by fields and trees. Helene saw horses and cows grazing, even a few late lambs in one field. She had a sudden nostalgic feeling for home. Not the house they lived in with her uncle these days, but the small country house they had rented while her father was alive.

Max shot a glance at her when she had been silent for some minutes. 'You look pensive, Helene—anything you wish to share?'

'I was thinking of my childhood in the country,' Helene told him. 'My father would take me to see the new lambs every year. Those we passed were late, I think?'

'Yes, perhaps. We had a cold spring.' Max turned back to the road. 'Do you enjoy living in the country? I know some ladies who would never set foot there if they had their way and prefer to be in Bath or London.'

'I do not think I should care to live always in town,' Helene replied. 'I love to dance and I enjoy the theatre. A visit to town must always be pleasant, but there is nothing so refreshing as a long walk in the country with dogs or a companion. Besides, I do not think I should care to be always at some society affair. Life should be about more than simply going from one engagement to another—do you not think so?'

'You censure society for being too thoughtless—too selfish and uncaring of others?'

'Not exactly. I see no reason why people should not enjoy themselves, but some part of life should be dedicated to more serious pursuits, do you not agree?'

'I do not see that it follows that you must be serious to lead a good life. Indeed, if one were to think only of the serious side of life, it would be very dull indeed. I fear I should find it intolerable—I must laugh at what I see or I might cry.'

'The poor have no choice. They have nothing to look forward to and nothing to sustain their spirits.'

'Yet, I think the poor are often happy with their lot.'

'No! How can they be when they do not know how

to find enough money to put food in the mouths of their children?'

'To be in that situation is hard indeed, but there are degrees of poverty and most working folk find something to bring pleasure into their lives, even if it is merely a chance to dance at harvest time.'

'Yes, that is true, but I was thinking more of those who have nothing—no home or work—the unfortunates who are forced to live on the streets or wherever they can find shelter from the rain. I believe that the government should work to alleviate the plight of the destitute. In the meantime people of fortune should do much more.'

'I cannot disagree with your point of view, but we cannot expect all our friends and acquaintances to feel the same, Helene.'

She blushed. 'You think me foolish, I dare say. I am no killjoy, I assure you. I take much pleasure in my friends, though I also like the quieter pursuit of walking in the country.'

'I agree with you there,' Max said. 'I particularly like to have a house party in the country, though I have not done so for some years. I spent some time in the army. My father died just before the last campaign in Brussels, my mother some years ago, as I believe I told you. I left my estate in the care of an agent and joined Wellington for the final fling against Boney. I think the estate may have suffered for it, though it thrives now. I shall go down again in a few weeks.'

'I suppose we shall return to my uncle's house,' Helene said and smothered a sigh. 'We have lived with him since Papa died last year.'

'You must miss your own home. Was the estate entailed?'

'I do not know exactly how things stood,' Helene replied and wrinkled her brow. 'Mama has never told me—but I know we had to leave almost immediately. My uncle took us in and Mama has a little money, but we could not have come to London had it not been for Miss Royston. She is a generous friend to us.'

'Yes, I think she understands what it is to live under someone else's roof and feel unwelcome.'

'She said something of the sort,' Helene said. She noticed that he had begun to slow the pace of his horses. 'Are we nearly there?'

'Yes, this is the house,' Max said, turning in at a gateway. There were some tall iron gates, which had been opened and fastened back before their arrival. 'It had fallen into disrepair before I purchased it. I made the repairs necessary and now it is a good solid property. As you have probably realised, it is a favourite project with me.'

'Oh…it is just like a large country house,' Helene cried as she saw the faded rose bricks of an attractive house. It was not huge by country-house standards, and of a similar size to her uncle's, but she thought nicer. 'Are the children expecting us?'

'They knew I would come one day this week,' Max told her. He shot a wicked glance at her. 'I hope that very fetching gown will wash, Helene. You are likely to be touched and admired, and young lads almost always have dirty hands.'

'Oh, I did not think to warn Emily,' Helene said. 'My gown will not show every mark, but hers will.'

'Perhaps she will have the good sense to stay out of

reach,' Max said. His eyes twinkled as he threw the reins to Jemmy and handed her down. 'Walk them, Jemmy—and give them a drink, please.'

'Yes, milord.' Jemmy saluted smartly and then winked at Helene. She wondered if he had once been one of Lord Coleridge's orphans.

She smiled at the lad, taking Lord Coleridge's arm as they walked up to the front door. It was flung open before they reached it and eight or nine children came streaming out, screaming and yelling with what was clearly delight. They threw themselves at Max, clinging to his legs and hanging on to his arms, their hands reaching for his pockets.

'These rascals have forgotten their manners,' he said but he was smiling. 'They think they may find something sweet in my pockets—but they have not bid my guests welcome.' He pulled one boy off him, took a handful of comfits wrapped in paper from his pocket and tossed them into the air. The children screamed and jumped to catch them. 'Enough, lads! Have you nothing to say to the guest I have brought to see you?'

'Good morning, miss,' the children chimed in unison. 'Welcome to our school.'

A woman in her middle years came to the door and clapped her hands. She was wearing a dark grey gown, her hair drawn back into a knot at the back of her head, but her smile was open and friendly.

'Now, children, that is enough,' she said and ushered them inside. 'Back to your places and allow our visitors to come in, please. My lord, forgive their excitement. You know how they love to see you.'

'There is nothing to forgive, Ann,' he told her. 'Miss

Henderson, this is my angel. I call her that because she cares for these little monsters with a devotion that is nothing short of angelic. Her name is Ann Saunders—and she is schoolmistress, mother and nurse to these brats.'

'Now, sir, none of that,' Ann said and smiled. 'You will be pleased to know that Arthur is settling well after a few tantrums, my lord. Miss Henderson, I am glad to see you. The children enjoy having visitors and I am always pleased that anyone should show an interest in what we are doing here.'

Helene smiled, for she could see that the children were well cared for and happy. 'I think that Lord Coleridge is right, ma'am. You clearly take great care of these children.'

'I do my best,' Ann replied. 'Would you like to see where they have lessons and where they sleep?'

'Yes, very much,' Helene said. Toby's curricle had come to a stop and he was handing Emily down. Helene followed the schoolmistress into the house while Max greeted the others.

'This is the schoolroom. We are very proud of it,' Ann said, taking Helene into a long room with several desks and a blackboard. The ceilings were high and the cream-painted walls were covered with maps, drawings and lists of words that were clearly used to teach pupils how to spell. At one end of the large room there was a rocking horse and a box of toys, which included lead soldiers and models of animals, also wooden swords and shields. 'We have school pageants to entertain our visitors sometimes. The children dress up as knights and ladies—we play mock battles and learn about the history behind them. I find they learn things they would reject if made to recite lists, as is often the case.'

'How wonderful,' Helene said. 'I wish you had been my governess, Miss Saunders. I was made to recite the kings and queens of England until I knew them by heart, but my governess never bothered to concern herself with their history. I read that for myself from books I borrowed from the lending library.'

'I am sorry that your governess did not see fit to make your lessons a pleasure. When Lord Coleridge offered me the post here I explained that I should want to make learning fun for my children and he agreed. If he had insisted on this place being run as so many others are, I could not have taken up his offer. I never use the cane and I do not force my pupils to do lessons they hate. Instead, I try to make them curious. Usually, the new ones hang back for a start, but after a while they come and ask about what we are doing.'

'How clever of you to let them come to you,' Helene said. 'I cannot believe how well the children look. If you had seen the climbing boy I recently rescued from his master…' Helene shook her head at the memory. 'Do you not think it should be the right of all children to go to school?'

'Oh, do not start me on politics,' Miss Saunders said and laughed. 'Lord Coleridge says I am a radical. My views are outrageous and I really should not harangue the guests. If ever women are allowed to stand for Parliament, you will find me on the hustings!'

'I think I might like to join you.'

Helene was amused. She liked Miss Saunders very much, and she gave Lord Coleridge credit for having found her and giving her the freedom to run her school as she chose.

* * *

After an hour spent looking round the house, Helene wandered out into the gardens where some of the boys had badgered Lord Coleridge and Toby into playing a game of cricket with them. She was laughing as she saw Toby catch Lord Coleridge out, and did not immediately notice the young lad at her elbow.

'Please, miss,' he said and tugged at her skirt, 'will you come?'

'Come where?' Helene asked, looking down. He had sandy hair, bright green eyes and a gap in his teeth. His face was streaked with dirt and she thought he might have been crying. 'Is something the matter?'

'It's Tiddler, miss,' the lad said and wiped his nose on his sleeve. 'He's in trouble, miss—will you come?'

'Yes, of course,' Helene said. 'Where is Tiddler?'

'Over here, miss.' The boy pulled at her gown. 'He's stuck, miss…he can't get down and it's too high fer me ter climb.'

Helene was intrigued. She allowed the lad to hurry her down the path to the far end of the garden where a small apple orchard bordered the garden. She looked round for the child in trouble, but could see nothing.

'Where is Tiddler?'

'Up there, miss.' The lad pointed into the branches of an apple tree. Helene looked and saw the small tortoiseshell kitten, its back hunched as it mewed in obvious distress. 'He can't get down and I can't reach the first branch.'

'No, I see it is too high for you.' Helene glanced back towards the game of cricket. Ought she to summon Toby or Lord Coleridge? She hesitated and then saw the ladder lying on the ground near by. No need to summon help. She could quite easily go up the ladder and rescue the kitten herself. 'Help me carry the ladder…then I will fetch Tiddler down to you.'

It was not a very long ladder and Helene was able to lift it easily, the boy balancing the end for her as she carried it to the tree in which the kitten was stuck. She leaned it up against the trunk, then, glancing over her shoulder to make sure she was unobserved, tucked her skirts up so that she could climb the ladder. She scrambled onto the most substantial branch, feeling sure it would hold her weight, and then looked for a foothold to climb to the next. From there she was able to see the kitten clearly.

'Come, kitty,' she coaxed softly. 'Here, Tiddler… there's a good kitty…'

The kitten arched its back, big round eyes looking at her suspiciously. She reached up and grabbed it, holding it to her breast as she tried to step backwards down to the substantial branch just below her. Her foot seemed not to be able to find it, so she turned her head, and let go of the kitten with one hand, still holding it close with the other as she tried to negotiate her way down to the ladder. The kitten suddenly hissed, dug its nails into her neck, causing Helene to cry out and wobble. The kitten made a bid for freedom and sprang down to the ground, shooting away into the bushes as if in fear of its life.

'Tiddler…' the boy yelled and set off after it. 'Come back 'ere…'

Helene grasped at a branch, which cracked and broke, leaving her floundering as she half-fell, and half-scrambled back to the sturdy branch that she knew would hold her weight. Now if she could just reach the ladder… Her foot touched it and sent it crashing to the ground.

'Oh, no!' she cried, annoyed because she had not thought to tell the lad to hold it. It was too far to jump, which meant she was stuck here until someone came. 'Lad…help me…someone…I'm stuck… I can't get down…'

The young boy had disappeared in pursuit of the kitten. Helene could hear the sounds of laughter and cheering as the cricket match continued. She peered down at the ground. Should she try to jump—or could she find footholds on the trunk? She leaned forward slightly and felt something holding her back. Her dress had caught on the broken branch. She gave it a tug, but it would not budge.

Now she really was stuck until someone came!

Max looked round and smiled as Miss Saunders approached him. He had been bowling for some minutes, but now it was Toby's turn and he was merely the outside fielder.

'I came to tell you that nuncheon is prepared, sir.'

'Very well. If you would like to summon the children, we shall join you.' He glanced round, looking for Helene. 'Is Miss Henderson in the house? I thought she was watching the cricket a few minutes ago?'

'I haven't seen her since she came out, sir,' Ann said.

Emily walked up to them. 'I noticed that Helene went off with one of the boys some minutes ago. I think she went in that direction—towards the orchard.'

'I shall go and find her,' Max said. 'Please go in, all of you. We shall join you shortly.'

He strolled in the direction of the orchard. It was a little odd that Helene should go off alone. He had thought she might like to join in the game as Emily had, but before he could ask she had disappeared.

'Please…someone help me…'

Max began to run as he heard Helene call. She was in the orchard somewhere. What could be the matter?

At first he could not see her, and then he heard her voice again and looked up. Seeing the ladder lying under the apple tree, he realised what had happened.

'What are you doing up there? Or shouldn't I ask?'

'There was a kitten in distress…'

'Of course, I understand perfectly,' Max said, his eyes dancing with amusement. 'Where is the poor creature now?'

'Tiddler scratched me and made off into the bushes—the boy ran after it. When I tried to reach the ladder, it fell and my dress is caught on a broken branch so I could not jump even if I wished.'

'Naturally,' Max said. 'It is all exactly as I should have imagined. You are impulsive, Miss Henderson. Did you not think that it would be safer to ask me or Toby for assistance?'

'The boy asked me to help. You were playing cricket. I did not wish to disturb you. I tried to climb down, but I am caught fast so I could not even jump.'

'No, of course not.' Max shook his head at her. 'Do not try anything so dangerous, Miss Henderson. You would break your ankle. Please stay exactly where you are. I shall come up and help you down.'

'Thank you. I thought I might be stuck here for some time, because no one knew where I was…'

Max did not reply immediately. He fetched the ladder and placed it against the tree, then looked for and found two large stones, which he wedged against the bottom, testing it to make sure it was safe. He then climbed up, reaching the branch Helene was now sitting on. He edged his way out to a position where he could pull her gown free. It tore slightly and he muttered his dissatisfaction, then came back to her.

'I am sorry, but there was no time to fiddle about. This branch will not bear both of us for long. I shall return to the top of the ladder. Turn so that your back is towards me and reach out with your right foot. I shall place it on the ladder and hold you as you descend—do you understand?'

'Yes, thank you. I shall be all right now the ladder is secure.'

Max stood on the ladder just below the top rung. When Helene's foot searched tentatively for the first step, he took hold of her ankle and placed it firmly in position.

'Now put your other foot on,' he encouraged. 'You cannot fall because I am right behind you. That's right… now hold the ladder and down we go.'

Helene obeyed. She came down steadily, Max's body steadying her until they reached the bottom. She turned to look at him, a smile of triumph on her lips and then saw what was clearly a scowl of displeasure.

'What on earth did you think you were doing?' he demanded. 'You might have fallen and injured yourself badly. You had only to call me and I would have fetched the wretched creature down. You are thoughtless and reckless. What would your mother have said if you had come to harm while in my care?'

'I am sorry,' Helene said, feeling as if he had slapped her. 'But there is no need to make such a fuss. I am not hurt and I should have come down myself had my gown not caught.'

'Do you make it a habit to risk your life for nothing?' Max demanded. 'Rescuing a donkey and then a stupid animal! The kitten would have come down itself in time, they usually do.'

'The boy was upset. I did not think,' Helene said defensively. Surely he had no need to scold her? 'I could not leave the poor creature up there. It was frightened.'

'So frightened that it scratched your neck,' Max said. 'You have blood on your gown. Come into the house and let Miss Saunders bathe it for you.'

Helene put her hand to her neck. 'It is only a small scratch. I can perfectly well tend it myself,' she said and set off towards the house. She was walking fast, her head bent as if in distress.

Max watched for a moment and then ran after her. He caught at her arm, swinging her round to face him. For a moment he stared at her, torn between anger, regret and amusement.

'Damn it, I'm sorry,' he said and then caught her to him. Helene's eyes widened as he bent his head and kissed her hard on the mouth. It was such an angry kiss that it aroused conflicting emotions in her. Almost immediately he drew back, an odd expression in his own eyes. 'Forgive me—that was most improper of me. I am sorry…sorry that I was harsh to you and sorry that I behaved so badly. I was shaken because you might have been seriously hurt, but I should not have spoken to you so sharply—and I should not have kissed you like that, either.'

'No, you should not,' Helene said, her expression one of pride. 'Excuse me, sir. I must tidy myself before nuncheon.'

'Yes, of course,' Max said. He stood watching as she walked towards the house. Damn it! He had been a complete fool! He could only hope that Helene had not completely lost her trust in him.

Helene rushed up the stairs to the room Miss Saunders said was kept for visitors to tidy themselves. She was relieved that it was empty when she entered. There was cold water in the jug on the washstand. Helene splashed a little on her face and neck. The scratch stung a little, but when she looked in the mirror she could see that it was only a very little one. Hopefully, no one would notice it after a few hours when the redness had gone.

She smoothed her hair into place and looked at the tear in her gown. Unfortunately, that was noticeable and Emily was sure to ask what had happened. Helene put her hands to her cheeks, feeling a hot rush of colour. Lord Coleridge must think her so foolish. She had acted like a hoyden—climbing into a tree after a kitten was something no properly behaved young lady would do. Helene hadn't hesitated. The child and the kitten had been in distress. How could she have done otherwise?

After a moment her feeling of embarrassment became anger. There had been no need for him to be so harsh—and to kiss her in that way, almost as if he wished to punish her. Just because she had climbed into a tree, it did not mean she was lost to all propriety, but he obviously thought so—a gentleman would not kiss a lady he respected in that rough manner. He had clearly lost all respect for her!

She felt close to tears, but she knew she must not give way to her feelings. The others were waiting for nuncheon. She must go down and join them. She lifted her head, pride coming to her rescue. She had been reckless and must simply take the consequences of her actions.

Helene went downstairs, making her way to the big dining hall that Miss Saunders had shown her earlier. The children were all standing behind their benches, waiting for her. She felt their eyes on her as she walked towards the high table, where the guests were already seated. Her cheeks heated, making her uncomfortable. She took a seat between Toby and Miss Saunders.

'Forgive me for keeping everyone waiting,' she said.

'She got Tiddler down,' a voice piped up as the children took their places. 'He were stuck up a tree and she got 'im down fer us.'

Helene was startled when the children stamped their feet and sent up a cheer. She blushed again, shooting a glance at Max at the other end of the table.

'Be quiet, children,' Miss Saunders said and a hush fell over the tables. 'We shall say grace and then you may eat.'

Helene looked down as the schoolmistress said the prayer. She felt embarrassed and uncomfortable. Whatever must everyone think of her?

'It was kind of you to rescue that wretched kitten,' Miss Saunders said as the children settled to their meal. 'I had to get it out of the lily pool the other day. The children thought it would drown. They do so love their pets—and they adore the donkey. Lord Coleridge sent it for them recently. He told them that a kind lady had rescued it from a cruel master and that they were to take good care of it. I think the beast will be totally useless after all the fuss they make of it.'

'Oh…' Helene glanced at Max again. He lifted his brows, as if to ask if he were forgiven. She gave a slight nod of the head and smiled. 'I should like to see Jezra. I understand that he is much recovered now.'

'Was it you that rescued the poor creature?' Ann Saunders asked. 'That explains it—I wondered why Lord Coleridge had taken a donkey under his care, but I see that you have a kind heart, Miss Henderson. I hope that you may take an interest in our little school in the future?'

'Yes, of course, though we are in town only for a short time,' Helene said. 'However, you already have the best patron you could have in Lord Coleridge.'

'Yes, indeed, we do,' Miss Saunders said. 'Would you care for some of this mutton, Miss Henderson? It comes from the Coleridge estate—or one of them, for I believe his lordship has more than one. Our patron makes sure that we never go short of anything here.'

Helene accepted a little of the pie, which was swimming in delicious gravy, the meat cooked slowly and very tender. She noticed that the children were being served the same foods as they had. In the workhouse they would have been lucky to be served bread and thin soup. The difference was so marked that she could not help feeling approval for the man who had provided them with this home.

Her anger had quite gone now. How could she be angry with Lord Coleridge when he was so generous to these children? He must think her very foolish for climbing that tree, but she would not hold the kiss against him. Indeed, it had made her tremble inwardly. Had she not been certain that he had meant to punish her, she might have found it enjoyable.

Chapter Five

After nuncheon, they were taken to see Jezra. The children took gifts of bread and carrots to feed their pet. Seeing how happy they were to have the donkey to fuss over and care for, Helene was completely satisfied that Jezra would do well in his new home.

Max told them it was time to leave after some minutes spent admiring the children's pet. They said their goodbyes and walked out to the carriages. Max glanced at Helene as they paused for a moment in the sunshine.

'Am I forgiven?' he asked. 'Or would you prefer Toby to drive you home?'

'I have forgiven you,' Helene said. 'I dare say I was foolish.'

'I would not say so. Reckless and brave, but not foolish,' Max replied. 'I was fearful for your safety but I should not have… behaved as I did. I hope it will not spoil our friendship?' His eyes quizzed her, making her look down quickly, her heart racing.

'It is forgotten,' Helene said and gave him her hand. Max inclined his head, helping her to climb into the curricle. 'I think, after what I have seen today, I should forgive you almost anything, sir.'

'You are pleased with our school?' Max glanced at her before giving his horses the order to walk on.

'How could I fail to be?' Helene said, but did not look at him. 'These children would be forced to live in the workhouse if it were not for you and I dread to think of their fate in that terrible place.'

'There are other decent homes. Miss Royston is the patroness of one in London, as I am sure you know.'

'Yes, Emily told me of it, but I doubt that it is quite like yours. You were fortunate to find Miss Saunders, sir. Her ideas and beliefs are very different, as I am sure you agree.'

'Yes, I was fortunate. I am glad you approve,' Max said, looking thoughtful. 'I trust you are satisfied with Jezra's new home?'

'How could I not be?' Helene said and smiled. 'I think those children will spoil the wretched creature.'

'I dare say Jezra will find it preferable to pulling an impossibly heavy cart and almost starving to death.'

'I am certain that he will,' Helene replied. She glanced at him, seeing that he was smiling. She had a warm feeling inside, because it seemed that their argument was forgotten. 'I think you are very kind, sir.'

'Do you, Helene?' he asked and turned to look at her for a moment. Something in his eyes at that moment sent a tingle down her spine. 'Jezra owes his good fortune entirely to you—and the children need help. Someone has to do something until the laws are changed to protect them. I am certain you agree?'

'Yes, of course.'

'I knew you would think as I do.' His dark eyes sent little tingles through her entire body. She remembered the way she had lectured him on the evils of poverty and felt embarrassed. He needed no such instruction from her! She was sure he knew far more about these things than she did.

Helene blushed and looked away. She had a strange feeling that something in their relationship had changed, though she was not sure what or why. Her heart raced for a moment, but she clasped her hands in her lap. She must not read too much into that kiss. She had thought he was angry, his kiss meant to punish…but that look in his eyes had seemed to say something very different.

Max stopped the curricle outside Miss Royston's house. He got down to help Helene alight, holding her hand for a moment, gazing down at her as they stood in the street.

'I have enjoyed your company,' he told her. 'I have taken a box at Vauxhall next week. If I were to send Mrs Henderson an invitation for all of you, would it be acceptable, do you think?'

'I am sure Mama would be pleased to accept. Amelia has spoken of taking a box, but we have had so many engagements that there has been no time.'

'You must visit Vauxhall,' Max told her. 'You will enjoy the fireworks, and the gardens are pleasant. I shall write to your mama—and perhaps we shall meet soon?'

'I expect we shall,' Helene said. She gave him her hand, her manner outwardly calm, though her heart was beating very fast. 'Thank you so much for today. I have enjoyed myself.'

'Despite my show of temper?' Max lifted his brows.

'I think it was more my fault than yours, sir.'

'Well, we shall agree to forget a disagreeable incident,' Max said and lifted her hand to kiss it. 'Goodbye for the moment…'

Helene walked into the house, leaving Emily to offer her thanks for the outing. She paused by the silver salver on the hall table. To her surprise there was a letter addressed to Miss Helene Henderson. She picked it up and slipped it into her glove as she went upstairs.

Her mother came along the landing towards her as she reached her bedchamber. 'Helene, my love. Did you have an interesting day?'

'Yes, Mama. Miss Saunders is the schoolmistress at the orphanage and she is wonderful with the children. I think it must be so satisfying to do such worthwhile work.'

'Yes, I dare say it may be more rewarding than life as a governess,' Mrs Henderson said. 'However, you are in the fortunate position of not having to work, my love. I am confident that you will receive an offer very soon, Helene. Mr Bradwell called today. He seemed most disappointed that you were not at home. Had you been, he might have had something to say to you.'

Helene nodded, but made no answer as she went into her bedroom. She thought that she would prefer to work, as Miss Saunders did, than marry a man she could not truly love. She was almost certain now that there could be no true happiness in marriage without love. She had not thought that she would ever wish to marry a member of the class that had treated her mama so badly, but Lord Coleridge seemed to think just as he ought about so many things.

Yet it was foolish to allow herself to dream, for she had no real reason to suppose that he had any intention of asking her to marry him.

Max took his leave of Toby with the promise to meet later that evening at a card party to which both were invited. Leaving his tiger to see to the horses, he went into the house. He stopped to glance through the calling cards and pocket a sealed letter before going upstairs to change for the evening.

Max's valet had laid out the clothes he would need, and a bath had been set for his use in the dressing room. His valet gave the order and servants began to fill the hipbath with hot water. Sinking into the fragrant water some minutes later, Max closed his eyes, allowing his thoughts to drift back to the moment he had seen Helene in the apple tree. Her skirt had been caught up, revealing shapely ankles and more. The glimpse of white silk stockings going right up to her thighs had been tantalising; she looked beautiful, the picture of lovely womanhood, making him very aware of his feelings for her.

Max thought that perhaps it was this awareness that had made him suddenly angry. The desire to crush Helene in his arms and kiss her had come swiftly, making him act in a way he would not normally have dreamed of doing. He had made her angry in her turn. Max knew that he was lucky she had forgiven him so easily. He did not doubt that it was Jezra who had worked that particular magic, and promised himself he would take the donkey an apple when they came in season.

Max admitted to himself that he was intrigued with Miss Henderson. She was a very spirited lady and courageous, though her compassion tended to make her reckless at times. She had rushed to the defence of the donkey without thought for her own safety, and she had not hesitated to attempt the rescue of the kitten, making nothing of either the scratch or her plight when the ladder fell. He could not help but admire her, and she was certainly both intelligent and beautiful.

If he wished to marry, he surely could not do better than to make Miss Henderson an offer. She would make a companionable wife and a good mother for his children. Seeing her in the apple tree had made him aware that he found her desirable. He was not certain that his feelings went deeper and because of that he was still hesitating about making her an offer.

Harry Pendleton had fallen deeply in love with Susannah, and she with him. Max had witnessed the moment when she risked her life for Harry's, running between Harry and Northaven at the very moment the marquis pressed the trigger. His ball had struck her in the shoulder and she had made a complete recovery, but she might have died—and she had done it out of love for Harry. They were the happiest couple of his acquaintance. Most of Max's friends had married for reasons other than love: fortune, property and consequence. He knew that two of his friends who married in the last eighteen months already had mistresses; bored with their wives, they looked elsewhere for their pleasure. That would not do for him!

Max stood up, water dripping off the body of a superbly fit Corinthian, his well-toned muscles rippling beneath the skin as he dried himself. It was too soon to think of making Miss Henderson an offer, even though he had experienced a flood of intense desire when he kissed her. Even now he could feel himself hardening at the memory of those shapely ankles. Yet desire was not reason enough for marriage. He would wait for a time, he decided, get to know her better.

Wrapping a robe about himself, he walked into the bedchamber. He remembered the letter he had thrust into his pocket on his arrival home and discovered that his thoughtful valet had placed it on the dressing chest before taking the coat away to brush and clean it.

Max broke the seal and read the contents. He frowned as he digested the letter, which had come from a neighbour. General Tyler had written to tell him of some unfortunate events that had taken place in the district of late. A young woman had been attacked when walking home from her place of work late at night, and another had barely escaped the same fate. Some other girls had reported that a man had followed them—and all the incidents had taken place in the last six months.

It was six months since his cousin, Mrs Heronsdale and the doctor she insisted was the only physician to care for her son properly had moved into the dower house. Max had an uncomfortable feeling about what his neighbour had not written. Could he be implying that one of the newcomers was responsible for these despicable attacks?

Max frowned as he dressed for the evening. It would be inconvenient to leave town at the moment. He felt that he was just beginning to get to know Miss Henderson. He thrust the disturbing letter into a rawer. Robert could surely have had nothing to do with these attacks, for he was never well. Max was not sure about the physician. He did not care for the man much, but he would not have thought him capable of such wickedness.

He would give the matter some thought. No doubt it would keep for a few weeks. The problem of his marriage was more important for the moment. He needed to make a decision.

Helene opened her letter. She read the contents quickly, frowned and then puzzled over the spidery script. What did the rather cryptic message mean?

Lady Annersley requests the pleasure of a private interview at her house in Berkeley Square tomorrow at three in the afternoon.

Helene recalled that Lord Coleridge had once mentioned the lady as being an acquaintance, and she had been introduced to her at an evening party. However, she had not been invited to the small dance given by that lady only a few days previously. Since they were not intimately acquainted, why would Lady Annersley ask her to call for a private interview? It was puzzling, for Helene could not think that she had done anything to arouse that lady's interest—or to upset her. However, she was already engaged for the following afternoon to some friends, and would be unable to oblige.

She sat down at the little desk in the window and took out some notepaper, penning a short note of regret. She would be happy to call on her ladyship at another date, but did not have a free afternoon for some ten days. Having sanded and sealed her note, she went downstairs with it and placed it on a salver with others waiting to be delivered by hand. One of the footmen delivered letters to houses in the near vicinity each morning, which saved the cost of some sixpences unless they could be franked. They also collected post from the receiving house, which was left in the hall together with hand-delivered post.

The letter had taken up more time than she had anticipated, and Helene had to hurry to dress. That evening they were attending the theatre with some friends of Amelia's and would call at their house for a glass of wine first. She must not keep the others waiting!

In her haste to be ready on time, Helene did not give much thought to the day she had spent with Lord Coleridge. It had seemed for a moment as he looked at her that something had changed between them. However, he had not pressed his advantage. Apart from the invitation to Vauxhall, which she was looking forward to, he had merely said that he would see her when they met in company.

Helene could not in honesty tell herself that he had done anything to give her reason to think he intended to offer for her. His kiss had been an impulse, she was certain, meant to punish, perhaps, or in frustration at her reckless behaviour. Her pulses had raced while he held her so fiercely, but she had decided that she should not dwell on the small incident. Had it meant anything, he would have spoken on the way home—if only to request an interview with Mama. One kiss meant nothing, even though it had left her shaken and breathless.

She must not expect anything. Helene knew that, despite his harsh tone, she had felt pleasure as he kissed her. She was not sure how it felt when you fell in love, for she had no experience of such things. However, she did know that she enjoyed being with Lord Coleridge more than any other gentleman of her acquaintance. Since she must marry for Mama's sake, she would accept an offer from Lord Coleridge should he make it, providing he could accept her humble background—but of course he would not. She would be foolish to let herself hope for such a thing.

Helene finished dressing, thanked her maid for making her look elegant, and then ran downstairs to join the others. She must put all her foolish notions from her mind! Perhaps there was someone else she could happily marry…

Helene was engrossed in the play; it was *The Taming of the Shrew* by William Shakespeare and vastly amusing. She laughed in delight, enjoying the performance so much that she did not become aware of being watched until the interval. As the curtain came down and people began to move about, Helene saw that some people in the box opposite Amelia's were staring at her hard. She felt an odd uneasiness as she saw that Lady Annersley was looking at her through a pair of opera glasses, which she then handed to a gentleman sitting beside her with a comment.

Helene shivered, a sliver of ice sliding down her spine. She was sure that she had seen the gentleman once before in his coach. He had seemed to stare at her then, though she had not been certain the first time, for he might have been looking at Emily. This evening she was sure that he was watching her—and had been for some time.

Helene picked up Amelia's opera glasses and lifted them, studying the gentleman. He was a man of advanced years, aristocratic with a proud face, his nose long and his lips thin. He was not unattractive even now and she thought he must have been very handsome when younger. He became aware of her scrutiny and bowed his head towards her, a slight smile on his mouth.

Helene put down the opera glasses at once. She did not know who he was or why he—and Lady Annersley—were taking such an interest in her, but she did not wish to encourage him. It was not unheard of for a gentleman of advanced years to take a much younger bride. Helene would not wish him to imagine that she was giving him encouragement.

She turned her gaze back to the stage, feeling glad that she had refused Lady Annersley's invitation. When she thought about it, the letter had been couched in terms that made it more of a command than a summons. A shiver went through Helene, because she was very sure that she would not wish to become that gentleman's bride!

'Is something the matter?' Emily whispered in her ear. 'Did you notice that gentleman staring at you, Helene?'

'Yes. I did not like it.'

'I am sure it is the Duke of Annesdale,' Emily told her. 'Lady Annersley is the wife of the late Marquis, Annesdale's daughter-in-law. She was married to his eldest son, but they had no children—at least none that survived infancy. Her husband died some years ago, but she has never married again.'

'I am sorry for her,' Helene replied. She might have told Emily about the lady's letter, but the curtain was going up and the play was about to begin.

Helene took the letter from her drawer and read it again that evening. The more she puzzled over it, the less she understood. Clearly both Lady Annersley and the Duke of Annesdale had taken an interest in her—but why?

Helene was uneasy as she blew out her candle and tried to sleep. She had never met the duke, so she could only imagine that he found her attractive. He was a widower and had been for some years. His sons had failed to provide him with an heir before they died. It was quite possible that he was looking for a young wife to give him the heirs he needed.

She could appreciate his feelings. His title was an old one and unless he married again and had a son it would pass on to some distant cousin—perhaps there was no one. The title would then die with him, his estate pass to whomever he chose or perhaps the Crown if he made no will. It was sad, Helene thought, and felt sympathy for his plight. However, she had no wish to be the Duchess of Annesdale.

No, she must be wrong! Helene laughed at herself as she snuggled down into the comfort of her feather mattress. She had imagined it all. He was merely curious about a new face or there was some other perfectly simple explanation.

Helene went driving with Miss Marshall and her brother Captain Paul Marshall the next day. He was a handsome man only a few years her senior, and of a teasing disposition. The afternoon passed so swiftly that Helene was reluctant to take leave of her friends, but felt happy in the knowledge that she was sure to meet them again that evening, for they were all to attend a small dance given by Mr Henry Marshall.

'My uncle does not often stir himself to visit town,'

Miss Marshall told Helene, 'but when he does he gives wonderful parties. Everyone has been sent a mask to wear this evening, and we shall unmask at midnight— is that not amusing?'

'Yes, it is,' Helene said. 'I have not been to a masked ball before, but I have heard of them. Amelia says that she shall give a costume ball for her charity at the end of the Season.'

'Oh, yes, I have received my invitation and I am looking forward to it,' Miss Marshall told her. 'Paul has a wonderful idea for us, but I must not tell you because it is a secret.'

'I am not sure I should have told you, Lily,' Captain Marshall replied with mock severity. 'Ten to one you will tell everyone and I shall have to think of something else.'

Miss Marshall denied it and they all joined in the laughter.

It was just gone four when Helene was taken home. She parted from her friends happily and went into the house, pausing to glance at the cards and letters on the salver in the hall. A little shiver went down her spine as she recognised the hand of the sender of a letter addressed to her. Snatching it up, she ran upstairs to her own room. She broke the seal and scanned the contents.

I urge you not to ignore my request. Please visit me in the morning tomorrow. It is of the utmost importance…

Helene felt cold all over. What could be of such importance? She stared at the letter for some minutes, wondering what best to do about it. Ought she to show it to Mama?

Helene was reluctant to do so, though she was not

certain why. Mama would certainly not even consider any offer the duke might make her. He was far too old to make a suitable husband.

Helene shook her head. She must be mistaken. The duke did not know her. They had not even met. He could not be thinking of making her an offer—and yet he had been staring at her in such an intent way.

Suddenly, Helene went cold all over. There was one very plausible explanation of why the duke and his daughter-in-law could be taking an interest in her! It had not occurred to her at first, but now she was wondering if the duke could be Papa's father. Mama had told her that his family had been unkind to her, refusing to accept her and cutting her father off without a penny when he married. She had never told Helene the name of her paternal grandfather and Helene had not thought to ask, but now things began to fall into place.

Mama had been upset by a letter she had received a few days earlier. Had the duke written to Mama? Had he threatened her? She had been so upset that she had gone to bed with a headache.

Why had she not told Helene the truth?

Helene knew Lord Coleridge as soon as he approached her, even though he was wearing a handsome black-and-gold mask over the top half of his face.

'My lady,' he said, bowing to her. 'I do not know your name, but it would give me pleasure if you would dance with me.'

Helene laughed and shook her head. 'I am afraid your mask does not hide your identity from me, sir. You would need to wear something to cover your whole face—and then your size would betray you. You are rather larger than most other gentlemen, Lord Coleridge, and your height gives you away.'

'Woe is me. I hoped to surprise you later,' Max replied and chuckled. 'You were too clever for me, Miss Henderson.'

'Not clever, sir, just observant,' she told him and smiled, glancing round at the assembled company. 'I believe Mr Sinclair is very fond of that blue coat, for I have seen him wear it before this eve-ning…and I know Captain Marshall is wearing a black mask—his sister told me. Hers is gold, I think—but there are certainly some others here that I would not recognise.'

'Perhaps one has to know the other person quite well to recognise them wearing a mask. I certainly knew you immediately, and I do not think I have seen this delight-ful gown before?'

'No, you would not—it is new,' Helene told him and laughed. 'I will not ask you to explain how you knew me, for it might embarrass us both.'

'Perhaps,' he agreed and his mouth curved. 'I should have known you as soon as you spoke. You have a most unusual way of cutting to the heart of things, Miss Henderson.'

'Am I too direct?' Helene asked. 'I am not always so in company, but somehow I have found myself able to talk to you without reserve. You must tell me if I am too free. I know that some gentlemen prefer a lady to have no opinions or at least to keep them to herself. It is the reason that I am often quiet, for I do not wish to offend.'

'Do they? More fool them,' Max said drily. 'I am not one of them. You may be as direct as you please, and your opinion will always weigh with me. You will certainly not offend me, whatever you say.'

'Oh…' Helene blushed beneath the mask. She was thrown into confusion by his manner, which she thought more intimate than before, and her heart raced. 'Mama says that she will be quite happy for me to be a part of your party at Vauxhall, sir. She says that she shall not come, but Amelia and Emily are both looking forward to the evening.'

'I am glad to hear it,' Max said. 'Does your mama not care for fireworks? I know that some people find them frightening.'

'I do not believe Mama is frightened of them,' Helene said. 'It is a little odd—she has cried off one or two engagements recently. I wondered if she found London tiring, but she says she is perfectly well. It is just that she prefers to stay at home sometimes—and I am well chaperoned with both Amelia and Emily for company.'

'Indeed you are,' Max said. He stopped dancing as the music ended, gazing down at her ruefully. 'Why is it that whenever I dance with you the duration is always too short? I must ask you to grant me at least one more dance this evening, Miss Henderson.'

'I have reserved the dance before supper, if that will suit you?'

'It will do very well,' he said and held her hand for a moment longer than necessary. 'I shall see you later, sweet Helene. Now I must see if I can guess the identity of some others. I think I see Sally Jersey. I shall discover if I am correct. Please excuse me…'

Helene smiled as he released her. She was about to rejoin her mother and Amelia, who were sitting at the side of the room, when a lady dressed in a dark blue gown and a mask of silver came up to her. Helene turned in enquiry as she laid a hand on her arm.

'Yes, ma'am—may I help you?'

'I have written to you twice, but you refuse to see me,' the lady said in a harsh tone. 'Has someone forbidden you to visit me?'

'Lady Annersley…' Helene gasped. 'Forgive me, I truly have been engaged every day. I am sorry if you feel that I have slighted you, but I could not break my engagements. Besides, I do not know why you would wish to see me, ma'am. I hope I have done nothing to offend you?'

'The only offence is in your stubborn refusal to meet him. He has the right to make himself known to you.'

'I beg your pardon—of whom do you speak?' Helene felt a shiver down her spine. Could she mean the Duke of Annesdale? 'I am not aware that I have refused to meet anyone.'

'You did not answer his letter.'

'I must ask your pardon once more, but I have not received a letter from a gentleman. If I were to receive one—which would be most improper—I should give it to my mother.'

'And she would of course destroy it,' Lady Annersley said. Her mouth drew into a thin line. 'This is not the place to discuss anything of a private nature. I must have your promise that you will call on me as soon as you have time. I have something of importance to tell you, Miss Henderson—something that could change your life.'

'Indeed? I do not know what that might be, ma'am.' Helene's manner was stiff. If this woman were a member of the family who had treated Mama so badly, she had no wish to know her!

'It is not for me to say, at least not here. Come to my house next Tuesday morning and all shall be revealed.'

'If that is your wish,' Helene said. 'If you will excuse me, ma'am, I see a friend approaching and I believe he means to ask me to dance.'

Helene walked to meet Toby Sinclair. He grinned at her and lifted his mask slightly. 'I dare say you knew me anyway, but I wanted to be sure you would dance with me, Miss Henderson.'

'I should be delighted,' Helene replied and went to him with relief. She felt safe with Toby Sinclair—her brief interlude with Lady Annersley had left her feeling uneasy.

Helene danced all evening, going from one friend to another. It was amusing to guess the identity of her partners, though she had little trouble with most of them—they all had some little mannerism or habit that made it easy. However, the company was enjoyable; she had begun to make many friends, both gentlemen and ladies, and she particularly enjoyed her time with Miss Marshall and her brother.

Dancing twice with Lord Coleridge made the evening perfect. The supper dance was a waltz and Helene felt that she was floating on air as he whirled her around the floor. Afterwards, he took her into supper and was so attentive that she felt people must notice. Her happiness was complete when he asked if he might join her when she walked with Toby and some others in the park the following afternoon.

'I should be delighted if you would join us,' Helene

said. 'I am to drive there with Miss Marshall and her brother. Mr Sinclair will bring Emily and Mr Osbourne is driving his sister. We shall listen to the band playing in the park. It has been arranged for some days, but one more will only make the afternoon more enjoyable.'

'I am grateful that you feel my company will add to your enjoyment of the afternoon, Miss Henderson.' His look was so intimate at that moment that butterflies set up a crazy dance in her abdomen.

Helene felt her cheeks becoming warm. She glanced down, for she could not quite meet his eyes. She felt that his attentions were becoming more particular, but she was not sure that anything would come of their growing friendship. It was rumoured that he had paid court to an heiress the previous year for a while, but that had fallen through. Perhaps he was fickle in his relationships, though she could not truly think it of him.

After supper, Lord Coleridge took his leave of her, promising to keep his appointment the following afternoon. Helene was sorry to see him go, though she knew she could not dance with him again that evening unless she wished for it to be thought that he was the admirer she favoured. She was not yet ready to make that commitment in public and she did not think Lord Coleridge had any intention of making her an offer just yet. They liked each other very well, and they enjoyed being together. Helene thought that perhaps there was more, because when he kissed her she had felt something stir inside her. Had his kiss been tender rather than punishing, she might have felt that he cared for her. As it was, she was still uncertain.

She danced the last of the evening with Mr Nicholas

Bradwell. It was he who was standing with her when the unmasking happened at midnight. Helene smiled and laughed as she removed her own mask.

'I think we had guessed long since, sir,' she said. 'I must admit it has been vastly amusing this evening.'

'Dancing with you must always be a pleasure,' he replied with a little bow. 'Will you be at home if I should call one day this week, Miss Henderson? I thought we might drive out one day.'

'I am sorry to disappoint you, sir,' Helene said. 'I have engagements all this week and some of next. Indeed, I do not have a free morning until Thursday next.'

'Then perhaps you will engage with me for that morning?'

Helene hesitated, feeling reluctant to commit herself to such an engagement. 'I am not certain of Miss Royston's plans,' she said. 'Pray let me consult with her and I shall give you my answer when we next meet.'

He looked displeased with her answer, but inclined his head, leaving her as her mother came up to her.

'Are you ready to leave, Helene?' Mrs Henderson asked. 'I think the others have already gone up to retrieve their cloaks.'

'Then I shall go at once—I should not want to keep Amelia waiting,' Helene said. She saw that her mother was looking tired, a little anxious perhaps. 'Is something troubling you, Mama?'

'I have a little headache,' her mother said and frowned. 'This is not the time or the place but I must talk to you alone soon, Helene.'

'Yes, of course, Mama. Whenever you wish.'

Helene leaned forward and kissed her cheek impulsively. She was startled to see what looked like tears in her mother's eyes, but in another moment they had gone.

'We must not keep the others waiting,' Mrs Henderson said and appeared to make an effort to be brisk. 'Come along, my dearest. I think you have had a good evening, for you have many friends now. You are enjoying yourself, Helene?'

'Yes, of course, Mama.'

'Then I must be content with that for the moment,' Mrs Henderson said. 'I just hope that I have not harmed you, my love. I thought only to secure your future…'

'Mama! What do you mean?'

'Not now, Helene. I must think about something and then I shall tell you what I have decided.'

Helene stood patiently that morning as the dressmaker pinned and pulled, moulding the new evening gown about her so that it fit her like a second skin. It was made of a flame-coloured silk and was quite the most sophisticated gown that Helene possessed.

'You have lost a little weight about the waist,' the seamstress remarked. 'The gown will require a little alteration, Mademoiselle Henderson.'

'I am sorry to put you to extra trouble,' Helene said. 'Will it be ready for the Duchess of Marlborough's ball next week? I believe it is meant to be the highlight of the season and I was hoping to wear this.'

'*Oui,* of a certainty,' the seamstress said. 'I assure you that the alterations will be made and the gown delivered before the ball.'

'Thank you,' Helene said. 'I dare say you have many calls on your time, *madame*?'

'*Oui,* I am busy all the time, but this is good—no?' She looked pleased. 'I believe the gown will be a triumph. I hope you will ask me to make your wedding gown?'

'I have not yet been asked to marry anyone,' Helene said, her cheeks pink. 'However, I shall certainly ask if I am…if you have time.'

'I should make time for you, *mademoiselle.* It is not always that the figure is so good. Of a certainty it will not be long before milord speaks. I have heard your name mentioned by one of my clients.'

'Someone spoke of my marriage?' Helene frowned. 'Surely not, *madame*! I do not think that I have done anything to occasion gossip.'

'Forgive me, I should not have spoken…' The Frenchwoman looked uncomfortable. 'It was a conversation I overheard. Perhaps I did not hear correctly.'

'What exactly did you hear?' Helene was both curious and annoyed that people should be discussing her.

'It was something about the marriage being suitable… and a name was linked with yours. I heard nothing more, Miss Henderson. I should not have assumed, but I imagined the engagement to be imminent.'

'Who mentioned my name?'

'I do not think I should say…'

'Please tell me. It will go no further.'

'I believe it was Lady Annersley. I called on her to fit her new gown. She was behind the screen and talking to the gentleman.'

Helene felt a sliver of ice slide down her spine. 'Do you recall the gentleman's name?'

'I think he was the Duke of Annesdale. He is her father-in-law, I believe. They seem close.'

'I see, thank you,' Helene said. She did not press the seamstress further, for she could see that she was embarrassed. She felt angry that Lady Annersley and the duke should discuss her in such an intimate way.

Why did they feel that her marriage was important enough to be discussed? If the duke was her grandfather, he had abandoned the right to influence her life. She decided that she would keep her appointment with Lady Annersley the following week. Before that, she would find a moment to speak privately with her mama.

After the dressmaker had gone, Helene went up to her mother's bedchamber. She knocked and went in, finding her mother still in bed, a tray with the remains of her breakfast on a table beside the bed. She did not appear to have eaten very much.

'Mama, are you unwell?' Helene asked, looking at her in concern. 'You have not been quite yourself of late. Last evening you spoke of wanting to speak with me alone. Is something on your mind?'

'Yes, dearest,' Mrs Henderson said and patted the bed beside her. 'Please sit down, Helene. I have searched my conscience and I think I must tell you. I had hoped that you would receive a suitable offer and none of this need have come out, but now I believe I must confess the truth.'

'Tell me what, Mama?' Helene frowned. 'What can be so dreadful that you have tortured yourself, for I know that you have been anxious for some days now?'

'Firstly, I must ask you if you have received any offers that you have not mentioned to me, Helene?'

'No, Mama...' Helene blushed. 'There are three gentlemen I think may make me an offer in time, but none of them have spoken.'

Mrs Henderson sighed. 'I was afraid of that. It is unfortunate, for if you had chosen wisely it might all have been settled to your advantage. I am afraid he will make things awkward for us.'

'Of whom do you speak, Mama?'

Mrs Henderson shook her head. 'Papa's father. He is come to town and wishes to see you, Helene.'

'I have thought…' Helene hesitated. 'You have not told me Papa's family name, Mama—was it Annesdale? Was Papa the duke's younger son?'

'Yes, though he never used his title.' Mrs Henderson frowned. 'Who told you? Have you see him?'

'He was staring at me at the theatre—and Lady Annersley has written to me.'

'Why did you not tell me?'

'I did not think it was important at first—and you did not tell me that my grandfather was in town.'

'I did not wish to have anything to do with the family. You know that I was not treated well as a bride, Helene. I was given the cold shoulder. One lady told me that she did not wish to mix with people of my class.' She fiddled with her lace kerchief, as if she found the words difficult. 'I have never forgotten or forgiven them.'

'Oh, Mama, I am so sorry,' Helene said. 'I know it still hurts you—and of course I shall have nothing to do with them if you do not wish it. I told Lady Annersley I would call, but I can cancel the appointment.'

'I wish it were that simple.' Mrs Henderson sighed. 'As you know, your father would have nothing more to do with his family. When they refused to receive me, he cut them out of our lives. Even when his father wrote and offered him a small allowance, he refused it. He was too proud to accept charity and we managed on what he earned from his copying. He had a beautiful copperplate hand, but the work did not pay much money.'

'That was hard for you, Mama.'

'I did not mind, though there were times when I wished we had a little more money. My father gave me five thousand when we married, even though we quarrelled. He did not approve of my marrying into the aristocracy and he cut me out of his will—but he still gave me something. Annesdale gave us nothing, not one penny. What little I had is almost gone, and if you do not marry well I do not know what we shall do.'

'Oh, Mama…' Helene did not know how to answer her. 'I am so sorry.'

'Well, it is not your fault. I had hopes that Mr Bradwell might speak. He seems to like you, and he is the kind of man that would make me an allowance—even provide me with a home of my own, perhaps. He is a gentleman, but not an aristocrat, and would make nothing of the fact that my father was in trade. I know that you like Lord Coleridge, but I fear his family might shun you, Helene. I do not want you to suffer as I did, my love.'

'I am sure something good will happen soon, Mama.'

'The duke is demanding to see you, Helene,' Mrs Henderson said. 'I have never told you, but he made me an infamous offer once…just after your father died. He said that he would take you into his family and give you everything that I could not—but that I must give you up entirely.'

'Mama!' Helene was shocked. 'How could he say

such a wicked thing to you? I hope you told him that I should not go?'

'To be honest I was nervous of telling you, Helene. Our lives have been hard since Papa died, and I was afraid you might be tempted by what Annesdale had to offer.'

'Mama! You should have known I would never leave you in such circumstances.'

'I have felt guilty over it. I refused without asking if you would like to live under his roof. You would have so many advantages…'

'None that would compensate for having to give you up,' Helene said. 'I shall certainly not visit Lady Annersley. How dare they write to me, knowing how they behaved to you in the past?'

'I think perhaps you should keep your appointment, Helene. Hear what they have to say. I thought if you married well you would be safe, but I do not think Annesdale will rest until he hears your denial from your own lips.'

'You are sure, Mama? I do not wish to have anything to do with these people—they do not deserve it.'

'Hear him first and then we may put an end to this business.' Mrs Henderson smiled. 'Go and change for your outing this afternoon, Helene. It is not your fault that you have not received an offer of marriage. I dare say I can live in Edgar's house a little longer if I am forced to it.'

'Is it so very bad, Mama?' Helene asked. 'If a gentleman asked for my hand, I should naturally tell him that my grandfather was in trade. I know it is not considered the done thing, but if there was genuine affection between us, it could not matter.'

'It might matter to others,' her mother warned. 'If a gentleman loved you for yourself, he might not care—but his family might think otherwise.'

'What are you trying to tell me, Mama?'

'Lord Coleridge…his father was second cousin to Annesdale…' Mrs Henderson put a hand to her face. 'It is the reason I tried to warn you from the start, my love. Max Coleridge is said to be fond of the duke—I fear that he would give you up rather than risk a breach with him. I dare say Coleridge may even be his heir…though I am not certain of it.'

'Oh, Mama!' Helene stared at her in dismay. The discovery that Max Coleridge was distantly related to Papa's father was shocking. How could she ever marry him in the circumstances? The duke had ruined her mother's life, thereby forcing Papa to work as a secretary for barely enough money to keep his family alive.

If she married Max, he would expect her to welcome his friends and family. How could she be civil to a man she must hate?

Helene dashed away the angry tears. She was being ridiculous, for Max had not asked her to marry him, and it was unlikely that he would—especially if she told him exactly who she was.

Chapter Six

'I do not know how much longer this weather can last,' Max said as they strolled together in the park that afternoon, waiting for the band to start. 'We have been lucky this year and it must rain before long.'

'I do not mind the rain,' Helene said. She directed an uncertain look at him, for her secret was playing on her mind. She felt that she was deceiving him, because he could not know that she was the daughter of a woman the duke had hated so much that he had cut his son off without a penny for marrying her. 'At home I sometimes walk when it is wet. Everything in the country smells so clean and fresh after the rain—do you not think so?'

'Yes, particularly new-mown grass,' Max said and gave her an approving look. 'I can see that you are truly a country girl at heart, Helene. Would you consider being a guest at my home when the Season ends? I am thinking of having a house party for friends. I have not done so for some years. Indeed, no one but Harry Pendleton and the Earl of Ravenshead have been there since my father died—apart from my widowed aunt and her son. They live in the dower house, but it is time that the main house was opened up to guests again.'

'I dare say you were away for long periods in the army, sir?'

'Yes, I was. My father was ill for a while, but he would not send for me and I did not know until I came home. I was with him when he died, but he was a very proud man. Had he asked, I would have resigned my commission and come home to be with him sooner. He was one of the old school. His name and family were everything to him. He was proud because I was doing my duty for my country. Pride and honour were all. He would not summon me simply because he had only a few months to live.'

'You must have been sad when you knew,' Helene said, the expression in her eyes thoughtful. 'My father died some years ago. We live with Mama's brother. I know very little of my family.' It was on the tip of her tongue to confess what she knew, but she held back.

'I was fortunate enough to know my grandparents well,' Max said. 'I recall that Grandfather was a stiff, cold man—but his wife was a sweet lady. She more or less brought me up after my mother died when I was a child. My mother's father died only last year. He left me everything. I was very fortunate to have such relations.'

'How sad for you that your mama should die, but fortunate that your grandparents were kind to you,' Helene said. She turned her head as they heard the music begin. 'I think we should rejoin the others, sir.'

'Yes, I am sure we should. I must not monopolise your time or your friends will not be pleased with me.'

Helene laughed and shook her head. 'Tell me, Lord

Coleridge— have you ever discovered who shot at you when we were at Richmond?'

'I fear nothing has been discovered as yet,' Max said and frowned. 'It may be that I shall have to go down to the country for a few days—but that will not be until after we have visited Vauxhall.'

'I dare say your estate takes a great deal of your time?' Helene glanced at him, noticing the tiny nerve flicking in his cheek.

'Yes, sometimes,' Max agreed. 'There may be some changes necessary before I can hold my house party. Nothing of any great moment, I assure you.'

'I see.' Helene nodded. 'I shall look forward to our visit to Vauxhall. I have been thinking that I might buy a few comfits and trinkets for the children. Shall you be visiting them again soon?'

'Perhaps on my return,' Max said. 'I see that Miss Marshall is looking for us. We'd best rejoin our party now.'

'So Lord Coleridge told you he may be going out of town for a few days? And he asked if we would join him at his estate at the end of the Season?' Mrs Henderson frowned when they spoke in Helene's room later that evening. 'He has certainly paid you some attention. I do not think he can be aware that you are Annesdale's granddaughter.'

'Oh, Mama—' Helene felt her throat tighten '—do you think it would distress him if he knew the truth?'

'I told you that they are close,' her mother said and sniffed. She waved her kerchief, sending waves of lavender water in Helene's direction. 'I am not sure what he would say, but I fear he might take Annesdale's part. If you married him, I might not be able to visit you often.'

'Do you want to go home, Mama?' Helene felt a strange ache in her breast. It was as if she had been stabbed to the heart, because all her dreams must end now.

'Not yet. There are other gentlemen, Helene. Could you not bring yourself to marry Mr Bradwell if he asked you?'

'I am not sure, Mama,' Helene said, her face very white. 'I do not truly like him, but if you say I must…'

'No, I shall not force you to take him,' Mrs Henderson said. 'But there must be someone else you've met that you like enough to marry—someone who will not be influenced by Annesdale?'

'I do not know…' Helene felt overwhelmed by her disappointment. 'I think I am in love with Lord Coleridge, but I am not sure that he loves me—or that he would accept me if he knew the truth.'

Helene went driving in the park with Miss Marshall and her brother Paul the next morning. She had decided that she must carry on as usual until they could leave town, but she had kept a distance between herself and Captain Marshall. Helene sensed that he was considering making her an offer, but she could not allow it— she knew she did not love him. Her heart belonged to another. When Captain Marshall suggested that she might like to attend a balloon race with a party of his friends the following week, she smiled and told him that she had a prior engagement. His expression showed that he was disappointed, and perhaps a little offended, but her pride would not let her continue as an intimate friend when she knew that she could never accept an offer from him.

She returned home just before noon, a little surprised to see a large travelling coach moving away from the house. A gentleman was staring out of the window, and he seemed to sit forward as the coach drew near to her. Helene frowned, for she knew that he was the Duke of Annesdale. How dare he call here? He must know he was not welcome after the way he had behaved to Mama.

She went straight upstairs to take off her bonnet, but she had not yet changed for nuncheon when someone tapped at the door. A moment later it opened and her mama entered.

'Helene dearest,' Mrs Henderson said. 'Did you enjoy your drive?'

'Yes, Mama,' Helene replied. 'Have you had visitors this morning? I saw a coach leaving just as I returned from the park. I believe it may have belonged to the Duke of Annesdale…'

'Yes, he was here. He asked to speak to you or, failing that, to me. I was lying down with a headache and refused him.'

'Was that wise, Mama? I think perhaps he might be a dangerous enemy.'

'What more can he do to me—except take my daughter from me?'

'He shall not do that, Mama.'

'Then I have nothing to fear.' Mrs Henderson smiled at her. 'I cannot blame him for wanting you—but I do not think I could bear to give you up, my love. I know I am selfish and—'

'You are not selfish!'

'Supposing it comes to a choice between Lord Coleridge and me?'

'If he could not see how unfair such a choice was, he would not be the man I care for.'

'You do care for him,' her mama said and sniffed. 'If I have caused you unhappiness, I shall never forgive myself.'

'Please do not cry, Mama,' Helene begged. 'Lord Coleridge has not asked me to marry him—and I dare say he will not.'

'You say it does not matter, but I know you will break your heart,' Mrs Henderson said. 'But I am being foolish. You must get ready. Amelia is taking you to visit her orphanage this afternoon...'

'Well, what do you think of my children?' Amelia said as they finished their tour of the house. 'I like to think that they are being taught to become responsible citizens of the future.'

'They all look happy and well fed,' Helene said. 'I enjoyed sitting in on their lessons, Amelia. Do you know, I think I could be content as a teacher. I know I could be a governess if I wished, but I think it must be more rewarding to teach in a school like yours. They have come from misery and poverty and yet they show such courage and resilience.'

'Some of the boys were very unruly when they first came,' Amelia said and looked thoughtful. 'I suppose the girls would do well with a woman to teach them how to sew—but surely you will not think of it, Helene? Would you rather not be married?'

'I suppose I might,' Helene said and wrinkled her brow. It was impossible to explain, for she could not tell Amelia about the duke or that infamous letter. 'But I cannot marry unless someone asks me—and I would only wish to marry if I could like the gentleman. I have not yet given up hope of meeting someone I can like well enough to wed.'

'I thought…' Amelia hesitated and shook her head. 'No, I should not say. You know your own feelings best, Helene.' She glanced at Emily, who had lingered to talk to the housekeeper. 'I believe we ought to be leaving, for we have an engagement this evening. I have thought of setting up another home in the country— somewhere I can send those who need a little extra care. Do you think that would be a good idea? I have been fortunate here for Mrs Rowley was looking for a position, and her husband is very good about the place. Mr Makepeace is an excellent tutor and he does not mind helping with other things. I am not sure that I should be as lucky again. I would not wish to employ someone who would treat the children badly, though I know they need a firm hand.'

'I dare say that is the difficult thing, finding the right staff,' Helene said and looked thoughtful. 'As you say, you have been lucky here, Amelia. Perhaps it is enough.'

'I do not think it will ever be enough,' Amelia replied. 'My brother thinks me foolish, of course. He says it is a waste of money and that the children are slum rats and will remain so whatever I do.'

'Oh, no,' Helene said. 'I think you are doing a won- derful thing, Amelia. More people of consequence should set up homes of a similar kind, there must always be a need for them, I believe.'

'There certainly is,' Amelia replied. 'There are few other places these children can go. Most of them would be sent to the workhouse if they were not here. Have you any idea of what happens to them there? They are given poor food, made to do physical, hard work, and when they are old enough they are sold to masters who will work them even harder. They have no choice, no control over their lives at all.'

Helene nodded agreement. She told Amelia about the climbing boy she had rescued at her uncle's house. 'His master demanded to be paid ten guineas for him. In the end I paid much less, but it was not right that he should be able to buy and sell the boy.'

'It certainly was not,' Amelia said and smiled at her. 'When you are married, you must set up your own charity, Helene. You may invite gentlemen of influence to your salon and try to influence them to use their power in government to change the laws. Until that happens, we can only do so much.'

Helene had enjoyed her visit to the orphanage, because the children had looked healthy, well fed and content. It was proof of what could be done when one had money. Lord Coleridge's orphanage was in the country, and Amelia's was in the poorest part of London, but they were both doing excellent work.

It would be pleasant to be the wife of a wealthy man, Helene thought, a little wistfully. She would have had many interests in common with Lord Coleridge, but there was no point in thinking of it. She could not marry him even if he asked. He was related to the Duke of Annesdale and fond of him. Helene could never accept that man in her life.

It was obviously best if she put all thought of Max Coleridge from her mind.

Mrs Henderson had decided to keep to her bed. On the Sunday morning, Amelia was worried and called the doctor to her. He came, prescribed a tonic and said that it was either a chill or an irritation of the nerves.

'I am well enough,' Mrs Henderson said when Helene took a tray of tea and comfits up to her. 'I think I have a summer cold and should stay in bed for a few days. You must not think of giving up your pleasures for my sake, Helene. If I feel no better in a few days, I may go home—but you will stay here with Amelia for the time being. At least until…' She sniffed and held a small bottle of smelling salts to her nose. 'Do not worry, my love. In a day or so I shall be better. If you would be so kind as to fetch me some books from the lending library, I shall do well enough here.'

'Of course, Mama,' Helene agreed. 'I have engaged to go to an art collection with Miss Marshall and Emily this morning. I can quite easily call in at the lending library on my way home.' She looked at her mother anxiously. 'Are you sure you do not wish for company? Emily may go in my stead and I could read to you.'

'You are a sweet girl to think of it, but I shall not hear of it. Run along now and make the most of your visit. I do not know when we shall come to town again.'

'Do not worry, Mama. I shall think of something,' Helene promised. 'If you are so unhappy living under my uncle's roof, we shall not live there for ever.'

'I wish things might be different.' Mrs Henderson shook her head, tears brimming in her eyes. 'Go away now, Helene. I want to rest.'

Helene was obedient to her wish. She collected her pelisse for there was a little chill in the air that morning—the first sign, perhaps, that the weather might turn. Joining Emily downstairs, the two of them went out to the carriage.

Miss Marshall was waiting when they arrived at the gallery. Her mother accompanied her, but there was no sign of her brother.

'Paul had another engagement,' she said. 'He says he has danced attendance on me long enough and has only a few days before he must leave for his regiment. They are based near Lyme Regis at the moment, but he expects a posting to India quite soon.'

'Oh, I did not know that.' Helene looked at the other girl as Emily fell into step with Lady Marshall. 'Does Captain Marshall mean to make a career in the army? I thought perhaps he might give up the life in time to help your father manage the estate.'

'Paul is my younger brother,' Miss Marshall told her. 'I have two older brothers, Helene. He has a small estate of his own, but employs an agent. He says that he shall stay in the army for some years to come…though he did think he might give it up soon. However, he has changed his mind.' Her look was a little accusing and Helene felt that she was being blamed for his decision.

'I think if I were a man, I should choose to remain in the army. It must be exciting to travel to foreign lands.'

'Do you think so? I should not care for it,' Miss

Marshall said. 'Oh, do look at this landscape. It is rather fine, is it not?'

Their conversation was concentrated on the pictures for some minutes after that, and when they parted company Miss Marshall seemed to have recovered her usual good humour. She kissed Helene on both cheeks and said that she looked forward to seeing her very soon.

It was as Helene and Emily were emerging from the library half an hour later that they met Lord Coleridge. He stopped and doffed his hat, smiling at them.

'I hope you are looking forward to tomorrow evening, ladies? I believe it may keep fine, though it is cooler today, is it not?'

'Yes, a little fresher,' Emily said. 'We are very much looking forward to joining you tomorrow, Lord Coleridge—are we not, Helene?'

'Yes…yes, we are,' Helene said. She could not meet Lord Coleridge's eyes, her cheeks hot as she glanced down at her shoes. He would not look at her so kindly if he knew the way things stood between her family and the Duke of Annesdale. 'I am sure it will be a very pleasant evening.'

'Have you visited the new art collection?' Max asked.

Helene risked a glance at him and saw that his eyes were serious as he looked at her. He must be able to sense the reserve in her, because she had always been so free with him. She tried to smile, but knew it was a woeful effort.

'We have been this morning,' she said. 'There were some fine landscapes after the style of Mr Constable— though not quite as good in my opinion.'

'You enjoy good art?' Max asked and Helene nodded. 'I have been collecting for a while, though most are in store until I am ready to hang them.'

'At your home in the country?'

'Yes, I think so. I stay at my club while I am in town—as yet I have no need for a town house, though that may change,' Max said. 'I think you must excuse me, ladies. I have an appointment and I am sure you have things to do.'

'We are going on to a poetry reading at Lady Jamieson's house this afternoon,' Emily told him. 'She is sponsoring a new poet—a gentleman by the name of Mr Tarleton.'

'Henry Tarleton,' Max nodded. 'I have read something of his—the man is a Cit and has no soul.'

'That is unfair, sir!' Helene cried. 'To say that he has no soul merely because he is in trade is abominable. I did not imagine you to be such a snob!' Her cheeks were flushed and she felt hot as his eyes dwelled on her.

'I beg your pardon if I have offended you,' Max replied. 'It was a careless remark. The man's poetry is dull and I find it without passion or soul. His being a Cit is certainly nothing to the point.'

'I should hope not,' Helene said. 'A man cannot help his birth and those born to privilege should respect others for their character and not their social standing.'

Max frowned, but said nothing in reply, his eyes reproachful as he gazed at Helene. Her cheeks were flaming, but she would not look at him.

'I believe we ought to hurry on or we shall keep everyone waiting for nuncheon,' Emily said, looking at Helene in concern.

'Then I must certainly not delay you longer,' Max said. 'I look forward to tomorrow evening.'

'As do we,' Emily answered, but Helene merely looked at the ground. Her feelings were in such disorder that she hardly knew how she felt and could not bring herself to speak.

The two ladies walked on in silence. After a moment Emily glanced at Helene. 'You have not quarrelled with Lord Coleridge?'

'No, of course not,' Helene said. She still felt hot and uncomfortable, and was realising that she had been unnecessarily sharp. 'I just felt that he was unfair.'

'When you have listened to several of Mr Tarleton's poems, you may feel that Lord Coleridge was less unfair than you imagine.'

'It was not his remark about the poetry that made me cross. However, you are right to censure me, Emily. I should not have been rude to him.'

'I do not think Lord Coleridge a snob. We are all in the habit of calling persons in trade by that name, but it is not necessarily meant to disparage,' Emily said. She looked at Helene's face. 'If something is troubling you, I would be happy to listen, Helene.'

'You have been a good friend,' Helene said. 'There is nothing to tell you, but I do thank you for the offer.'

Helene's eyes stung with tears, but she refused to let them fall. She had made so many good friends and it made her sad when she thought about the future. When they left town she would probably never see any of them again.

Lord Coleridge's remark might not have been meant to disparage, but it showed what he must think of persons in trade. What would he say if he knew that Helene was the granddaughter of a tanner?

Helene had never believed that she was at a disadvantage because of her background. Even when her mama had warned that Lord Coleridge's family might find it objectionable she had believed that Max was above such things—but now she was not as sure.

Supposing he decided that she was beneath his touch! To see him turn away in distaste would be so hurtful, she did not think that she could bear it.

When Helene woke the next morning she was aware of a heavy feeling, as if a cloud hung over her. She wished that she had not promised to visit Lady Annersley, but Mama had told her that she must keep her word and of course it would be rude to cry off at the last.

Helene dressed in a dark blue walking gown; it was severe but elegant and made her feel equal to the task. Lady Annersley's house was in a fashionable square near by. She did not need to order the carriage, and she had no intention of asking Emily to accompany her. Instead, she summoned her maid.

'I have a morning call to pay,' she told the girl. 'You will accompany me and wait in the hall. I dare say I shall not be more than a few minutes.'

Tilly dropped a curtsy. 'Yes, Miss Henderson.'

Helene chose an elegant pelisse of deep yellow, which went well over the gown of dark blue, matching the ribbons on her bonnet. She was determined not to appear cowed. Whatever the lady had to say to her, she would remain polite and dignified and she would not lose her temper!

Lord Coleridge's opinion of Mr Tarleton's poetry had proved justified in part. Helene would not go as far as to say he had no soul, but his work was certainly without passion. She was uncomfortably aware that she had been hasty in her condemnation; her temper was sometimes volatile and she must learn to control it!

She held her head high as they reached their destination, standing back while her maid knocked at the door and then announced to the footman who answered that her mistress had come to call on Lady Annersley. Helene had had visions of being sent to the tradesman's entrance, but the imposing front door was held wide and the footman inclined his head.

'You are expected, Miss Henderson.' He looked at Tilly. 'You may sit there, girl. I shall take your mistress upstairs.'

'I shall not be long.' Helene looked apologetically at the girl, for she was a little apprehensive now that they were inside what was obviously a much grander house than Miss Royston's. 'Remember we are going shopping later. We shall buy you a new bonnet.'

'Yes, miss.' Tilly summoned a grin.

Helene followed the footman up the wide staircase. It was hung with paintings of men and women, possibly past Dukes of Annesdale and their ladies, she thought, since it was the duke's house.

At the head of the stairs the footman turned to the right. They walked to the end of the landing and he threw open a pair of magnificent mahogany doors.

'Her ladyship will be with you in a moment.'

'Thank you.' Helene walked into the room. It was furnished with heavy pieces of mahogany with richly brocaded upholstery. The walls were hung with more paintings, some of them landscapes, and there was a cabinet filled with what Helene thought must be gold objects at the far end. Everything was slightly opulent, almost decadent; it was clearly the home of a very rich and important family.

She was studying one of the landscapes when she heard footsteps behind her. She drew a deep breath and turned slowly to face the woman who stood there, dipping in a slight curtsy.

'Ma'am, I am come as you requested.'

'I am glad of it,' Lady Annersley replied. 'I wish to talk to you for a moment alone—and then I should like to make you known to my father-in-law.'

'Why?' Helene lifted her head. 'I do not know what the duke can have to say to me, ma'am. I certainly have little to say to him.'

'He has wanted to make himself known for some time,' Lady Annersley said. 'We were not informed of your birth, but it was brought to our attention some years later. Until recently it was not thought of any consequence. However, my husband died soon after the stillbirth of my last child.'

'I am very sorry to hear that, ma'am,' Helene said, her hackles rising at the woman's arrogance. 'I do not see what it can have to do with me?'

'Has that woman told you nothing?' Anger glittered in Lady Annersley's eyes. 'She ruined your father by marrying him and she has deliberately withheld the knowledge of your birth from Papa—and now she has withheld Annesdale's offer from you. I do not know what your father ever saw in her. She was the daughter of a common tanner. Passable to look at, I dare say, but he could have done much better!'

'You are wrong, ma'am. I know that I am the duke's granddaughter—but still I have nothing to say. Because of the arrogance of Papa's family, Mama has had much to bear.'

'She is the daughter of a tanner. How your father can have been so lost to his duty as to have married such a person I do not know!'

'I do not think you should say such things to me, ma'am,' Helene said, feeling angry. 'Mama has done you no harm…'

'No harm? She brought our family into disgrace—'

'You are the disgrace, ma'am,' Helene cried as her good intentions fled. 'I will have you know that I am proud of my mama and her family. I have had more kindness from them than from—'

'You are insolent. If I had my way, you would not even have been invited here—'

'Sarah, if you please…' A gentleman had walked into the room. Helene knew at once that he was the duke. She was quivering with anger, stung by the unfairness of Lady Annersley's attack. 'You may leave us now, if you will.'

'She should be made aware of her duty to you—to the family,' Lady Annersley began angrily, but he lifted his hand and she was silenced. 'Very well, have it your way…' She walked from the room, clearly angry.

Helene looked at the gentleman. His hair was white, his eyes a faded blue, his cheeks lined with age and perhaps illness. However, he stood straight, unbowed, pride in every line of his body. She made him a curtsy while keeping her head high and her expression proud. He nodded, a faint smile in his eyes.

'Forgive my daughter-in-law, she is very loyal to me and she has a temper, which I think perhaps you have, too, Miss Henderson.' He was silent for a moment, his gaze intent. 'You are something like my second wife—your father's mother…' Helene gave a little shake of her head, as if in denial. 'I called on your mother and I have written to you many times. You did not receive any of my letters?'

'No, sir. I believe my mother may have kept them from me—and I imagine you will understand her feelings in this matter. She has been treated ill by you and others.'

He frowned, but did not reply, going on as if she had not spoken. 'Your father was my youngest son, but my favourite. I suppose that was why I was so angry when he threw his life away.'

'By marrying my mother?'

He inclined his head. 'Yes, by taking a wife who was not of his class.'

Helene was silent for a moment, then, 'Is a man less for having been born poor, then? My grandfather was one of a family of six boys and five girls. He had nothing but his wits and his hands, but he built a considerable business, which he passed on to his children. My uncle was sent to a good school and is generally thought a gentleman, and my grandmother was the daughter of the younger son of a country squire. I have every reason to be proud of Mama and Grandfather. I shall not hang my head in shame because he happened to be a tanner by trade.'

'You are very proud. In that you are like me.'

'Mama's father was also proud. He did not wish her to marry into a family who would not acknowledge her.'

'You think we acted unfairly towards your mama?'

'I am certain of it.'

'You do not understand. Our family goes back to the Conqueror.'

'So?' Helene's eyes glittered.

'We could not admit your mother to the family,' he said heavily. 'It would not have been acceptable. You may think me hard, but I had no choice. I had my sons to consider, their wives and children. I did not know then that I should lose them all. It is a hard thing for a father to lose all his sons, Helene. I should have died with my grandchildren around me, secure in the knowledge that they would succeed me. I have no one—at least only Sarah. I am grateful for her company. She might have married again, but she has refused to desert me.'

'That was noble of her.'

'Ah, you speak bitterly. You are angry because I have told you the truth. I could not lie to you, Helene. If we are to trust one another, we must be honest from the start.'

'Why should I trust you?'

'You have little enough reason. I know that your situation is precarious. I could make things so much better for you. If I acknowledge you as my granddaughter, you will make a good marriage. Houses that have not yet been opened to you will receive you. You will inherit most of my disposable fortune when I die—and if your husband is willing to add my name to yours, I will make your children my heirs.'

'Why would you do this for us now?' Helene looked at him suspiciously.

'I offered your mother an income if she would give

you up to me as soon as I learned of your father's death. It was only then that I knew I had a granddaughter.'

'If she would give me up? You are saying that you want me—but not Mama?' Helene felt the disgust choking her. 'She told me of your offer, but I could hardly credit that you would dare to make me such an offer to my face.'

'I see you do not mince words. I think you get that from me. Your father was honest also. He told me that if I would not accept his wife, he would have nothing to do with me—and he kept his word.'

'What makes you imagine that I would be less honourable than my father, sir? Why should you think that I would give up my mother for your sake?'

'You have much to gain—and perhaps even more to lose.'

Helene's gaze narrowed as she saw the glint in his eyes. 'Are you threatening me, sir? Mama feared you. She has been in great distress of late and now I understand why.'

'She has tried to keep you from me. You are my only grandchild, Helene. My only hope of an heir.'

Helene felt the anger rising inside her. 'Then why did you not offer her a home? I should have come with her and you might have known me as a child. Why did you make her wait in the kitchen while my father spoke to his mama? Why did your family treat her as if she were nothing?'

'Your mother is a tanner's daughter. I am a proud man, Helene.'

'And I am a tanner's granddaughter.' Helene raised her head and looked him in the eyes. 'I am not ashamed of who I am, sir. If I am ashamed of anything, it is that I carry your blood.'

His face went white and he seemed to stagger for a moment, but he righted himself and his eyes were hard. 'Then you refuse my offer? Your mother would have her own home somewhere in the country, and you have my word that the estate would go to your heirs.'

'I am not for sale,' Helene told him proudly. 'Had you offered us both a home when Papa died, I should have honoured and loved you—but you are despicable. Excuse me, I must leave.'

'If you go, you may ruin yourself. I know that you have hopes of Lord Coleridge. His father was a proud man. You may not know it, but we are close, almost as father and son. A word from me and your hopes would be at an end. He is distantly related and I had intended that he should inherit the Annesdale estate, though my private fortune would have come to you had you not refused me. Do you imagine he would give that up for the granddaughter of a tanner?'

Helene did not turn her head to look at him. His words were like a dagger thrust into her heart, but she would not allow him to see her pain. He could do his worst—she had already made up her mind that honour must make her walk away from the man who might have brought her so much happiness.

'Do not go, Helene…' The duke's voice held a world of pain. 'My wretched pride…you are my only hope…'

Helene walked down the corridor and then the stairs. Tilly was sitting in the hall, flirting with one of the footmen.

'We are leaving,' Helene said and forced herself to

remain calm. 'I think we should go shopping, for I may not be in town much longer.'

Helene paced the floor of her bedchamber. She felt so angry that she did not know how she would face her friends or her mother. She could not bring herself to tell Mama that she had quarrelled with the duke. Mrs Henderson had done all she could to avoid the confrontation, but Helene had walked straight into it and had behaved recklessly. Her anger had made her speak out and now he would ruin Helene's chances.

Helene knew that she did not wish to marry any man of her acquaintance save one. That must be at an end! So she would not marry.

Poor Mama! She had not deserved to be treated so scurvily. They would have to return to Uncle Edgar's house, and her mother would continue to be unhappy.

Helene would have to find work, somewhere they could both live. She knew that she would enjoy working with children as Ann Saunders did. Amelia had spoken of setting up a second home in the country if she could find the right people to take care of the children. Perhaps she would offer the chance to them.

Helene would do most of the work. Her mama could keep accounts and perhaps help with the cooking. It was the only way out of this mess as far as Helene could see.

But first she had to get through this evening. Helene was almost certain that Lord Coleridge had planned the evening for her benefit. It was exactly the kind of thing she loved, but tonight it would be difficult to keep a smile in place. It would be difficult to face Max Coleridge knowing that she had quarrelled with a man he thought of almost as a father. Perhaps the duke had already summoned him? It might be that he would cancel the outing that evening rather than spend time with her.

Chapter Seven

Helene dressed in a gown of emerald silk that evening. Her maid styled her hair back in a complicated twist, allowing tendrils to fall about her face. Afterwards, Tilly looked at her doubtfully.

'You are pale tonight, Miss Henderson. Would you like me to apply a touch of rouge to your cheeks?'

'Thank you, but no,' Helene said and touched her hand. 'Do not worry, Tilly. My looks do not matter. You have dressed me most elegantly and I am satisfied with my appearance.'

The ache in her heart had been steadily growing all day, and she thought that the only answer for her pain was that she was indeed in love with Max.

Clearly she could not go on seeing him. Her quarrel with the duke had put an end to any hopes she might have had in regard to Lord Coleridge. Helene was determined to speak to her mama the next day and ask if they could go home. However, she could not bear to give up her last chance to see Max. She would make the most of this evening, and then she would refuse all future invitations from him.

It had been made clear to her that she was not to be allowed her happiness. The duke had sufficient influence with Max Coleridge to put an end to her hopes. Mama had warned her that they were close, but Helene's temper had led her astray. The quarrel with Annesdale had sealed her fate. Max would not give up friendship and fortune for her sake—nor would it be right to expect it. Helene had believed that he might just accept the fact that her grandfather had been in trade, though his careless remark about Mr Tarleton had made her wonder if she knew him as well as she had thought. She had intended to tell him the truth when they next met and take her chances, but now she saw that a marriage between them would be impossible.

Max dressed with care that evening. He smiled as he used his third neckcloth in an effort to perfect a style he had been toying with for a few days, achieving his aim at last. He looked tolerably well—respectable and wealthy, in the prime of his life. He had a comfortable home in the country and the wherewithal to buy a town house if his chosen bride wished to visit often. Was it enough to tempt her?

Max had come to the conclusion that Miss Helene Henderson was the lady who would best fill the position of his wife. There were other beautiful ladies, some of them heiresses—but none of the others had captured his attention as Helene had. He enjoyed her company, missed her when he did not see her, and he found her very attractive, desirable. He had kissed her on impulse when he rescued her from the apple tree and the fierce hunger that seized him as he held her had surprised him. He was not sure whether his feelings amounted to being in love, for he had never felt more than a passing desire for any other woman. However, he had come to the conclusion that he should ask Helene before someone else stole a march on him.

Vauxhall was an ideal place to propose, because there were many secluded areas. He could draw her aside into a pretty arbour and make his feelings known to her. If she indicated that she would be happy to accept, he would call on her mama the next day.

Smiling because he was relieved to have made a decision, Max added a magnificent diamond stickpin to his cravat and slipped his signet ring on his little finger. This evening would, he believed, settle his future.

Helene smiled apprehensively as Max greeted her. He had called to collect them in his carriage, an impressive vehicle with his family crest emblazoned on the side panels and a team of the most magnificent horses Helene had ever seen. She knew that he was a member of the prestigious Four-in-Hand club, though he was not driving his team himself that evening.

'You look beautiful,' Max told her as he handed Helene into the carriage and climbed in beside her. 'I have been looking forward to showing you Vauxhall. The gardens are lovely at this time of the year, and there are some interesting booths. We may see artists and even playwrights offering their wares for sale, as well as other merchants.'

'I am looking forward to the fireworks,' Helene replied, dropping her gaze. He was staring at her in such an intimate way that she could not doubt he meant her to know he liked her very well. If only she had not agreed to meet Lady Annersley! If she had not quarrelled so dreadfully with the duke, she might have gone on as before.

'Oh, so am I,' Emily said from the opposite seat. 'No matter how often I see them, I am charmed.'

Helene nodded and smiled. She would not allow herself to think of the future this evening! If it were to be her last in Max's company, she would make the most of every second.

Toby Sinclair joined them as they strolled past the booths, glancing at various trinkets displayed for sale. They stopped to glance at some enamelled snuff boxes and scent flasks, and Toby considered buying a fine example of Bristol blue glass, but did not part with his blunt in the end.

It was as they lingered at a booth displaying some rather exquisite miniature paintings done on porcelain, which could be made up into jewellery or set into picture frames, that a gentleman came up to them. Helene had never met him, but she saw at once that the gentlemen all knew each other well. Amelia also seemed to know the newcomer, but Helene could not tell whether she was pleased to see him or not, for her face did not reflect any emotion, though her hands curled into tight balls at her sides for just one moment. In another second she was smiling as she turned to Helene.

'Helene dearest, may I introduce the Earl of Ravenshead—my lord, this is Miss Helene Henderson. She is staying with me in town.'

'Delighted,' the earl said, nodding his head towards

Helene. He looked a little puzzled as his gaze returned to Amelia. 'I have just today arrived in town. Max was good enough to invite me to join you all, for I have no engagements as yet.'

'I am giving a card party on Saturday,' Amelia said. 'Perhaps you would like to join us, sir?'

'Yes, thank you, I should,' he replied and arched one eyebrow. 'I may call before that if you have a free moment. I have something I should like to discuss with you concerning my daughter. Max has been telling me that you are the patroness of an orphanage, Miss Royston. I should be most interested in seeing it.'

'Yes, of course. You may call tomorrow morning if you wish.'

Somehow they had separated into three couples. Amelia walked a little ahead with the Earl of Ravenshead. Toby Sinclair followed with Emily and Helene walked at Max's side.

'You are a little quiet this evening,' Max said and glanced at Helene's face. 'Is something troubling you?'

'Oh, no, certainly not. I was just thinking of our visit to your orphanage. I very much admire Miss Saunders and my thoughts return often to her and her wonderful work. I think it must be very satisfying to do such work with children—especially those who have come from poor homes.'

'You are very right. When I first took them there, some of the lads had been starved and beaten, forced to do work that even a grown man would find tiring. It is unbelievable what some masters expect of their apprentices. I think the boys find it difficult to believe that their new life isn't just a dream.'

Helene nodded. 'I dare say it must seem that way to them. With an education behind them, they will find it much easier to gain employment of a more congenial kind when they are older.'

'We shall have clerks and bankers, and tailors—perhaps even the new prime minister,' Max said, laughter in his eyes.

'I do not think it likely, though of course there is no good reason why not,' Helene said. 'Though I believe such honours go more usually to a more privileged class.' She arched her brows at him.

'Do I detect a note of disapproval in your voice?' Max looked at her, gaze narrowed. 'I know there are rotten boroughs where the rich and influential bribe people to vote for their candidate, and of course my seat in the House of Lords is hereditary—but I think on the whole we are honest and well meaning, even if we make mistakes.'

'I did not mean to question such privilege,' Helene said. 'I dare say there is nothing wrong with it, providing someone does not abuse their position. However, I have often wondered why a lady may not vote or stand for a seat in parliament.'

'Have you indeed?' Max chuckled deep in his throat. 'I see you are a radical, Helene—but I shall not harangue you with all the reasons why it would not work. Perhaps if you invited ladies of like mind to your salon, you could bring about the changes you desire.'

Helene's cheeks flushed. 'I did not say that I wished to change things, sir—only that I have wondered why it is so. Besides, I do not think that I shall ever be in a position to have a salon of my own.'

'Do you not?' Max's gaze was soft as it dwelled on

her face. 'I believe it might be arranged quite easily if your husband chose to help you—and I am sure that a liberal-minded man would not object to his wife taking an interest in politics and good works. I know that I should not.'

'Oh…' Helene's gaze flew to his face. What she saw there made her heart race. He was going to speak. She was certain he was about to propose to her. He must not! She had to stop him somehow! 'But I do not intend to marry.' The words were out before she could stop them, falling over themselves in an effort to save them both embarrassment. 'I have decided that I shall find myself a position similar to that of Miss Saunders and devote my life to looking after deprived children.'

Max's eyes narrowed; the laughter was gone from his face. Helene felt as if a knife had struck her in the heart as she saw his expression become closed, a little angry, hurt—even offended. She almost wished the words unspoken, but knew that this was how it must be. The duke hated her now. He would certainly forbid the marriage even if she agreed to it.

'Are you sure that is your wish?' Max asked in a careful, guarded tone. 'You must know that as a the wife of a wealthy man who cared for you, you could help children by giving them your patronage—as well as other things that might be near to your heart.'

'Yes, I am aware of that,' Helene said, her manner strained. She looked down, because she could not bear to see the glow fade from his eyes. She could not doubt that he liked her, but marriage was out of the question. 'If it were possible for me to marry, I should have considered it and I think it might have made me happy.' Her voice was close to breaking, but she held her misery inside, pride making her lift her head though she could not meet his gaze. 'However, it is impossible. Circumstances—there are reasons why I shall never marry. It is quite impossible.'

'Would you care to tell me those reasons, Helene?'

Something in his tone compelled her to look at him. 'I am unable to do so, for they concern others, as well as myself,' she said, her composure remarkable considering the rending pain in her heart. This was the hardest thing she had ever had to do! It hurt her so very much. 'I am sorry…'

'You need not apologise to me,' Max said, and his eyes were once again intent on her face. 'I must tell you that I shall be leaving town shortly. I have to pay a visit to my estate. I may not be back for some days.' He hesitated, then, 'In the matter of a position of the kind you envisage…I may have an opportunity in the future. If you were willing to receive me when I return, I could have some news that might interest you. If you are quite determined on your future?'

'I am certain that it is for the best,' Helene said and swallowed hard. She could see the others had turned to look at them. 'I believe Amelia and the others are waiting for us. I dare say they are ready for their supper.'

'And I am remiss in my duties as the host,' Max said. 'Please do not be distressed by anything that has occurred this evening, Miss Henderson. I hope that we shall continue as friends?'

Helene murmured something appropriate. He had taken her at her word and seemed to have recovered easily from his first shock and anger. Perhaps he had not truly cared for her at all, merely thinking her a suitable wife. If that were the case, he would soon forget her and turn his attentions to another young lady.

Max watched Helene for the remainder of the evening. She hid her emotions well, but he sensed her distress, though he did not know the reasons for it. Her prompt action in preventing him from speaking had saved them both embarrassment, but he did not think that she was embarrassed. Something else was making her look sad whenever she thought herself unobserved.

She conducted herself well throughout supper and the remainder of the evening, though she declined to dance with Toby when he asked. Max thought it might be that she did not wish to dance with him and had made some excuse about having eaten too much supper. She had eaten only a few mouthfuls and was clearly ill at ease, though when the firework display began she seemed to forget for a while and her delight was genuine. Once she turned to him and smiled when a particularly fine display made her clap her hands.

'Oh, this is so much fun. Thank you for bringing me, sir.'

'It was my pleasure.'

Max wished that he had waited to speak. He had arranged the evening for her pleasure and then spoiled it for her. It might be that she was frightened because she did not know him well enough—and yet he did not believe that anything truly frightened her. What reasons could she possibly have for saying that it was impossible for her to marry?

His emotions were mixed: anger, disappointment and

hurt pride warring in his mind. Yet, despite his feelings, something was telling him that Helene's distress was at least as great as his own.

He knew that ladies often said no the first time in the hope that they would be asked again, or by someone more important or richer. However, he acquitted Helene of playing games or of hanging out for a more prestigious title. She genuinely believed that she ought not to marry—but why?

He had told her that he would be out of town on impulse, wanting to give them both a breathing space before they met again, but it made sense. He had delayed his journey because he wished to continue his friendship with Helene. Now was surely the right time to make the visit to his home and to think about the future. Helene's refusal had made Max all the more certain that she was the only woman he wished to marry.

Damn it! He would not give up at the first fence. If he withdrew because his feelings were hurt, he would be a fool. If Helene had a problem, he would do what he could to discover it and see if it could perhaps be solved in some way.

Helene had no way of knowing Max's thoughts. She had managed to put on a brave face all evening, but alone in her room later that night she gave way to tears. Oh, how awful it all was! Had she been able to accept Max's proposal, she would have been the happiest of women! If she had been in any doubt of her feelings for him, she was clear now. She loved him so much that it had broken her heart to refuse him—at least, to prevent him from speaking. It would have been cruel and heartless of her to allow him to continue knowing what her answer must be. If only the Duke of Annesdale had never come to town! If she had controlled her damnable temper…

Helene cried herself to sleep at last.

Her dreams had been wild and made her toss and turn, crying out in anguish. She awoke, shaking, for she had seen Max lying on the ground with blood seeping from a wound to his chest. The dream was vivid, leaving her cold and frightened.

'No…oh, no,' she wept. It was a foolish dream— there was no reason to suppose that the rogue who had fired at him in Richmond park would do so again. Surely it had been just someone intent on robbery or some such thing? Helene forced herself to put the dream to the back of her mind, for there was nothing she could do and it was merely a dream.

She washed her face, dressing herself in one of her plainest gowns. She went downstairs and found her way into the walled gardens at the back of the house. It was very warm again and she thought it might turn out to be one of the hottest days of the year so far. She knew that she had engagements for most of the day. At some time during the day she must speak to Mama—beg her to take her home. Max had told her that he would call when he returned to town and perhaps have news of a position for her, but she did not think she could bear to work for him. It would mean she would have to see him, talk to him—and all the time she would be conscious of what she had lost. It would be best to make a clean break.

Perhaps Amelia would be willing to offer her a position? If Mama could come, too, it would be better for her than living in her brother's house—if she did not wish to, then Helene would take the position herself. If Amelia could not help her, she must either seek work as a governess or advertise for the kind of position she would most enjoy.

She hoped that she would not have to meet Max in company again, because to see that look of disapproval in his eyes would break her heart. She sighed as she went back upstairs. She must get ready for her first engagement of the day, and if her mama were awake she would tell her that she wished to go home as soon as possible.

'Go home? Why, Helene?' Mrs Henderson was sitting propped up against a pile of pillows, a tray of chocolate and soft rolls with honey beside her. 'We have at least another three weeks in town. It would seem rude if we were to break all our engagements and leave. No, we shall most certainly not go home, Helene.'

'We may be forced to…'

'What do you mean?'

'I visited Lady Annersley yesterday morning, Mama. The Duke of Annesdale is staying with her and he came into the room. He offered to make me his heir if I would live with him and abandon you. I told him that I wanted nothing to do with him—I am afraid we quarrelled dreadfully.'

'Helene!' Mrs Henderson looked at her in horror. 'You should not have done it, really you should not. You should at least have considered, dearest. You would have clothes, jewels and consequence—all the things I cannot give you. You would be foolish to give all that up.'

'Do you think those things mean anything to me?

Had he offered us both a home with him I should have thought him generous and kind, but he made it plain you would not be included in our world, though he did say he'd grant you a comfortable home to stay in. You are my mama and I love you. I would not live with that man now if he were the last man alive!'

'He could have given you so much, Helene,' Mrs Henderson told her. 'Sometimes I have felt so guilty for denying you what might have been yours—but your father would have nothing to do with the family after the way they treated me, and I could not betray his memory.'

'And nor shall I,' Helene said. 'But I think we should go home, Mama. The duke was furious when I refused his offer. If he were to cut us in public, it might be uncomfortable, for some people would be sure to take his side.'

'But your only chance of a future is to marry well, Helene.'

'I have decided I shall not marry. Instead, I shall seek a position as a housekeeper in a children's home. I shall ask for Amelia's help to find a place.'

'Helene, please do not! You are behaving very foolishly. I am sure that some of our friends would remain loyal and you might still marry well. Lord Coleridge—'

'No! It is impossible. He is too close to the duke.'

'But a position as a teacher...it is not what I wanted for you.'

'Mama, I must do something. I cannot continue to live at my uncle's expense—and I would prefer not to be married at all.'

'But you like Lord Coleridge. I know you do.' Mrs Henderson looked at her in distress. 'I know I have warned you against him, but if the marriage was arranged perhaps the duke would relent.'

'Lord Coleridge was about to ask me last night, but I told him I could not marry.'

'Helene! Why did you do such a foolish thing? I do not understand you.'

'The duke said that he had planned to leave the Annesdale estate to Max, but would disinherit him if I accepted an offer of marriage. I could not cause a breach between them, Mama.'

'Oh, Helene…I am so sorry. I have ruined your life…' She reached for a kerchief and dabbed at her eyes. 'Forgive me, my love. I have always disliked that man, but I did not imagine even he would be so vindictive.'

'I made him angry, Mama.'

'I warned you to be careful.'

'I know, but he made me so angry—the things he said…' Helene's head went up, her eyes moist with tears she would not shed. 'I should not have lost my temper, but it is done and there is nothing I can do to change it. I have made up my mind, Mama. I cannot marry Lord Coleridge and I shall marry no other.'

'Helene, dearest,' Mrs Henderson said, 'there are other gentlemen…you might find one you could care for if you gave yourself time.'

'Perhaps one day, when I have forgotten all this unhappiness,' Helene said. 'I know this is hard for you, Mama, but I think it is for the best.'

'Give me a few more days,' Mrs Henderson said. 'I have longed for this visit for your sake, Helene. I have dreamed of seeing you as the wife of a good man with a home and family of your own—let me come round to your new idea gradually.'

'Very well, Mama—a few more days,' Helene agreed reluctantly. 'But please understand that I shall not marry anyone—and if you prefer to return to my uncle's house, I shall find work for myself alone.'

Helene returned from her walk with friends to discover that a posy of roses had been left for her in her absence. The note said that they were from Mr Nicholas Bradwell, and asked if he might call on her in two days' time.

Helene frowned as she took the flowers to her room. She poured some water into a silver vase and arranged them on the dressing table. She had just set them down when her mama walked in.

'The roses are lovely,' Mrs Henderson said. 'Who sent them to you, my love?'

'Mr Bradwell.' Helene frowned at her. 'He has asked if he may call the day after tomorrow.'

'I am sure he means to offer for you,' Mrs Henderson said. 'Would you not consider taking him, Helene? It would be so much better for us both. I do not wish to live with Edgar—nor do I wish to become the matron at a children's home.'

'I am sorry, Mama. I could not bear to marry Mr Bradwell, even for your sake. I really could not.'

'Perhaps you need not give up all hope of Lord Coleridge. I have written to the duke and begged him to forgive you.'

'Mama!' Helene stared at her in horror. 'How could you do such a thing to me? I would never have asked him to relent. You know that I would not.'

'Perhaps you should give him what he wants?' her mother suggested. 'I have refused him for the sake of your father's memory, but perhaps I was wrong.'

'Never say such a thing again! I shall not give him what he wants and I shall write and tell him that you did not have my permission to write as you did.'

'Then marry Mr Bradwell. It must be either one or the other. You are my daughter and I shall not give you permission to work as a governess or a housekeeper.'

Helene stared after her as she walked from the room. She sat down on the edge of the bed, feeling sick. How could Mama make such a threat—and what was she to do?

Mama did not truly mean it! She was distressed and Helene did not blame her for her little show of temper. Neither of them wished to return to live under Uncle Edgar's roof again. The only alternative was for Helene to find work. Mama might resist the idea, but she would relent in time—because Helene would never consent to marry Mr Bradwell.

'I am going down to my estate in the morning,' Max told Toby as they sat drinking a glass of wine together that afternoon. 'I asked Gerard if he would care to come, but he has other things on his mind for the moment. I do not suppose you would care to accompany me?'

'It would be my pleasure,' Toby replied. 'I can stay for a few days, and then I should go home. Mama says there is something she needs to discuss with me, but it is not urgent.' He frowned. 'You have something on your mind, I think?'

'I had a letter some while back,' Max told him. 'It has

disturbed me and I think I ought to make some inquiries. And then there was the attack on me in the park...'

'You have had no more incidents?'

'None. I am not even certain that the shot was meant for me—though it certainly passed close by. My agents have discovered nothing, and I have searched my mind for a name, someone I have offended. I can think of no one who would want me dead or who could benefit from my death...'

'Except your cousin. I believe you told me that, as things stand, he would inherit everything?'

'Yes...though I have left a letter of intent should I die violently or in mysterious circumstances.'

'He does not know this?'

'No. I might make Robert aware of what I have done. It depends on how I find him—and if there is any truth in what my neighbour wrote to me.'

'Do you care to tell me what the letter contained?'

Max looked at him thoughtfully, then got up and went to the drawer. He opened it and took out the letter, handing it to Toby. The younger man read it through and whistled.

'These are serious accusations, Max. He does not lay the blame on anyone, but you can see where his thinking lies.'

'It seems that my cousin may have been behind these vicious attacks on young women,' Max said and frowned. 'I have to discover what I can. The attacks might go on—and I need to know the truth.'

'It is very odd that they should have begun just after your cousin moved into the dower house. Who else lives with him?'

'My aunt and her physician. He is a gentleman and

seems everything he ought. I do not like him—his manner is too smooth—but he does not look like a man who would attack young girls. I would have thought he would not find it difficult to find a willing wench if he chose.'

'But your cousin… It is a serious charge, Coleridge.'

'One that I should not bring lightly,' Max agreed. 'The devil is in it either way, Toby! I have decided that I must discover the truth. Besides, I have some serious thinking to do about the future—and I shall do it best out of town.'

'Yes…' Toby looked thoughtful. 'I know exactly what you mean. Sometimes it is hard to make your choice when you are too close to things.'

'That sounds as if you have a decision of your own to make, Toby?'

'Yes, I have,' Toby replied and shook his head. 'It will keep for the time being. Your problems are more pressing than mine, Max. I am at your service. I may not have served under Wellington, but I am pretty handy with a pistol.'

'I pray that it will not come to that,' Max said and laughed. 'I am thinking of spending the evening at White's—do you care to come or have you another appointment?'

'I said I might look in at Lady Annersley's soirée, but I don't care if I give it a miss.'

'The duke is staying with her. I know that people think him stiff in the neck—and he did cut his youngest son off without a penny when he married a girl of whom he disapproved. However, I believe that he has suffered for it. He was great friends with Father and has always been good to me. I had a letter from him yesterday, asking me to call today, but I have not had the time. I must do so as soon as I return to town, however.'

'Unfortunate business, that—cutting his son out of his will,' Toby said. 'I should not care to be in that position, but it would not happen. My father would give me a lecture and then accept my decision.'

'Quite right, too,' Max said and smiled at him. 'Thinking of putting him to the test any time soon?'

'I am not sure,' Toby said, trying to look innocent, but failing badly. 'I have a call to make, Max. I'll see you at White's later.'

Max nodded. He frowned as his visitor left. His agents had come up with nothing in the matter of the attack on him, but before he left town he would set them another puzzle to solve.

Helene frowned as she looked through the notes on the salver in the hall and found one addressed to her. She did not recognise the hand, but when she turned it she that it had been sealed with the crest of Annesdale. She thrust it into her glove as she went upstairs. She had written to the duke, as she had told her mama she would—was this his reply? She had hoped that he would simply ignore both letters and she wondered if it would be best to destroy the letter without reading it.

Two days had passed since the argument with her mother. Helene had not yet spoken to Amelia about the position as a teacher, but she felt that she could not bear to go on like this for much longer. Mama was still cross with her, but she really could not bear to marry Mr Bradwell.

Perhaps the worst of all was that Mr Bradwell was

calling that afternoon at three. Helene had not written to him herself, but she knew that her mama had sent him a note inviting him for tea. He was sure to take it as encouragement. It was too bad of Mama!

Alone in her room, the tears suddenly welled up and began to trickle down her cheeks. How could she marry someone she did not like when her heart belonged to Max Coleridge? Yet if she did not, she must find work and Mama was against it. Helene did not wish to be at odds with her mother, but she could not bend to her will in the matter of this marriage.

A sob broke from her as the door of her bedchamber opened and someone walked in. Helene hurriedly brushed the tears from her eyes as she saw Amelia.

'Helene, my dearest,' Amelia said, 'whatever is the matter?'

'Oh…nothing…' Helene said and reached for her kerchief, wiping her face. 'I am being foolish…please ignore me.'

'No, I do not believe you would cry for nothing,' Amelia said and sat down on the bed beside her. 'Will you not confide in me, Helene? I would help you if I could, you must know that, dearest?'

'Mama is so cross with me…'

'What have you done that is so very terrible?'

'She wants me to marry Mr Bradwell, but I cannot. I really cannot—even though it means we must return to Uncle Edgar or find work.'

'You know you are welcome to live with me.'

'I know, but we could not expect more of you, Amelia. You have been so very generous.' Helene lifted her head. 'You know that Mama's father was a tanner—

and that the Duke of Annesdale is my grandfather? Oh, it is such a coil! I do not know what to do.'

'Yes, I know. Your mama told me her story long ago. I do not see why any of this should distress you, Helene.'

'The duke wanted me to live with him. He offered to leave me a lot of money—but I should not be able to see Mama, at least in public.'

'That was an outrageous offer. I imagine you refused?'

'I—quarrelled with him,' Helene said and sighed. 'I should not have done, for it has made things worse. He…he threatened me…'

'What did he say?'

'You know that he and Lord Coleridge are close?' Amelia nodded. 'Well, he says he shall leave Max his estate—but not if I refuse to live with him and give up Mama. He is so proud! He thinks Mama unfit to belong to his family because her father was a tanner.'

'Ah, I see,' Amelia said and frowned. 'Annesdale is a fool! What did you say to him?'

'I told him that…my shame was in having his blood, not Mama's.'

Amelia looked shocked. 'That was a little reckless, Helene. Annesdale is a proud man. I imagine he was angry?'

'Very angry indeed. It was after that the threat to Max was made.' Helene looked at her in distress. 'Mama is reluctant to go back to her brother's house. I wanted to find myself work, perhaps in an orphanage taking care of the children, but Mama will not permit me. She says that I should accept Mr Bradwell if he asks me—and I am sure he means to do so this afternoon. I do not wish to quarrel with Mama, but I truly cannot marry him.'

'Now I understand your tears,' Amelia said and nodded. 'Marie has been a little unfair to you. I understand how she feels. She has had a hard life and she wants you to have a better one, Helene.' Amelia's gaze was thoughtful. 'It is a pity that Coleridge did not come up to scratch before he went to the country. You might have been happy with him.'

'He…almost did, but I prevented him,' Helene said, her cheeks slightly pink. 'I could not let him speak after what the duke threatened.'

'No, you could not have done differently in the circumstances.' Amelia stood up and went over to the window, glancing out into the street. 'I must think about this, my love. My advice is to go to bed with a headache. I shall tell your mama that you cannot come down for tea this afternoon—and I will tell her something that may make her less eager for you to marry Mr Bradwell.'

'Do you not like him, Amelia?'

'I have heard rumours that he is in debt from gambling. How bad his situation is I have no idea, but it may give your mother pause for thought.'

Helene hesitated, then said, 'You once seemed as if you did not quite approve of Lord Coleridge.'

'Did I? If I gave you that impression, I am sorry, Helene. Max is a good friend. Something happened years ago, but I know he was not involved. I did think he might be interested in someone else, but then he began to pay attention to you.' She smiled. 'I should have liked to see you wed to a decent man. You have behaved in an honourable manner, my love—but I rather think something may be rescued from this mess. For the moment I believe you should plead a headache and let things rest.'

'You are so kind,' Helene told her. 'I thought you might be angry because I have wasted my chances.'

'I brought you to town because I like to have my friends about me. You owe me nothing, Helene—as for returning to a house where you are not welcome, I think there will be no need. I am sure I can find a home for you in one of my properties.'

'For Mama,' Helene said. 'If I cannot marry where I choose, I would rather work for my living in a children's home, where I might do some good for others.'

'That would be an easy solution to both your problem and mine,' Amelia said, 'but I do not give up so easily.'

'I am not sure I understand?'

'Do not bother your head, my love. Go to bed and rest—and then I am sure things will seem better.'

Helene undressed and crept into bed as Amelia left her. Her crying bout had given her an unpleasant headache so Amelia would not be telling Mama a lie.

The letter from the Duke of Annesdale lay forgotten with the gloves she had taken off when she came in.

Chapter Eight

It was late in the evening and dark when Max and Toby arrived at the Coleridge estate. Max frowned as he saw there were no lights in the windows of the house. He rapped sharply on the door, but it was a minute or two before someone came to open it. The sleepy footman stared at them in dismay, his mouth falling in dismay, his candle flame wavering in the breeze from the open door.

'Forgive me, my lord,' he apologised as he realised who it was. 'Mr Hale did not tell us that you were expected, sir.' He stood back to allow them to enter. 'The letter announcing your arrival could not have reached him.'

'I did not send one,' Max replied. 'My orders were that this house should be kept ready at all times. I did not expect to arrive and find it in darkness at this hour, even though I know it to be past ten.'

'Mr Hale took to his bed a few days ago, for he had a chill, and Mrs Hale has been busy running after him, sir.'

'Do I employ no other servants?' Max said angrily.

'You will inform Mrs Hale that I have arrived. I shall expect her to wait on me in the morning. I trust the bed-chambers have been aired recently?'

'Yes, my lord—at least, that is Mrs Hale's department. I shall ask her.'

'Please do so, and light some candles. Let's have a little life in this house. We shall want something to eat and drink before we retire. If the chambers are not ready, rouse some of the maids and have them made ready immediately. We shall want to retire in an hour.'

The footman sprang to life at once, lighting a branch of candles from his own and then another. As the light began to brighten the gloom a little, Max picked up one branch of candles, leading the way into a small parlour to the left of the door.

'We shall manage here for the moment,' he said and began to light more candles. 'Damn Hale! Even if he is unwell, he should have made certain that the house was running as it ought.'

'I dare say it would have been better prepared if they had known of your imminent arrival,' Toby observed with a wry smile. 'Mama says servants will get away with doing as little as they can, unless you have a good butler and housekeeper.'

'I thought Mr and Mrs Hale were reliable,' Max said with a frown. 'Even when I came back after the war the house was as clean as a new pin. I do not understand it. Forgive me. I think this is poor hospitality and I shall want an explanation in the morning.'

'It does not bother me,' Toby said, though his mother always had the family home running like clockwork.

Mrs Hale came bustling into the parlour a few

minutes later. She was all apologies for the welcome they had been given.

'I am sorry, sir. Hale has been ill and I gave the servants permission to go to bed early. Mrs Heronsdale gave orders that candles were not to be wasted so I thought it best to close the house at nine. Of course, if we'd known you were coming…'

'Since when has Mrs Heronsdale been the mistress here?' Max glared at her. 'I gave Hale my orders. The house was always to be kept in a state of readiness for visitors.'

'Well, I'm sure I'm sorry, sir—but she seemed so sure…' The housekeeper paused and looked bothered. 'Mrs Heronsdale comes to the house most days and she gives us orders, sir. We were told not to clean the guest chambers every week, because they were not needed— and she let two of the footmen and the upper parlour-maid go, my lord.'

'Indeed?' Max was angry, a little nerve flicking at his temple. 'You will bring the staff up to its original level as soon as possible, Mrs Hale—and in future you will refer Mrs Heronsdale to me.'

'Yes, sir,' the housekeeper said, a little smile of satisfaction on her lips. 'I did tell Hale to write to you, but he didn't want to bother you, my lord.'

'If you should have a similar problem in the future, I want to know—but I dare say it will not happen, for I shall speak to my aunt. She may do as she pleases at the dower house naturally, but this house will run as I see fit. I should like some wine, and something to eat—if you have anything in the house?'

'Oh, yes, sir. There is a cold ham in the pantry, bread

cooked this day and a bit of mutton, if that will do you with some relish this evening? Tomorrow I'll draw up some menus for you to approve. May I ask how long you will be staying this time, sir?'

'A few days. I must be back in London by the end of next week, but certainly three days, ma'am.'

'Hale will be pleased, sir. It always seems better when you're down, my lord.'

'Yes, well, I dare say I may bring a party of friends down later in the summer,' Max said, his anger fading. He had purposely not sent word of his visit, but he had not expected to find his orders countermanded. 'I shall let you know in good time.'

'Why did you not let them know this time?' Toby inquired as the still-anxious lady went away to see to their supper. 'I am sure they would have had everything just as you like it.'

'I had a reason for not doing so,' Max told him with an odd look. 'I am sorry we came to a closed house, but I was hoping to take my aunt by surprise. It seems she has taken the role of chatelaine on in my absence. It will be interesting to discover what else has been going on.'

Toby nodded. 'You need not apologise to me, my dear fellow,' he said. 'I shall be quite comfortable. As you say, perhaps it was for the best, otherwise you might not have known what was going on down here.'

'Precisely,' Max told him. 'After that incident at Richmond, I believe it is time that I made some changes here.'

'Coleridge.' Mrs Heronsdale came rushing into the parlour where Max was having breakfast with Toby the following morning. She was a large lady, heavy boned but thin, her face all angles and planes, her skin sallow against the black of her mourning gown. 'Why did you not let me know you were coming down? I could have made sure that everything was in order.'

'Aunt Tilda,' Max said as he and Toby both rose to their feet. 'May I introduce you to a friend of mine, Mr Sinclair—Toby, my aunt, Mrs Heronsdale.'

Toby murmured something and bowed his head. The lady looked a little surprised to see him, a flicker of what might be annoyance in her eyes.

'Forgive me for disturbing your breakfast, sir. Please carry on.'

'Will you not join us, Aunt?' Max asked. 'At least sit down so that we may also sit. May I give you some coffee?' He signalled to a footman, who set a chair for her, and another poured some of the fragrant liquid into a cup and set it before her. 'I am sorry if it disturbs you that I arrived unannounced, but I do not make it a habit to inform others of my movements. I expect my servants to obey my wishes and have my house ready at all times.'

A faint flush appeared in Mrs Heronsdale's cheeks. She glanced down at her delicate porcelain coffee can, her hands moving nervously in her lap. 'I may have spoken out of turn, Coleridge. I have been used to practising economy and I hate to see waste.'

'You may order the dower house as you please, of course, but I prefer to make my own arrangements here,' Max said smoothly. 'However, no harm was done. And we shall forget it. Did my cousin not accompany you this morning? I have come down on purpose to see him.'

'Then you have had a wasted journey,' Mrs Heronsdale told him. 'Robert has been ordered to his bed. He has been very ill, Coleridge. We truly thought we might lose him this time.'

'I am very sorry to hear that,' Max said and looked grave. 'I know you trust your own physician, but I really think you should let Dr Clarke advise you, ma'am. My cousin is a young man. He should not suffer from such frequent bouts of illness. I shall ask Dr Clarke to call later today.'

'No! You must not,' Mrs Heronsdale said and looked agitated. She jumped to her feet, obliging the gentlemen to rise, too. 'Oh, do sit down! I am going. My son is too ill to be troubled by a new physician. Excuse me, I must return to him at once. I left him only because I thought it my duty to welcome you home.'

The gentlemen remained standing until she had left the room. Toby threw Max a look of enquiry. 'Is she usually so agitated?'

'Whenever I suggest that Robert should see a different doctor she makes the same excuse. Robert is too ill to see anyone. I accepted it at first, for it might be true—but you saw the letter I had. I think I must make an effort to meet my cousin this time. I do not believe that a visit from me would endanger his life—do you?'

'I cannot think it,' Toby said and frowned. 'It seems an odd situation, Max. When shall you go?'

'Almost immediately, I think,' Max said. 'If you have finished your breakfast, Toby, perhaps you would care to walk down with me? I have tried to visit my cousin with my aunt's permission several times, but been refused. This time I thought I might use a little subterfuge and you may assist me, if you will.'

'Naturally—please explain, dear fellow.'

* * *

'Ask Mrs Heronsdale to show you the garden,' Max said as they walked through the gardens towards the dower house. 'It is the one thing she seems to have a passion for other than her son. I shall make an excuse to leave after we have been there for a few minutes— but you must keep her talking for long enough for me to slip up the back stairs to my cousin's room.'

'Do you think you ought?' Toby said and looked uncomfortable. 'It is a little deceitful. Could you not just demand to see Robert?'

'I have tried it before,' Max said. 'If this makes you uneasy, I'll find another way—but I am determined to see him for myself.'

'I'll do it, of course,' Toby said at once. 'I imagine she will be very angry when she discovers what you've done. It may be unpleasant for you.'

'I do not mind her anger,' Max said, looking concerned. 'Something is being hidden from me, Toby. I have to discover what it is and this is the only way I can do it. She defends her son like a dragon and there has to be a reason for it.'

'Yes, I do see that,' Toby agreed. 'Besides, you have to know if it was your cousin that took a pot shot at you in Richmond park.'

'That, too,' Max agreed. 'It points that way, of course, but I am not certain. I need to talk to Robert myself. So you'll keep her busy while I slip upstairs to Robert's room?'

'I will do my best,' Toby said. 'What excuse will you give for coming like this, so soon after her visit?'

'I shall apologise for my abruptness earlier, beg her

to forgive me—and then you will show interest in her garden. She has been asking me if she can change some things in the main gardens, so I have no doubt that she will try to influence you if she can, because so far I have resisted her plans.'

Toby looked thoughtful, then inclined his head. 'I am interested in gardens so it will not be too hard. If she has some unusual plants, we could be talking for hours.'

Max smiled. 'Half an hour should be sufficient. Well, here we are. Leave the talking to me for a start. I think that there are a few repairs needed to the house. I had set them in hand, but I shall enquire about the roof and a damp patch at the back of the house.'

'I was intrigued by what you are doing with the gardens here,' Toby said after they had been talking for some ten minutes or so. 'Would it be too much trouble to ask if I could see your gardens, ma'am? If I am not mistaken, I believe you have a new variety of magnolias, one I have been wanting to purchase.'

'Are you interested in gardening?' Mrs Heronsdale turned her sharp gaze on Toby. 'I have been trying to persuade Coleridge that he should have a magnolia walk.'

'Do you know, I have that very thing in mind at my own estate,' Toby said quite truthfully. 'Of course, my estate is quite small, nothing like this place, but I think it could be improved and I should like to plant a walk. I should like to talk to whoever has been planning your garden, ma'am.'

'I do it myself,' she replied, her mouth softening slightly. 'Would you care to see some of my rarer plants?'

'Yes, very much so,' Toby told her. 'May we go now?'

'I shall leave you. I must speak to someone about estate business,' Max said. 'Do not mind me, Sinclair. Spend as long as you like looking at plants. I shall see you later. Ma'am...I will speak to someone about that damp patch at the back of the house immediately.'

'I am not sure that I wish to speak to you,' Mrs Henderson said when Helene went to her bedchamber that morning. 'I had to make excuses to Mr Bradwell yesterday—and despite what Amelia said to me, I still believe he might be a good match for you, Helene.' She gave her daughter a look filled with reproach. 'Amelia was so kind as to offer me a home with her. It is quite lowering to be in my position, Helene. I accepted this visit for your sake, but I cannot take more from Amelia, though she swears I should be doing her a favour by living in a house that would otherwise be left empty.'

'Amelia is truly generous, Mama. She found me crying and would not rest until I told her why. I really could not bear to marry Mr Bradwell. I would much prefer to work for my living—as Papa and Grandfather did.'

'Well, I suppose you will have your own way. I hope that you will never have to live as I have, Helene. I do not think you have considered what your life will be if you do not marry.'

'Oh, Mama,' Helene said, 'I am so sorry for all you have suffered and I did not like to be at odds with you. I truly wish that I could make things better for you. It is because of the way that the duke has treated you— would continue to treat you!—that I do not wish to be taken up as his granddaughter. Had he acted towards you as he ought, I should have honoured him and loved him.'

'You are a good girl and I am sorry if I made you cry,' Mrs Henderson said, pulling at her delicate lace kerchief in an agitated manner. 'Run away now and make the most of the time we have left to us. You will not get a chance like this again.'

Helene left her mama's room with a heavy heart. She wished that she might have married and obliged her mother, but she simply could not marry Mr Bradwell.

For a moment Helene allowed herself to think of Max Coleridge. How long would he be away—and would she ever be able to meet him without feeling that deep ache in her heart?

Max walked round to the back of the house and let himself in by a little-used door. He could hear voices in the kitchen, but he passed it without being discovered and used the servants' stairs to gain access to the landing, which led to the main bedchambers. He knew that he had to be quick, because if he were discovered it would be awkward and he might be forced to leave without achieving his purpose. The first two doors were slightly ajar and a quick glance inside told him that they belonged to the mistress of the house. The next door opened at his touch, but it looked unoccupied. The fourth door was locked, which made him frown—if Robert were locked in, it would seem to confirm his fears. He tried the last door and immediately the smell of sickness told him that he had found the right room.

He went through the sitting room into the bedchamber behind. The windows were tightly shut, which accounted for the slightly unpleasant odour, and the blinds were drawn. If he had his way, he would pull back the blinds and open the window, but he did not wish to impose his authority as the head of the family—unless it was strictly necessary. As yet he did not know the nature of Robert's illness.

The man in the bed was lying on his back, the sheets pulled up to his chin. As Max approached, he could see that Robert looked pale, his eyes tightly closed. He bent over him, studying his face for a few moments.

Robert's sleep seemed odd…as if he were heavily sedated. When someone was ill, the bedcovers were normally messy, as if they had been tossed back. These were too tidy. He laid a hand on Robert's forehead. The young man opened his eyes and looked at him; for a moment he just stared and then he smiled.

'Cousin Max…' he said. 'You have come to visit me. I am glad to see you…'

Max gazed down at him. 'I am sorry to disturb you, Robert. I was anxious, for you have been ill each time I visit. I wanted to make sure you were being well cared for.'

'Have I been ill?' Robert seemed confused. His eyelids flickered and closed.

'Robert…' Max touched his shoulder. 'Robert…can you talk to me?'

'Robert had a disturbed night,' a voice said from behind Max. He turned and was in time to see the physician enter the room. 'I was forced to give him something to ease him earlier this morning. It makes Robert a little tired. You must forgive him.'

'Doctor Clarke.' Max inclined his head. He was immediately aware of a prickling sensation at the nape of his neck. The man's manner seemed genuine, but there was something about him that he instinctively disliked.

'Would you be good enough to tell me the nature of my cousin's illness? He is a young man and his appearance, though sickly, is not truly that of an invalid.'

'Robert is prone to violent chills and inflammation of the lungs,' the physician said, but he avoided looking at Max as he spoke. 'You may leave him to my care. I have cared for Robert since he was this high.' He held his hand waist high. 'He is as a son to me.'

Max stared at him, eyes narrowed. He had never liked the fellow; he thought him sly and he was certain something was not as it should be, though he could not quite decide what was wrong. Both Mrs Heronsdale and this man were hiding something!

'Nevertheless, I believe it will be best if I ask my own doctor to call and see him. Robert has been ill too often. I shall call in the morning. If there is no improvement, I shall return with my doctor.'

'That is your privilege, my lord.' Doctor Clarke inclined his head, his eyes glittering with a suppressed anger he dared not show. 'You will find nothing wrong, milord. I assure you that his mother is very satisfied with my care.'

Max inclined his head. 'I shall call in the morning. I expect Robert to be able to receive me.'

He saw the physician's eyes narrow, hiding his anger. Max smiled inwardly as he walked past him and down the stairs. In the hall he saw his aunt, who had just come into the house.

'I have seen Robert, but he was under the influence of some drug and unable to speak to me,' he said. 'I have told that fellow who calls himself a physician that I shall call tomorrow, ma'am. If there is no improvement in my cousin's condition, I shall have him taken to the house so that my own physician may take care of him. I am not satisfied that he is receiving the proper care here.'

'Coleridge!' Mrs Heronsdale stared at him, seeming dismayed and nervous. 'I thought you had left…'

'I am sorry it was necessary to deceive you, ma'am, but I am convinced something is wrong here. You may trust that fellow, but I do not. Robert should not be for ever ill. He is my cousin and I intend to take an interest in his health in future. Do not try to deny me, madam— if you wish to continue living on my estate…'

Mrs Heronsdale turned pale. She put a hand to her throat. 'I do not know why you should speak to me thus, my lord. You cannot think that I would harm my own child?'

'Something is not as it should be, ma'am. As yet I do not know what it may be, but I am determined to find out. Expect me in the morning—and remember that I wish to speak to Robert.'

Max walked past her and out of the house before she could recover her powers of speech. He was thoughtful as he left the dower house. What were she and that sly fellow hiding from him?

Max decided that he would not return home just yet. He would visit the neighbour who had written to him about the attacks on village girls that had begun to happen in the past few months. He needed to get to the bottom of this affair, because if his cousin were guilty— but that did not bear thinking about!

He knew that the evidence was stacking up against Robert, but to his mind something smelled wrong. His instincts were telling him that he should look to others and that Robert might need his protection.

* * *

'Tyler apologised for troubling me,' Max said as he and Toby sat drinking a glass of wine that afternoon. 'He says a man from a village some ten miles away has been taken into custody after molesting a girl and they believe he may have been responsible for what happened here. He had been drinking and apparently has a history of violence.'

'I am glad to hear that the attacker has been apprehended,' Toby said. 'That must have relieved your mind, Max. You were concerned that those attacks might have had something to do with your cousin, were you not?'

'Perhaps and perhaps not...' Max said. He frowned. 'I am certain they are hiding something from me concerning my cousin. I told you that he had been drugged, though he did open his eyes for a moment. He knew me and smiled, but then he fell asleep once more—and Doctor Clarke arrived. For some reason he and my aunt seem not to want me to speak with Robert.'

'What reason could they have for keeping you apart?' Toby asked and looked puzzled. 'It is a mystery, Coleridge. I do not see what they could gain from it.'

'No, it is difficult to imagine a reason, but there must be something. However, I have issued an ultimatum. Either I am given access to my cousin when he is properly awake or I shall have him brought here where my own physician may care for him.'

'At least you know it could not have been your cousin who shot at you,' Toby said. 'If he is being kept a virtual prisoner in his room, it is unlikely that he took a pot shot at you.'

'Most unlikely,' Max said. 'I am relieved on that score, of which I am heartily glad. I should not have enjoyed the feeling that Robert wished to murder me so that he could step into my shoes. However, it does make me wonder who did fire at me—or could it be that someone else was the intended victim that day?'

Toby stared at him. 'Good grief! You do not mean Miss Henderson? Surely not? Why would anyone wish to kill her?'

'I have no idea,' Max replied. 'But if I was not the intended victim, it must have been Miss Henderson, though I cannot imagine why. Or who could possibly want her dead.'

Toby shook his head. 'I do not think it, Max. Miss Henderson is not an heiress. I believe she has something, but not enough to make anyone wish to shoot her so that they could inherit her fortune. I dare say you will find that the mystery lies closer to home. Are you sure Robert was drugged when you saw him?'

'You think my cousin may have been faking it this morning?' Max looked at him oddly. 'I had not considered it, but it is one possibility. Yes, you are right about the shooting. I believe I was the one meant to die at Richmond, but as yet I cannot decide who was behind the attempt or why someone wants me dead.'

Helene had been to the lending library. Tilly was with her and they were walking home when the carriage drew to a halt at the side of the road just ahead of them. A groom jumped down and spoke to someone through the window, then approached Helene.

'Miss Henderson. Lady Annersley asks if you will step inside her coach for a moment.'

'Lady Annersley...' Helene glanced at her maid. 'Stay close to me. Tilly.' She looked at the groom. 'I will speak to her through the window.' She approached and saw that the lady had the window down. She was heavily veiled so it was impossible to see her face. 'You wished to speak with me, ma'am?'

'You are an ungrateful wretch,' Lady Annersley said harshly. 'How could you refuse Annesdale's generous offer? If you had the sense you were born with, you would do as he asks.'

'Indeed?' Helene looked at her coolly. 'Had my grandfather seen fit to apologise for his behaviour to my mother I might have been more inclined to think about his offer, though I cannot approve of the way it was made.'

'And who do you think you are, miss?' The older woman was plainly furious. 'If it was left to me, I would treat you with the disdain you deserve. You and that mother of yours should be drummed out of society for pretending to be something you are not, but his Grace wishes to see you again. I was on my way to request you to call on us.'

'Then I have saved you a wasted journey,' Helene said. Her pride was hurt and she felt angry. How dare this woman speak to her so! 'If the duke cares to call on my mother to apologise, I may consider a part of his proposal—but it will be on my terms. I should certainly not agree to a settlement that did not include an invitation to my mother. I dare say we have nothing more to say to one another, so I shall not detain you.'

'Vixen! I dare say you imagine Coleridge will offer for you and that you can afford to ignore the duke—but I assure you that once he knows the truth he will withdraw.'

Helene's eyes flashed with anger. 'Indeed, then perhaps you should tell him yourself, ma'am. Good day, my lady. I have an appointment I must keep.'

Helene walked on, head in the air, face proud. She was angry that Lady Annersley had chosen to interfere in something that did not concern her and that she had lost her temper. It was very wrong of her, and something she seldom permitted herself to do, but she did not regret it. Lady Annersley's threat did not worry her—if it had not been for her own pride and sense of honesty, she would already have become engaged to Lord Coleridge.

She had wanted to leave town before he returned, but both her mama and Amelia seemed determined that she should finish her Season.

She had no idea when Max would return, but it could not matter, for he would hardly bother to call. He had behaved as a perfect gentleman that night, but he must have resented her refusal to listen. No doubt he would despise her now.

Max walked down to the dower house alone that morning. Mrs Heronsdale greeted him, her face pale and anxious. She greeted him politely, but did not smile, a look of resentment in her eyes.

'I hope that Robert is awake and ready to receive me, ma'am?'

'It seems that you know your own way, sir. I shall not come up with you.'

'As you wish, ma'am.' Max inclined his head. Clearly he would have some fences to mend with his aunt, but firm action had been necessary if he were to get to the bottom of this mystery.

He went up the stairs, walking along the hall to his cousin's bedchamber. He noticed that the smell was different. Someone had used lavender polish and, as he went into the bedroom itself, he saw that the blinds were partially drawn and the window was open a crack to let some air in. Robert was sitting propped up against a pile of pillows. His face was pale, but he looked slightly better than he had the previous day.

'Robert,' Max said. 'I trust you are a little better today?'

'I think I must be,' Robert said and looked puzzled. 'Doctor Clarke tells me I have had another bout of sickness, though if truth be known I do not remember much of it. I am sorry that I was sleeping when you called yesterday.'

'I am relieved to see you so much better,' Max said. 'I should like to have my own doctor call on you—just to make sure you are receiving the right treatment. I intend to bring some friends down to Coleridge to stay in a week or two and I had hoped that you might be well enough to join us.'

'I should like that…' Robert frowned, his eyes drawn across to the physician who stood near the window. 'Clarke—shall I be well enough, do you think? Should I have this other quack to take a look at me?'

The physician inclined his head, his eyes lowered. 'It must be your decision, Robert. If you think I have neglected something in your treatment, you must say.'

'He's sulking,' Robert said and laughed. 'Clarke has

looked after me since I first became ill. I dare say I might have died had he not nursed me devotedly. I thank you for your concern, Max. I am sorry that you should have been denied access when I was in the fever—but I dare say Mama thought you might despise me for my weakness.'

'How could I?' Max said. 'Illness strikes the best of us. I am sorry that you should have so many bouts of sickness, Robert. My offer remains if you should change your mind—and I hope you will be well enough to join my guests when we dine.'

'I think I shall be well for a while now,' Robert said. There was an odd, slightly defiant look in his eyes as he stared at his physician. 'If I am in any doubt, I shall avail myself of your physician's advice, Max.'

'I am glad to hear it,' Max said. 'Are you comfortable here? Is your allowance enough for your needs?'

'I have very few needs,' Robert said and once again there was an odd, militant expression in his eyes as he looked at the physician. 'Do I, Clarke?'

'I think perhaps you should rest now,' the physician said, looking grave. 'It will not do to exhaust yourself, Robert—or you may have a relapse.'

'I told you, he is sulking,' Robert said and laughed. 'You had better go, Max. I am sure I shall be well enough to join you when you have guests.'

'I am glad,' Max said. 'If you need anything more, you have only to send me word.' He nodded his head to the physician. 'Good day, sir. I shall see you again in two weeks, Robert.'

He walked from the room. He was frowning as he left the house and made his way home. Everything had appeared quite normal, but Max's intuition was telling him that the situation here was far from what it ought to be. However, with the man who had been attacking girls in custody, and his cousin seeming to be well enough to talk sensibly, there did not seem to be much to keep him here beyond the morrow.

He would be glad to get back to London, for there was something he needed to do…and if things went as he hoped he would not be alone when he returned in two weeks' time. Helene had prevented him from speaking when they last met, but he had decided that he would review the situation when they met again. Of course, it was possible that she might truly prefer not to marry and that would be a shame.

Helene spent the morning walking with friends in the park. She had wondered if Lady Annersley would drop a hint of her background to her friends, but it seemed the lady had kept their secret so far. If anything, Helene seemed to have more friends each day. She mentioned the fact to Amelia, who smiled at her.

'You have a quiet manner and you do not put yourself forward, Helene. I believe that is the reason you have become popular with the ladies as much as the gentlemen.'

'People are very kind, but of course they do not know my background.' She was unsmiling. Lady Annersley's spite had made her very aware that she did not belong in exalted circles.

'I believe you would find that most people would accept you despite it,' Amelia told her. 'Your father was a gentleman—and you are related to Annesdale.' She smiled. 'Your mama had such a bad experience that she has allowed it to cloud her judgement, but I do not think it would weigh with many of your friends.'

Helene was thoughtful. Her mother's father had been an honest working man. She lifted her head proudly. She would not allow a spiteful woman to make her ashamed of her grandfather!

A part of her wished that she had opened her heart to Lord Coleridge that night at Vauxhall Gardens. The duke had told her that Max would not wish to marry her once he knew it would disoblige him, but she had not given him the chance to choose and she had never ceased to regret it.

Max glanced through the notes and cards handed to him when he returned to his rooms at his club in London. One of them was from Amelia Royston, asking him to call as soon as he returned to town. He frowned over it for the tone seemed urgent, but decided it could wait until the morning. He would send a note to tell her that he would call tomorrow, and then pay a visit to a gambling house that he sometimes frequented. In the meantime, there was a call he must make. He had ignored Annesdale's letter asking him to visit and he must certainly put that right without delay.

His valet had put up a change of clothes for him, his manner of dignified silence reminding Max that he had offended the man by dispensing with his services for the past few days.

'Do not look so stiff, Carter,' Max said and grinned. 'You will be coming with me next time—and, if things go as I plan, we shall be acquiring our own house in town. I am thinking of settling down and taking a wife.'

'If I may say so, it is not before time, my lord.'

'You are very right,' Max said and grinned. 'I am not

certain the lady will have me, but I mean to make a push with her.'

'I dare say most ladies would consider it an honour, milord.'

'No? Do you?' Max said and chuckled softly. 'This one is not so easily convinced, believe me. I shall not be late back, Carter—but I shall want my best coat tomorrow. The new blue one...'

'Ah, yes, sir. That is very suitable. I shall have it ready in the morning.'

Max nodded and took his leave. He went out into the gathering gloom. It was after he had been walking for a few minutes that Max had a sense that he was being followed. He glanced over his shoulder, but could not see anything. He might have imagined it, but he was alerted to danger, his instincts telling him that someone had been following at a discreet distance. He touched his pocket, where the pistol was heavy, already primed for use. He did not intend to be taken unawares again. Then, seeing a hackney waiting for a passenger drawn up at the side of the road, he hailed the driver. It was better to be safe rather than sorry.

He was smiling as the cab set him down in front of Annesdale's house a little later. The duke was an irascible old devil, but he happened to like him.

Chapter Nine

'I am going to the lending library with Emily,' Helene said that morning as she met Amelia on her way downstairs. 'Mama has requested a book—is there anything you require? Unless you wish to accompany us?'

'Thank you, dearest,' Amelia said and shook her head. 'I have several things to do. I must go through the list of acceptances for my costume ball, which is next week. It is amazing how time has flown. The ball seemed such a long time away and now it is almost here.'

'I am looking forward to it,' Helene said, for she had decided that she must make the most of things since she was forced to remain in town. 'I think it should be amusing to guess the identity of one's friends.'

'I am glad you are looking forward to it. Run along now, Helene. I have much to do…'

Helene felt that Amelia's manner was a little odd, for it was almost as if she wanted to be rid of her, but, no, she must be imagining things. Amelia was the kindest of friends.

Emily was waiting for her when she reached the hall. She picked up a small parcel of books she was returning.

'Are you ready, Helene? I was hoping we might have time to visit the milliner's shop after we have been to the library. I ordered a new bonnet and I think it will be ready.'

'Yes, of course,' Helene agreed. 'I am sure there will be plenty of time. We have no other engagements until this afternoon.'

They spent half an hour choosing the books they had come to find and then left, carrying two each. Another twenty minutes was spent in the milliner's shop. Helene tried on three pretty bonnets, but could not decide between them. She was uncertain if she wished to spend her pin money on a new bonnet, because if she returned home without finding a new position she would have to make what little money she had last until she could find herself work. Uncle Edgar would not be too pleased to have them back, especially if he learned that she had turned down a suitable offer.

They had left the milliner's shop and were on their way home, just crossing the square to Amelia's house when it happened. Helene saw the man coming towards her and her heart took a flying leap. She felt her throat tighten with sudden longing. Max looked even more handsome than she remembered; he was wearing a very smart blue coat that fitted him so well that it could only have been made by Weston, that most exclusive of tailors. Her heart began to beat very fast and she was feeling a little confused, which was why she did not immediately notice the odd behaviour of the man behind

Max. It was only as he raised his arm that she was alerted to danger. He was holding a knife in his hand. When she saw what he meant to do she cried out, but her warning was a second too late. The man's arm was raised poised to plunge a long, thin dagger into Max's back; Max's interest was fixed on her and he seemed unaware of the danger.

Afterwards, Helene did not know if it was her cry of alarm or Max's instinct that made him turn in that instant. He grabbed for the assassin's arm, tackling him as the knife struck. Because of his action, the knife slashed through the arm of his coat; she was sure that it would otherwise have been plunged into his back. She screamed as they struggled, rushing towards them and crying out for help. The assassin became aware of her and suddenly broke free, dropping his knife as he ran off. However, the alarm had been raised and at least two men set off after him.

'Stop! Foul murder!' The cry was taken up all around them and several passers-by set up a hue and cry. Two burly costers went running after the rogue who had attacked Max. Helene rushed towards him, her embarrassment at this meeting forgotten in the shock of seeing what had happened.

'My lord—Max,' Helene cried. 'That wicked rogue! He tried to kill you…I saw the knife…' She gave a cry of distress as she saw the blood seeping through the slash in the arm of his coat. 'You are hurt…you must come back to the house and let me tend it for you.'

'Be careful, Miss Henderson,' Max warned. His face was a little white, but he seemed steady on his feet and able to think clearly. 'You will get blood on your clothes if you come too close.'

'What can that signify?' Helene asked. 'I insist that you come with us. Your arm must be bound, for it is bleeding a great deal. It may be best if you allow us to send for the doctor.' She glanced at Emily. 'Please take my books and warn Amelia. We shall need linen and salves.'

Emily took her books and ran across the square. Helene watched Max anxiously. He refused to let her assist him, holding his right hand over the wound to his left arm. She could see the blood oozing through his fingers and knew that it must be causing him pain, but he said nothing as she hovered, ready to catch him if he should faint.

'Do not look so anxious,' Max told her. 'I have suffered worse, believe me.'

'In the war, I dare say,' Helene said. 'I fear your coat will be ruined, but we must be glad if that is all.'

'You may be glad,' Max grated with an attempt at humour. 'I will have you know that this coat was made by Weston. If he could see what I have done to it, he would never waste his time on me again.'

'Oh, you are funning as always,' Helene said, her throat tight with tears. 'But you are losing too much blood…' She grabbed him as he staggered. He righted himself in a moment, but she could see that it was costing him to stand upright. 'We should go through to the back parlour, sir. There is a wooden floor and it will wipe clean.'

'I should not want to damage the carpets,' Max said and smiled just before he swooned.

Fortunately, a footman had come out to see what was happening and helped Helene to catch him. Between them they managed to support Max into the house and set him on a wooden settle in the hallway.

Amelia had come down the stairs. 'Good lord! When did this happen? I was expecting Lord Coleridge to call before this.'

'Someone tried to kill him with a knife,' Helene said. 'They stabbed him in the arm. It is bleeding terribly and he is a little faint, but had he not fought back, the knife would have entered his back...'

'Not dead yet,' Max said. 'Sorry, my love. I have bled all over your gown.'

'It does not matter about my gown, Max,' Helene said, her throat catching with the tears she refused to shed. 'We must get that coat off, Max—and bind your arm to stop the blood.'

'The best thing will be to cut it,' Amelia said. 'The coat is ruined anyway—and it will be easier to bind his arm without it. I think we should attempt it ourselves now, and then put him to bed. The doctor may do more when he comes.'

Max made a murmur of protest, but Amelia was in charge. She summoned her footmen, had them bring what she needed and bound the wound tightly, before instructing the men to carry him upstairs. He attempted to walk, but could not have managed it without help. Amelia followed the little procession with an anxious Helene close behind.

Max had recovered his senses by the time the doctor arrived. He suffered the man's probing in silence, and waited until his arm was stitched and bound once more. However, he was provoked into speech when told that he must stay in bed for a week.

'I thank you for your attentions, sir, but I must tell

you that I have no intention of staying in this bed. If Miss Royston will be good enough to call for a cab, I shall take myself off.'

'No, sir, you shall not,' Amelia said from the doorway. She came towards the bed, smiling, but looking determined. 'You were murderously attacked outside my door and you nearly passed out before they could bring you here. You are weak from loss of blood and need to rest. I insist that you stay until you are feeling better—at least tonight and perhaps tomorrow. The doctor will call in the morning, and we shall see how you go on.'

'If you will take my advice, you will stay here for at least a week,' the doctor said and went out.

Amelia lingered. 'I know you feel that you will be a trouble to us, sir—but I assure you it is not the case. Besides, I believe that you should take full advantage of what has occurred. It is not my place to say this, but Helene was very upset when you were attacked. If you wish to break down that foolish reserve she has built up against marriage, you could not do better than stay here for a day or two.'

'Miss Royston, I believe you are a devious schemer,' Max said and grinned at her. 'If you will put up with me, I believe I shall stay.'

'I have learned that sometimes one must dissemble to gain one's way,' Amelia replied. 'I am aware that you think this wound is nothing, for you have suffered worse injuries, sir. That much was obvious when we tended your arm—there were old scars…'

'We?' Max said and frowned. 'I was out of it at the start and cannot quite remember. Do you mean to tell me that you allowed Helene to help you?'

'She was there and helped as much as she could,' Amelia said. 'I am certain her feelings for you are genuine. It is her stupid pride that makes her say she will not marry. I may not tell you the whole, but if you were to ask her she might be prevailed on to speak. I know that she has been breaking her heart over something.'

'You need say no more, ma'am. I visited Annesdale last night and he was kind enough to tell me everything. Including his own infamous behaviour, for which I believe him to be truly sorry.'

'Annesdale told you—and you still intend to wed her?' Amelia looked awkward. 'Forgive me, I have gone too far, but I care for Helene's happiness.'

'No, you have not gone too far. I shall make her my wife—if she will have me,' Max said and frowned. 'Though I am not sure it is wise—it is obvious I have a dangerous enemy. I had thought the first attempt at Richmond might have been nothing more than an opportunist or even a mistake—but now I know that someone wishes me dead.'

'At Richmond? Did something happen there?' Amelia exclaimed as Max recounted what had happened. She shook her head. 'Neither Helene nor Emily breathed a word of it to me. It seems clear that someone does indeed intend to kill you if they can. You must take some precautions, sir—but I do not think you can allow this rogue to ruin your life.'

'I have no intention of letting the rogue have his way, though I shall need to take more precautions.'

'You cannot think who your enemy might be?' Amelia asked, but he shook his head and looked thoughtful.

'I recall that an attempt was made to kidnap you last summer,' Max said. 'Gerard had you watched for months afterwards—but nothing more occurred. Have you ever wondered why that should be?'

'I have tried to think of a reason, but can find none—none that satisfies me anyway,' Amelia told him. 'I have been careful not to go for long walks in woodlands, but otherwise I do not let it disturb me.'

'It is curious, none the less,' Max said and his eyes narrowed. Something had occurred to him, which he might mention to Ravenshead when he saw him, though he was not certain enough of his theory to put it to Amelia just yet. 'I am not certain who would wish me dead. The obvious person is my cousin, for as things stand he would inherit the most, but he suffers bouts of ill health. I cannot think it was he—and I have never seen the ruffian who stabbed me before in my life.'

'A hired assassin, I imagine,' Amelia said. 'Would you like me to send for your valet? He could stay here to attend you if that would make you more comfortable.'

Max arched his right eyebrow. 'I see I have no choice, but I shall not stay in bed above one day, Miss Royston.'

'I dare say that may suffice,' Amelia said and smiled. 'You helped both Susannah and I last year, Lord Coleridge. This is my chance to repay you if you will let me.'

'I think I should be a fool if I did not,' Max said and grinned. 'Now that I understand Helene's situation, nothing is going to prevent me asking her to marry me—but I shall make sure that my back is protected in future. I should not wish her to become a widow before she is a wife.'

'I think that is very wise,' Amelia said. 'Now I shall

go and find Helene. You are bored in bed and threatening to get up. To do such a foolish thing might cause your wound to open. I dare say a little light reading might help. Helene has an understanding of books. She will find something suitable and bring it to you.'

'How can I thank you, Miss Royston?'

'By inviting me to your wedding,' Amelia said and went out.

Max laughed softly, then the smile faded, his own problems forgotten for the moment. It was odd that no more attempts had been made to kidnap Amelia since last summer. What had changed in her circumstances that might make someone feel that it was no longer necessary to kidnap or dispose of her?

Max could think of only one thing. He needed to talk to Gerard Ravenshead about certain things, but that could keep for the moment. Max had two rather more pressing problems on his mind. The first was to discover who had paid to have him killed, for he was certain that Amelia was right—it had been a paid assassin who had tried to stab him in the back. Two failed attempts on his life had been made so far. When would the third happen? He was certain there would be another attempt. Someone clearly wished him dead—but why?

Nothing had happened while he was at his estate. He had walked alone there without harm. It had been the perfect opportunity if someone had wished to dispose of him and yet no attempt had been made to kill him. Why? Was it because it was too close to home? Was the person behind this afraid of being discovered?

A convicted murderer could not inherit property. If Robert wanted Max dead so that he could inherit the estate, he would not want suspicion to fall on him. The explanation made sense and there was certainly some mystery surrounding his cousin. Max could not make up his mind whether Robert was the sort of person likely to entertain murder to gain what he wanted. He hardly knew his cousin—or his aunt, come to that—but he instinctively disliked the physician. No, he would not believe that Robert could be behind these cowardly attempts. There must be some other reason...

He thrust the unwelcome thoughts from his mind. When inviting him here this morning, Amelia had obviously planned to ask him his intentions towards Helene, and perhaps reveal something of her background, but Max's visit to Annesdale had made that unnecessary. He had spoken forcibly to the duke, who now understood him very well and had made his apologies. Whether it would be as easy to convince Helene was another matter. Max was vexed that she should have believed he would be swayed by the duke's threats, yet he understood her pride and her reasons for thinking she must prevent him from speaking.

He knew her to have spirit and that she could sometimes be provoked to a show of temper. Her reprimand when he had spoken disparagingly of the poet had only made him admire her the more. Helene was not afraid to stand up for what she believed. She seemed to imagine that he was the kind of snob Annesdale could be on occasion, and he wondered how he could convince her that he was no such thing.

If she cared for him, she must see that the matter of her mother's birth was not important beside the way they felt about each other. Even if it became generally known, which at the moment it was not, it should be easy enough to drop a few hints in society; the fact that one grandfather had been in trade could be balanced by the knowledge that she was also Annesdale's grand-daughter. Max looked grim. Once Helene was his wife, no one would slight her. He would make certain of that!

Would the foolish girl realise that these things were of no importance? Or would he have to take drastic measures to persuade her?

Helene took her time choosing between the books she had borrowed from the library. She did not know what kind of poetry Max preferred, and she was almost sure he would not enjoy the Gothic romance she had brought for Mama. Perhaps he might care for Miss Austen's work, she thought, and smiled to herself as she took the book upstairs. She knocked at the door of his bedchamber and was invited to enter. Max was sitting propped up in bed, looking annoyed and frustrated, just as Amelia had told her. He was still wearing his breeches, though his shirt had been removed. Amelia had found him a silk dressing robe, which he wore around his shoulders. His frown was replaced by a smile as he saw her.

'I am once again grateful for your help,' Max said, a gleam in his eyes. 'Are you destined to keep saving my life, Helene?'

'I did nothing of the kind, for I was too late to warn you of the attack,' Helene said. She was very aware of the bronzed and muscled torso exposed by the opening at the front of the dressing robe. A spasm in her stomach made her uncomfortably aware of the physical reaction the sight of him caused her. Heat was flooding through her body. She swallowed hard, licking her lips with the tip of her tongue. He was so very handsome and masculine! 'I merely assisted you to Amelia's house. Her footmen carried you here.'

'And you both bound my arm to stop the blood,' Max said. 'Amelia told me and the doctor said that it had been done very well. I fear I must have ruined your dress.'

'Well, if you did, we ruined your coat by slitting the sleeve—and it was a particularly fine coat,' Helene replied. 'I care nothing for a little blood, sir. Someone has tried to kill you twice now and I find that disturbing. I should be very distressed if this rogue were to succeed next time.'

'Would you?' Max's gaze was intent on her face. 'I vow it was worth the inconvenience if it has made you aware of me as something more than a friend. You must know that my greatest happiness would be to have you as my wife. I tried to ask you before I left London, but you did not wish me to speak. Have you changed your mind? Will you allow me to make you an offer—not at this moment, but when I am on my feet again?'

'My lord…' Helene stared at him. She was so startled that she hardly knew what to say. 'I did not mean to say that—at least… You must know that I have a high regard for you. I know I told you…I mean…' She floundered and looked flustered. 'Well, perhaps I do think more of you than is proper, but it can make no difference. I could not accept an offer of marriage.'

'Because your mama was the daughter of a tanner—or because Annesdale had the effrontery to say that he would cut me out of his will?' Max asked and saw her eyes widen in shock. 'Do you really believe that I care two farthings if your grandfather was in trade? As for Annesdale's fortune, he may leave it to whomever he desires—I do not need a penny of it! I do care for the man, but not if he persists in such abominable behaviour towards the woman I adore. He is now aware of my feelings and I believe he will not make such a mistake again. Next time you meet, I think you may discover that he wishes to apologise. Foolish Helene! How could you think me so shallow?'

'Forgive me. I did not at first, but then…'

'I called that damned poet a Cit and you assumed me to be a snob?'

'Well…yes, at first, though afterwards I realised that I had been hasty. I should not have spoken to you as I did. Amelia says that it is a term often used, but not necessarily a disparagement.'

'Unfortunately, too often it is,' Max admitted ruefully. 'And I fear I am as guilty as the next man. However that does not mean that I have no friends amongst persons who find their living from trade or that I despise them—and since your father was a gentleman, your grandfather's trade is too far in the past to be a problem, Helene.'

'Do you think so? Mama has never forgotten the way she was treated and Lady Annersley said—'

'That lady is a vixen. She is not well liked, Helene. You should ignore anything she said to you.'

'Oh…' Helene's heart fluttered as she looked into his eyes and saw them flame with passion. 'Does it truly not trouble you that Mama's father was a tanner?'

'Not one jot. I love you and would love you if you

were a tinker's daughter. Nor do I care for the opinions of others. As my wife, you will be accepted by my friends,' Max told her firmly. 'Anyone who snubbed my wife would no longer be my friend. I think we should have as much company as we cared for, both in the country and in town.'

'Oh, but you cannot…' She shook her head as Max swung his legs over the side of the bed. 'You must not get up. You may harm yourself.'

'Come here and sit beside me, then,' Max said. 'I want to hold your hand and kiss you. I think it is time I told you how much I love you.'

Helene moved slowly towards him, her heart beating wildly. The shock of seeing him so near to death had broken down her defences. If he did not care that her grandfather came from the lower classes, why should she? She sat next to him on the edge of the bed and he reached for her hand with his uninjured arm.

'Really, you should not. I ought not to be here. Amelia said it was perfectly proper because you were not well, but I do not think Mama would agree. I fear she would be most shocked…'

The words died in her throat as Max leaned towards her, kissing her softly on the lips. There was such sweetness and tenderness in his kiss that Helene sighed and sat perfectly still, her lips parting as his tongue probed between them. She felt a tingling sensation inside, warmth spreading through her and a joy she had never experienced before.

'Oh…' she whispered as he drew back and looked at her. 'Are you sure?'

'Perfectly sure, my foolish love.'

'Mama did not wish me to marry a title.'

'We must see what we can do to change her mind,' Max said and held her hand, caressing it with his thumb. His touch set off little butterflies of sensation inside her, making her feel very strange. She wanted to melt into his arms, to be kissed until she could think of nothing else. 'I shall ask you properly another time, my dearest girl—but you will make me happy, won't you?'

'If it is truly your wish,' Helene replied, looking at him shyly. 'I have been very unhappy since that evening at Vauxhall, but I could not let you ask me. It would not have been fair or right.'

'I understand perfectly,' Max said. 'It was honourable, but foolish, my love. I knew what was in your mind the moment Annesdale told me what he had said to you.'

'I should have told you myself. Indeed, it was in my mind that I would do so when you were well again.'

'I wish you had told me at the start. Promise me there will be no more holding back, Helene. If something upsets you—you must tell me.'

'I am afraid that the duke will not be pleased if you marry me and allow Mama to visit us—you will allow it?'

'Of course. She may live with us or have her own home, but she will always be welcome.'

'Oh, Max…' Helene's throat caught. 'The duke will be so angry—and you are fond of him.'

'You may leave the duke to me,' Max said, such a grim look in his eyes that Helene almost felt sorry for her grandfather. 'If he wishes to visit us, he must learn to respect you and your mama.'

'You are so determined—' Helene stopped as he

kissed her once more, her throat tight with emotion. 'I do care for you very much, my…Max…'

'That is very much better,' he said and smiled. 'I have decided to ask some friends to stay at my country home in two weeks' time. I think we should announce our engagement in *The Times* as soon as possible and then we shall go to the country—if the idea pleases you?'

'Yes, please,' Helene said. 'We could leave after Amelia's masquerade ball. If that is suitable for you?' She glanced at him uncertainly. 'You will have to speak to Mama…'

'I shall as soon as I am on my feet again,' Max told her and winced, clearly in pain. 'My arm is still a little sore. Perhaps I should rest for a while.'

'I shall go and leave you to sleep,' Helene offered, rising to her feet.

Max lay back against the pillows, his eyes soft with laughter as he looked at her. 'I would rather you stayed and read to me from that excellent book you brought with you. If it makes you feel easier, you may sit in the chair. I assure you I am not strong enough to ravish you, my love, even if I wished to, and I would much rather you gave yourself to me when you are ready. Love is mutual and should be enjoyed equally by both parties— do you not think so? Now I have made you blush. Read to me and I shall behave—as best I can.'

'Oh…' Helene gave him a look of admonishment. 'You love to tease, Max. I was not sure if you liked Miss Austen's work?'

'I think everyone enjoys her stories. I know Prinny is very fond of them,' Max told her. 'No, I am not one of the Regent's set, though we have visited the races at the same time and sat down to cards more than once.'

'Lie back and rest,' Helene said and opened the book to begin reading. 'I have not read *Pride and Prejudice* yet, but I have been told that it is vastly amusing...'

'Is it true that you spent almost two hours with Lord Coleridge?' Mrs Henderson said when she came to Helene's room that evening. 'It is all very well to assist in a sick room when someone is injured, but it is improper for a young girl to visit a gentleman's bedchamber.'

'I knew you would think so, Mama,' Helene told her. 'I assure you that nothing improper took place.' *Well, almost nothing, anyway!* 'Besides, we have an understanding. When Lord Coleridge is better, we shall become engaged. He will announce it in *The Times* soon and he has invited us to go down to his country house and stay for a while when we leave town.'

'Coleridge came up to scratch?' Mrs Henderson looked at her with a mixture of disbelief and dismay. 'You told me that you had refused him—why did you change your mind? Did you tell him what the duke said to you?'

'I did not tell him, Mama. However, the duke must have done so, for I believe they have had words,' she said. 'However, Max says that he does not care two farthings that Grandfather was a tanner. Nor does he care for Annesdale's fortune. You are to have a house, if you so choose—but you will always be welcome to stay with us, and we shall visit you. Max says if the duke wishes to know us and our children, he must acknowledge you in public.'

'Helene...' Tears stung the lady's eyes. 'This is more

than I could ever hope for—but are you sure, my love? There will be some who may whisper behind your back—you will be envied your good fortune.'

'It does not matter,' Helene said. 'Max says that anyone who will not accept me will no longer be his friend.'

'He must truly love you, Helene. You are fortunate, my love.'

'I know.' Helene kissed her cheek. 'Shall you like your own home, Mama—or would you rather live with us?'

'That would not be right. I should like my own home, though I shall visit often—at least when you are in the country. I do not care for London so very much.'

'I dare say we shall spend much of our time in the country. You will not insist on a long engagement, I hope? I know Coleridge means to ask you as soon as he is better.'

'Well, we shall see,' Mrs Henderson said. 'But what of these attacks on his life? Amelia says it has happened twice—and you were there both times. What does he mean to do? You can hardly marry until this unfortunate business is cleared up, Helene. You might have been hurt yourself. Lord Coleridge will have to convince me that he is able to protect you before I give my consent. However, I shall consent to take you down to the country, if I am certain he respects you as he ought, I shall allow the marriage to go ahead—perhaps at Christmas.'

'Coleridge will discuss all the details with you, I am sure. We have only spoken of our plans—he did not feel it appropriate to make me a formal offer in his present situation. I am sure he will do so as soon as he is able.'

'Yes, I suppose he will,' Mrs Henderson said and her frown eased a little. 'I shall be satisfied once I have heard what he has to say—but I suppose I should wish you happy, dearest.'

'Thank you, Mama,' Helene said and smiled. 'I am very happy.'

'I was a little done up yesterday,' Max said and kissed Helene's hand when he took his leave of her the next morning. 'However, I am much recovered this morning. I could not quite squeeze my arm into the coat my man brought with him, but I may find something a little more accommodating at home. I have things to do—one of them to send a notice to *The Times*. I shall ask them to announce it the morning after Amelia's costume ball. We shall let it be known to our friends that evening. By then I am determined to be wearing a decent coat—and to have my ring on your finger.' He smiled down at her anxious face. 'Is there any particular stone that you have a fondness for, my love?'

'I shall love it whatever you choose,' Helene told him. 'You are quite sure you are well enough to go home?'

'Quite sure. I may not call tomorrow—but it will be the day after for certain.'

'I shall look forward to it,' she told him. Her grey eyes were still uncertain, deeply thoughtful. 'You will take care? Two attempts have been made on your life…'

'I shall be escorted home, by my man, and my groom, also Jemmy,' Max said, gazing down at her. 'Do not worry, my love. I promise I shall be safe—and before I walk anywhere again I shall make certain arrangements to protect my back. I am not that easy to dispose of, believe me.'

'Then I suppose I must let you go,' Helene said with a reluctant sigh. 'I shall count the hours until we meet again.'

'They will seem long to me,' Max told her and kissed her fingertips. 'I would stay longer, but I need to be at my lodgings. I have people to talk to, things to arrange. I promise you, nothing will happen to me, my darling.'

'Go, then,' Helene said and stood back. 'I shall not keep you since you wish to leave.'

'I hope it will not be long before I need never leave you again.'

Helene watched as he left the house, his valet close behind him. It was not likely that the assassin would make another attempt on Max's life so soon, but she would be uneasy until they were in the country. He had been safe there. His enemy had attacked him soon after his return from the country, so it made sense that whoever the rogue was, he lived in London.

Helene frowned as she wondered who wanted Max dead and why. He had offered no explanation other than saying that it might have been robbery, but Helene did not believe it and she did not think that Max did, either. If he had his own suspicions, he was not sharing them with her.

'What made you think of it?' Gerard asked as he shared a bottle of wine with Max after dinner that evening. 'Do you really think that someone tried to kidnap Amelia last summer because they thought she might marry me?'

'It occurred to me and it seemed to fit,' Max told him. 'We were all staying with Harry at Pendleton. You had paid some attention to Amelia at Susannah's dance— and then again at Pendleton. Someone who was not of our party might have thought you intended to ask her to marry you. Indeed, I wondered myself. I believe you knew her some years ago?'

'I suppose Harry told you?' Gerard frowned. 'I was in love with Amelia when we were younger. I asked her to marry me and I approached her brother. He refused me for reasons he never explained—and when I said that I would not take no for an answer, he set his grooms on me. They bound my hands and then…he took his riding crop to me. Some of the scars remain to this day.'

'Good grief! The man is a scoundrel! Does Amelia know?'

'I did not tell her.' Gerard frowned. 'He told me that the beating was a gift from her to punish me for my impertinence. Even in my anger and humiliation I did not believe him, but I left a letter for her in our secret place. The letter was found and taken, but she did not meet me as I begged her. I thought that she must wish for our affair to be at an end. It was only later that I wondered if the letter had gone astray. I think Amelia loved me once…though that was long ago and forgotten now.'

'What had you done to upset her brother?' Max frowned. 'Royston is a bore and a bully, but I would not have believed he was capable of such behaviour if you had not told me.'

'I believed at the time that it must have been because he thought me impertinent to ask for her in marriage,' Gerard said. 'My father had near ruined us. If it had not been for a lucky inheritance, the estate might have had to be sold. Yet I would swear there was something more—something more personal to Royston.'

'You still do not know why he hates you?'

'I have no idea,' Gerard said. 'Unless…I saw something once, but I have never been sure what happened. I shall not tell you, because I prefer not to malign someone if I do not know the whole truth. Royston could have thought I knew more than I did.'

'From what I have seen of Amelia Royston, she would never have been a party to something of that nature, Gerard. She could not have known what her brother did to you.'

'I am certain of it,' Gerard replied. 'At first I was bitter. I needed time to lick my wounds and I joined the army. I came to realise that I had been a fool to let Royston drive me away, but by then I was married and my daughter was born.' He frowned. 'I did have thoughts of asking Amelia to marry me last summer, but I am not certain that she wishes for it. Or that it would suit my plans. Besides, there were other things to settle…' Gerard frowned. 'You have given me something to think about, Max. However, I would say your own problems are more pressing.'

'They are certainly something I could do without,' Max agreed. 'You are the first to know, but I have asked Helene Henderson to be my wife. She has agreed. We are going down to Coleridge after Amelia Royston's costume ball. I intend to ask Sinclair and a few others to stay, you included, of course…make a party of it. Mrs Henderson has not yet agreed the date of the wedding, but I hope it may be sooner rather than later.'

'I begin to understand,' Gerard said. 'I see your thinking, Max…why you put two and two together in the matter of Amelia's little fright in Pendleton woods. I suppose the situation is somewhat similar in a way.'

'Amelia is quite an heiress these days…'

'Unfortunately.' Gerard grimaced. He laughed as Max raised his brows. 'It is a part of the reason I hesitate to ask her. Pride—foolish, I dare say. In your own case, your thinking may be sound, my dear fellow. Once it is announced that you are to marry, there may be some urgency in someone's mind. Another attempt is almost certain to be made quite soon.'

'They might wish to make certain that I do not make it to the altar.'

Gerard looked thoughtful. 'Yes, I see that it might spoil someone's plans if you should marry. It could be dangerous, Max—and not just for you.'

'That is why I need your help, Gerard. Last year you arranged protection for Amelia. I rather think I may need a similar plan.'

'Yes, of course.' Gerard's mouth settled into a grim line. 'I am at your disposal, my friend. You know you may call on me. As Harry once said, we are bound together by a single thread after what happened out there in Spain. You will not ask him to assist you?'

'He is settled in the country with Susannah, and she expects her first child. I should not want to take him away from his wife at such a time.'

'No, indeed, that would be inconvenient—and we shall do very well with Sinclair, a few fellows I know, and ourselves, of course. I have a lot of time for Sinclair.'

'Yes, I think he is coming along nicely,' Max agreed with a smile. 'Well, that is settled. We shall go down at the end of next week.'

'Shall you invite Amelia Royston?'

'I was considering it. She has been a good friend to Helene—and me.'

'Then please do so,' Gerard said. 'It will be interesting to see if anything happens, if nothing else.'

Max managed to squeeze himself into a size larger coat than he normally wore the next morning and set out for his destination. He drove himself in his curricle with his groom beside him and Jemmy up on the back as usual. It was unlikely that he would be attacked again so soon, but he certainly would not be walking alone for a while.

Max had given his situation much thought; someone wished him dead and the obvious suspect must be his cousin. Yet Max could not quite believe that Robert was behind the attempts on his life. There was something more…something hidden. It was difficult to see what benefit his death would be to anyone else…unless… Yes, of course!

Max's brow cleared as he began to see the fiendishly clever thinking at the root of the plot. He must be very careful—the mind that had formed this devious plan was dangerous.

Robert would inherit if Max were dead, but if he should marry things would be different. The title might still pass to Robert unless Max had a son, but Max's estate was not entailed and he would be making a will that would make certain that his wife and children inherited everything. Therefore a further attempt must be made before it was too late.

He was taking a huge risk, which might lead to his death. Max could take certain steps to make sure that Helene would be wealthy even if he died before their wedding; it should not happen if he could help it, but some risk could not be helped. If he left things as they were, something worse than his own death might occur.

Arriving at Miss Royston's house a little over an hour later, Max asked for Mrs Henderson. He was shown into one of the best parlours and asked to wait. The lady arrived, looking anxious, some twenty minutes later.

'Forgive me for keeping you waiting, sir. I was dressing.'

'I am sorry if I called too early,' Max told her. 'Had you sent word, I could have returned later.'

'It is best to get this over with,' Mrs Henderson replied. 'You may tell me your intentions towards my daughter, sir—but I must warn you that I have reservations.'

'I have learned of some injustice towards you when you were first married,' Max replied. 'I am sorry that you were treated so harshly. It will not happen again. I have spoken to Annesdale. He knows that if he wishes to attend the wedding—or any other function that my wife may care to hold—he must treat both you and her with respect. I do not believe that that gentleman or his daughter-in-law will cut you in future. I cannot promise that they will welcome you to their homes, but they will behave properly in mine.'

Mrs Henderson looked a little disbelieving, but there was an air of authority about Lord Coleridge at that moment that was very impressive. 'I should not wish to be invited to their homes—but I shall wish to see Helene and her children sometimes.'

'Whenever you please,' Max told her. 'At the moment my aunt and her son occupy the dower house. I may find another house for them somewhere. It would then be made ready for you, if you wished to live there—or you may live in Bath if you choose and visit us when you wish.'

'I should be able to see my family most days if I lived at the dower house,' Mrs Henderson said. 'But I should not wish to take your aunt's home from her.'

'Let me see what I can arrange,' Max said. 'Something will be agreed that will suit us all. In the meantime, I shall be pleased to have you stay with us—if you care to?'

'You are generous, sir,' Mrs Henderson said and then frowned. 'But what of this other business? I have not asked how your arm goes on, sir.'

'Very well,' Max said. 'I was fortunate. It is little more than a scratch. If I had been stabbed in the back, I dare say I should be dead.'

'You will take better care in future—of yourself and Helene?'

'I assure you that Helene will be watched over,' Max said. 'I should not want anything to happen to the lady I love.'

'You do love her, I know.' Mrs Henderson studied him for a moment and then nodded. 'Very well, you have my consent. When do you wish to marry—at Christmas?'

'I think I would prefer the wedding to be in one month's time,' Max told her. 'The church at Coleridge is not large, but I dare say it could hold more than a hundred guests. If you wish for a larger wedding, we could come back to town…'

'I have only one brother and a couple of real friends,' Mrs Henderson said. 'I dare say you may have many friends, sir.'

'Only a few I truly count as friends,' Max replied. 'We shall have a family wedding and then hold a large reception in town a month or so later.'

'Yes, I believe that would suit both Helene and myself,' Mrs Henderson replied. 'It seems that things have been agreed between us. You will, of course, settle something on Helene?'

'Helene will be wealthy even if I die before we marry,' Max told her. 'There is no need to mention this to her, for she would not care to know such things—but you may set your mind at rest, ma'am.'

'Thank you. I did not want her to be left in poverty as I was when my husband died.'

'If Annesdale had been any kind of a man, he would have made you an allowance,' Max said. 'In future you will be secure, ma'am. The papers are already in hand.'

'You leave me nothing to say but to offer my sincere gratitude.'

'That is unnecessary. You are giving me your daughter—and she is more precious than any marriage settlement.'

Mrs Henderson smiled. 'In that case I shall go upstairs and send her down to you, sir.'

Chapter Ten

Helene touched her fingers to her mouth. She could still feel the tingle of Max's kisses, which had made her body throb with what she now understood was desire. The feeling was so new to her, her joy so complete that she felt she must be dreaming. Surely it was not possible to feel as happy as she did now? She glanced at the magnificent diamond-and-sapphire ring on her finger. She found it difficult to believe that she was actually engaged to be Max's wife. He had left her for a few hours, because he had some business to arrange, but he would dine with them that evening. They had no other guests, because they had decided on a quiet evening at home on the eve of Amelia's costume ball.

Helene could not help smiling as she glanced at herself in the mirror. It was really true! She would soon be Max's wife, because her mama had agreed that the wedding should be set for the following month. Only a short time ago she had resigned herself to a life of service, because she was certain nothing good could ever happen to her again, and now she was to marry the man she had come to love so very much. It was far more than she had ever expected!

Helene knew that she owed her happiness to Amelia's generosity. Not only had she made this Season in town possible, she had also made Helene's mother see that it would be unjust to deny her the happiness of being married to the man she loved. Helene owed her so much. She was filled with a desire to see Amelia and tell her how truly grateful she was for all she had done.

Having dressed for the evening, Helene went along the landing to Amelia's room. She tapped in the door, which was opened by Amelia's personal maid.

'Oh, Miss Henderson,' the woman said. 'Miss Royston has gone down to the parlour. I am sure you will find her there.'

Helene thanked her and went down the stairs, still feeling as if she were floating on a cloud. The door to the parlour was slightly open, and as Helene approached she heard a man's angry voice. Helene would have turned away immediately, for she would not have dreamed of eavesdropping, but the words were so harsh that she was frozen to the spot.

'I hear that you have been seeing that rogue again, Amelia. I told you last summer that I shall not stand for it. If you continue to defy me, you will be sorry!'

'You may be my brother, Michael—and I would not wish to show you disrespect,' Amelia replied in a much calmer tone. 'I believe I told you last year that I should not stand for this dictation. Aunt Agatha made me her heiress and because of that I am independent. If I wish to count the Earl of Ravenshead as one of my friends, I shall do so.'

'On your own head be it!' Sir Michael thundered at her.

Helene was startled as the door to the parlour was thrown back and Amelia's brother came storming out. She had retreated to the stairs, but he did not even glance her way as the footman opened the front door for him.

Helene ran back down the stairs. She knocked at the parlour door and then entered. Amelia was standing by the fireplace, leaning her head against it, her shoulders hunched as if in some distress.

'Amelia…are you all right?'

Amelia straightened. She paused for a moment before turning to look at Helene, her face pale but determined.

'Yes, I am perfectly well, Helene. You may have overheard something my brother said to me. Michael sometimes forgets himself. He will shout and that is foolish—a quiet word is often more effective.'

'It was unkind of him to be so harsh to you,' Helene said. 'It was not my business to listen and I would not have done so had he not shouted so loudly that I could not help hearing.'

'I acquit you of eavesdropping,' Amelia said. 'My dearest Susannah did so quite deliberately at times—she was concerned for my sake—but I know you did not mean to pry.'

'No, I did not,' Helene said. 'I am, however, concerned for your sake. I came to thank you for what you have done for me, Amelia. Had it not been for your kindness—your generosity—I would not have met Max. I know I owe my happiness to you and I wanted to thank you.' Helene took a step towards her, impulsively kissing her cheek. 'I do thank you from the bottom of my heart—and if there is ever anything I may do for you, you have only to ask.'

'Thank you, Helene,' Amelia said and smiled. 'Helping others to find their happiness brings me a great deal of pleasure, you know. However, you must not be concerned for me, because I am well able to stand up to my brother. His visits can be unpleasant, but I know that I have good friends to support me. Now tell me, when do you leave for the country?'

'It is your costume ball tomorrow. We shall leave at noon the following day for Max's home. I know he has asked you to stay with us—I hope you will do so.'

'I shall certainly come down in a couple of weeks and then stay until the wedding,' Amelia told her. 'Emily and I have decided to go down to Bath a day or so after you leave us. I have some business to set in hand there. When it is complete we shall come to you.'

'And after we are married—you will stay with us sometimes?'

'Yes, I hope so,' Amelia told her. 'I am not certain of my future plans. It is possible that we may travel for a while—but I shall certainly be at your wedding.'

Helene nodded. Amelia had made light of the incident with her brother, but she suspected that Sir Michael's visit had upset her friend more than she would admit. She wished that there was something she could do to help Amelia, but it was not her place to meddle in Amelia's affairs.

Helene considered telling Max about what she had overheard when he came to dinner that evening, but after some consideration she decided that it would be wrong of her to discuss what was a private family affair. Amelia would not have spoken of it to her had she not happened to hear Sir Michael shout at his sister. Besides, Max was full of his plans for the wedding and their honeymoon, and the incident was soon put to the back of Helene's mind.

She had already sent word to the seamstress who had made several beautiful gowns for her, and received a message that the lady would wait on her on the morning of Amelia's ball to discuss materials. She was prepared to make the journey into Hampshire to do the final fitting and finish Helene's wedding gown in time for the wedding.

'You may wish to order a few new gowns for the honeymoon,' Max told Helene. 'But I want to show you Paris, my love—and we shall visit the best couturiers to buy your wardrobe. You look well in rich colours and I shall enjoy helping you choose.'

Helene's pulses raced as she gazed into his eyes and saw the love reflected there. How fortunate she was to have found a man like Max Coleridge.

Helene did think about the argument she had overheard when she undressed for the evening, but plans for her wedding pushed it from her mind as she snuggled down into her feather mattress and fell asleep.

Amelia's costume ball was a brilliant affair. Everyone was masked and their disguises ranged from pirates to eastern sheikhs and sultans, pharaohs and even one Viking for the men. The ladies ranged from Roman vestal virgins to Marie Antoinette and Elizabeth I—and one daring lady came dressed as a pageboy in satin breeches, silk shirt and fancy waistcoat. Her face was completely masked, her hair covered by a wig. All the gentlemen were trying to discover her identity, but she was deliberately disguising her voice.

'I should think she will disappear before the unmasking,' Emily said to Helene. 'I doubt she will dare to reveal her identity.'

'Oh, my dear, it is not half so shocking as what Lady Caroline Lamb wore—or rather did not wear!—when she masqueraded as Lord Byron's little black pageboy,' Sally Jersey said. 'Now that was totally beyond the pale and it began her downfall, you know. Poor Caroline. I wonder that she ever dared to show her face in society again, but she continued her scandalous behaviour until she sank into a decline. Her behaviour was outrageous, but I have always felt a little sorry for her.'

Helene listened, but did not join in the conversation. It was a little shocking to appear in public wearing a man's clothing, of course, but she did not think it so very wicked.

Helene danced for most of the evening, often with Max or his particular friends, who wished to congratulate them both. It was almost supper time when she went to stand by the open window for a moment, because the room was so warm and her own costume of an early Tudor lady was a little heavy. Max was dancing with Emily and Helene was waiting for Toby to claim her. He was wearing a pirate costume, but there were several gentlemen wearing similar costumes and as yet Toby had not found her.

'Will you dance, lady?'

Helene turned and saw a man wearing a pirate costume. She smiled, thinking it must be Toby at last, though it was difficult to tell.

'Would you mind very much if we just stood and talked for a few minutes?' she asked. 'It is rather hot in here.'

'We could go on to the terrace if you prefer?'

'Yes, I think—just for a moment,' Helene said. She turned and went outside, drawing a breath of air. It was so much fresher out here! 'This is fun, isn't it? I cannot guess who some people are—can you? I knew you were wearing a pirate costume of course, because Max told me, but—'

She broke off as the man grabbed her arm, his fingers digging into her flesh so deeply that she winced. 'Stop gabbling, you little fool!' the man's voice was harsh and it struck a chill into Helene. Something was wrong! This was not Toby! Now she thought about it, he was of a different build. 'Listen to me, girl! I shall give you one warning. If you go through with this marriage, you will be a widow before you have hardly become a wife!'

'What do you mean?' Helene tried to break away from him, but his grip was too strong. 'Let me go! Who are you? Why do you say such a wicked thing?'

His grip tightened so that she cried out in pain. 'I told you to listen. You must break off this engagement or you may be the next.'

Helene struggled, but she might not have been able to break away from him had someone not come out on to the terrace at that moment.

'Miss Henderson…is that you?' Toby's voice called.

'Remember, I shall give only this one warning,' the man hissed in her ear. Then he let go of her and made off across the lawns.

Helene sighed and swayed slightly. Toby was at her side in an instant.

'Who was that fellow? Did he threaten you?'

Helene breathed deeply. 'It was a mistake. I thought it was you and told him I needed a little air. We came out and…but he has gone and you are here. Shall we have what remains of our dance?'

'Damned fellow!' Toby growled. 'These affairs are all very well, but not when some rogue threatens a lady. Shall I go after him and give him a thrashing?'

'No, please do not cause a fuss,' Helene said. 'Let us go back inside. I should have made certain it was you before I came out. Thank you for coming in search of me, sir.'

'You are very welcome. You must know that I am always at your service should you need me.'

'Thank you, I shall not forget your kindness,' Helene said.

She tried to dismiss the incident, but it was difficult; the pirate's words had frightened her—not for herself, but for Max. She was confused and distressed, but determined not to show it. However, the threat was serious and she must speak to Max as soon as possible.

Helene wished that she had not gone to the terrace with the pirate. His threats had spoiled the evening, even though she tried not to let her unease show as she went to join Max.

'Is something wrong?' Max asked as he sensed her agitation.

'I have something I must tell you…' She glanced over her shoulder. 'This is not the right place or the time, but it is important.'

'Something has happened?' She nodded. 'Tell me now, Helene.'

'I have been warned not to marry you.'

'Damnation! Who said such a thing to you?'

'I do not know who he was, for he wore a mask, but he said that if I did not break off my engagement I should be a widow before I was a wife.' Helene caught his arm, her eyes dark with emotion. 'I am sure he meant his threat, Max, though I do not know why he threatened me.'

'You have told no one else?'

'No, of course not. It was a little frightening, but Toby came and the man ran off.'

'You did not know him?'

'He was wearing the costume of a pirate. I thought he was Toby, but then he grabbed my arm and said… horrible things. Who could it be—and why does he wish to stop our marriage?'

'I have a good idea…' He shook his head. 'It is best if you do not know for the moment. Tell me, Helene— do you wish to break off the engagement in the circumstances?'

'No. If he wants you dead, he will try to kill you whether or not we are married—unless you…?'

'No, of course not. We shall not give him the satisfaction, Helene. I suspected something like this might happen and I am prepared for it, but I did not expect it to happen so quickly.' Max frowned, hesitated, then, 'I do not think you are in danger for the moment, Helene—and I think we have no choice but to carry on as if nothing had happened.'

'You will take care, Max?'

'Of you and myself,' he replied and smiled. 'Will you trust me, my love?'

'Yes, of course,' she said. 'But Mama must not

know anything of this or she will say we must abandon the wedding.'

'Mrs Henderson must certainly not be told—the fewer who know anything at all the better.'

Helene found it impossible to sleep as she tossed and turned on her pillow later that night. The pirate had told her she must break off her engagement to Max or he would die—but two attempts had already been made on his life. She was relieved to have told Max and he had taken the news in his stride. Indeed, he seemed to have been expecting something of the sort.

Who was his enemy and why did he want Max dead? Helene wished that Max had told her more, but she knew he was playing his cards close to his chest. All she could do was wait and pray that he would be safe.

Helene slept at last and it was past eleven in the morning when her maid woke her. She ate a light breakfast and then dressed, ready for the journey to Max's estate. They could not accomplish the whole journey by nightfall and were to stay at a good posting hotel for one night. In the rush of making sure that everything had been packed into her trunks, Helene had no time to think about the previous evening.

She took a lingering farewell of Amelia, hugging her and wishing her well. 'Thank you so very much for everything,' she said, tears stinging her throat. 'You have been the best friend anyone could ever have.'

'You have been a delight,' Amelia told her. 'I look forward to your wedding, my dear.'

Emily came forward to kiss Helene on the cheek. 'I

shall miss our walks and the conversations we had,' she said. 'I, too, look forward to your wedding.'

'You must come and stay with us sometimes,' Helene said and hugged her tightly. 'You have been a real friend, Emily. Please write to me when you have time.'

'Of course I shall, but you must go. I am sure that I heard the carriage pull up a moment ago.' She smiled as the doorknocker sounded. 'Lord Coleridge has arrived.'

Helene went to greet Max as he was admitted, giving him a searching look, but he only smiled and kissed her cheek.

'You look beautiful, my love.'

'Max…we must talk. I have been anxious.'

'Believe me, there is no need. Everything is in hand.'

Mrs Henderson came up then, looking expectant. The last goodbyes were said with thanks expressed to the servants, and then they were outside on the pavement. Max handed both ladies inside his travelling carriage, and then climbed in himself, tapping the roof with his stick to let the coachman know that they were ready to leave.

'Well, this is very comfortable, Coleridge. You looked a little concerned just now, Helene—is anything the matter?'

'Nothing at all, Mama,' Helene said. 'I was merely apologising for having so many trunks and bags.'

'And I was assuring Helene that my grooms will bring everything on the baggage coach,' Max said smoothly. 'As for having too many trunks, my love, I am sure your mama will agree that a lady can never have too many pretty clothes. I dare say we shall have twice as many when we return from Paris.'

'You will spoil her, Coleridge!' Mrs Henderson said and looked satisfied. 'Well, I dare say I may leave everything to you now. It is amazingly pleasant to have a gentleman to take care of one.'

'And I intend to take good care of both you and Helene,' Max told her with a smile. 'I think we should send out invitations to the wedding almost at once, do you not agree? A month is not so very long after all.'

Mrs Henderson's attention was immediately turned to all the preparations, and she passed the first of several miles happily discussing the various dinners, receptions and the dance that was to be held just before the wedding at Coleridge House.

Helene allowed her mama to talk, smiling at Max as he answered all Mrs Henderson's questions patiently, and occasionally glancing out of the window.

It was just after they left London that a curricle moving at speed came up behind them and then overtook them, passing so close to their carriage that the wheels almost touched. Helene caught a glimpse of the man driving, but it was impossible to see much of his face, for he wore a black hat pulled low over his face and a muffler that covered his mouth and nose.

'Damned idiot!' Max remarked and looked out of the window at the back of the curricle as it disappeared into the distance. 'Why must people be in such a hurry?'

'Some people have no manners,' Mrs Henderson said. 'He could easily have caused an accident.'

'My coachman had the sense to pull over to the side of the road and let him pass,' Max said with a slight frown. 'Besides, the coach is heavier and more substantial than that light rig. He must have come off the worst, and I dare say he knew it.'

Helene studied Max's face. A little pulse was flicking at his temple. She had a feeling that he was more concerned about the incident than he would allow. They had been in no danger, because the curricle had been too light to inflict substantial damage on their coach. However, something had made Max thoughtful, for he was silent for several minutes, clearly deep in thought. Had they been alone, Helene would have asked what was concerning him, but she did not wish to alarm her mama. Mrs Henderson had taken it as the thoughtlessness of a careless driver, but Helene could not help wondering if the driver of the curricle had hoped to cause an accident.

They stopped for the night at a prestigious posting inn. Helene and her mama were immediately shown to their rooms and Mrs Henderson declared that she would rest for a while before supper.

'I shall come down to the private parlour in half an hour,' she said. 'You should not go down too soon, Helene. It will not do for you to be alone with Max in a public place. I know you are engaged, but you must still observe the niceties of polite behaviour, dearest.'

'Yes, Mama. Do not worry, I shall do nothing to arouse censure,' Helene promised. However, she took no more than ten minutes to tidy herself before going down to the parlour. As she had expected, Max was already there.

'I wished for a moment alone before Mama came down,' she said. 'I hope you do not think it improper in me?'

'You could never do anything improper in my eyes,' he told her with a warm smile. 'You are worried about the incident in the carriage?'

'Do you think it might be him—the man who threatened me?'

'It is possible—even probable. He may have wished to cause an accident or perhaps just frighten us.'

'Who can it be?'

'I am not yet certain, though I believe I know what is going on. Forgive me, dearest. Believe me when I say it may be best for you not to know.' He took her hands, gazing down at her intently. 'You must not let this overset you. I promise that all will be well.'

'He shall not prevail,' Helene said and raised her head proudly. 'I am not afraid for myself, Max—but you must know that any threat against you distresses me.'

'Yes, it must,' he said, his expression grave. 'If a threat were made against you, I should be anxious. He did not threaten you?'

'No, at least only vaguely,' Helene replied, not meeting his eyes.

'Damn him!' Max was angry. 'Something about that rig made me feel I should know the driver, though he had made sure to hide his face. I have a feeling that that curricle belongs to someone I know.' His gaze narrowed. 'If I thought you were in danger, I would call the wedding off until the rogue has been caught and punished.'

Helene moved towards him, her expression urgent. 'I am not afraid of him, Max. I was startled when he threatened me, but I shall be alert from now on. I believe that our wedding angers him. The thought of your marriage might be enough to bring him out of the shadows. It may be that you can turn the tables, use it against him in some way.'

'That would mean a certain amount of risk on your part, but if the rogue is who I think he is, he will be watched constantly. If you have any doubts, please tell me now, for I do not wish to distress you, my love.'

'If this person believes he has his way he will take his time and perhaps strike when you have relaxed your guard—but if he feels that time is short he may grow careless in his urgency. Besides, why should we sacrifice our happiness?'

'You are very brave,' Max said, reaching out to touch her cheek with his fingertips. I am sorry that you should have been exposed to two attempts on my life.'

'I am glad I was there for the first time, you might not have noticed the man with the pistol,' Helene told him. 'However, I must ask you to keep even the merest hint of danger from Mama. She would insist on postponing the wedding if she thought I might be in danger.'

'She would be anxious for you and rightly so,' Max said. 'It will be much better if she knows nothing—I think she might unconsciously betray us if she were aware of what may happen.' He tipped her chin to look at her. 'You realise that this rogue may try anything to ruin our plans?'

'Yes, Max,' she said and raised her eyes to his. 'I know that he will try to thwart us if he can.'

'But we shall not let him?'

'Certainly not!'

Max laughed softly, and then bent his head to kiss her on the lips. For a moment he held her close, the kiss becoming hungry, demanding. Helene felt as if she were melting into his body, becoming one with him. It was a blissful sensation and she pressed herself closer. They were both breathing hard when he released her.

'Forgive me,' Max said. 'I should not have done that here, for someone might have walked in on us, but I could not resist. You are one of the bravest ladies I know and I adore you.'

'So I should hope,' Helene said and laughed up at him. 'It is quite expected of new husbands, you know—though in some instances it does not last too long.'

Max arched his brows. 'I hope that does not mean you will tire of me too soon?'

'No, sir—it means that I accept that some gentlemen tire of marriage. I hope that you will not be one of them, and I shall do my best to make sure that you prefer your wife's bed to that of a mistress.'

'Helene?' Max's eyes danced with mischief. 'Do you think that quite a proper statement for a young lady of quality?'

'I dare say it is most improper,' Helene replied demurely. 'However, it is the truth—I think that marriage is more than the exchange of contracts and duty. I hope for a lifelong love match.'

'That is exactly my own wish,' Max said. 'I think I need to k—'

His words were lost as the door opened and Mrs Henderson entered. 'Ah, there you are, Helene,' she said. 'I went to your room, but as you were not there thought I should find you here.'

'You are just in time, ma'am,' Max replied. 'I believe our supper should be here at any moment.'

Helene met his eyes, a tingle of pleasure running

through her as she saw the reflection of his desire. She knew that he wanted to kiss her again and she felt his frustration. It was difficult for a young lady to be alone with her fiancé in society, but perhaps when they reached Coleridge it might be possible sometimes.

They reached Max's estate in the early afternoon the next day. Grooms came running to help with the horses and open the door when the carriage pulled to a halt. By the time Max had helped Helene and her mama to alight, the front door was opened and a welcoming party of servants came out to greet them.

A lady dressed all in black apart from a neat white collar came forward and dipped a curtsy. 'I am Mrs Hale, the housekeeper at Coleridge House,' she said. 'We are delighted to have you here, Miss Henderson— Mrs Henderson.'

'Thank you,' Helene said and smiled at her. 'We are very pleased to be here.'

'May I introduce you to the servants, Miss Henderson? This is Hale, our butler and my husband, your own personal maid, Vera, the parlourmaids, Jenny, Susan, Jane and Millie. The upper footman Jenkins, his under footmen, Rawlings, Phillips…'

Helene was taken along a line of smiling men and women who all inclined their heads and murmured something about being pleased to see her. Obviously, they had been told she was their master's fiancée and were eager to welcome her. She tried hard to memorise their names but knew she might forget one or two until she became accustomed to their faces. However, she would not forget Vera, who was to be her own maid.

'Shall I take the ladies up now, sir?' Mrs Hale asked Max as he stood watching benevolently. 'Or would you wish for refreshment to be served immediately?'

'I would think the ladies would prefer to see their rooms first,' Max said. 'Shall we say half an hour?'

'That will be much better,' Mrs Henderson said. 'Come along, Helene. I am anxious to change this gown for a fresh one after so much travelling.'

'Yes, Mama.'

Helene followed her mama, listening as the house-keeper talked about the house and how good it was to see it come to life again now that the master was home from the wars.

'We thought at one time that he might settle else-where,' she said. 'It will be good to have a party of guests again…and to see his lordship happily settled at last.' Mrs Hale looked at Helene with approval. 'I do my best here, but the house needs a mistress.'

'A house like this needs a great deal of order,' Mrs Henderson said. 'However, I must say that it looks just as it ought.'

'His lordship put the repairs needed in order some months ago. He has spoken of further improvements, but I dare say he was waiting for the right time. Colour schemes are sometimes the better for a lady's eye— would you not say so, ma'am?'

Helene did not join in the conversation. She was too busy looking about her at what was to be her new home. Coleridge House was a fine building of pale yellowish brick, with long-paned windows and three storeys. From what she had seen so far, the décor was both stylish and comfortable, which was not always easy to achieve.

However, the entrance hall and staircase were not enough to judge the whole. She was curious to see the room she had been given, and when she was shown into a suite of three rooms, all of which were decorated in shades of green, white and gold, she thought them luxurious.

'These are the best guest apartments,' Mrs Hale told them. 'I thought that you would like to be together, Miss Henderson.'

'Yes, thank you,' Helene said, lingering in the sitting room. 'They are lovely. I am sure we shall be very comfortable here.'

'His lordship's apartments are in the west wing, Miss Henderson. We always used to house guests in this wing. His lordship had this part of the house refurbished first. I believe he means to have his own apartments done next.'

'I see,' Helene said. 'Thank you for telling me, ma'am.'

'I shall leave you to refresh yourselves,' Mrs Hale said. 'If you need anything please ring. I think you will find warm water in your rooms, and Vera will be here to assist you in a moment.'

Helene thanked her and she went away, leaving them to make themselves at home. Mrs Henderson walked round the sitting room, nodding her approval before going through to the bedrooms.

'Which would you prefer, Helene?' she asked. 'They are both very comfortable—but this one has a better view. You can see a water feature beyond the lawns.'

'You have this one,' Helene said. 'I have a view of the woods.'

'You should have the best view,' her mama said, but since she was standing by the window, clearly entranced by the view, Helene chose the slightly smaller room, which was over a small courtyard that backed on to what looked as if it must be a park.

She took off her pelisse and deposited it on the bed. She was just attempting to unfasten the back of her gown when someone knocked at the door and Vera came in, carrying a yellow silk teagown.

'May I do that for you, miss?' she asked. 'Some of your things were sent on ahead and arrived earlier. I took the liberty of unpacking the small trunk and I pressed this for you. I hope it will do, Miss Henderson?'

'Thank you,' Helene replied. 'That was kind of you, Vera. It will do very well. In the largest trunk you will find a dark green evening dress. I would like to wear that later—if you can manage to press it for me?'

'Of course I can,' Vera replied. 'I am so happy to have been chosen as your maid, miss—and I hope you will be pleased with me.'

'I am sure I shall,' Helene said. She wriggled free of her gown as the girl finished unfastening her. 'Thank you. I want to go down as soon as I have changed, because I should like to take a look at the gardens, though I am not sure if there will be time before we have tea.'

Helene did not wait for her mama. She had caught sight of some beautiful gardens and was eager to explore. A footman was standing by the door when she returned to the hallway.

'I should like to explore the pretty rose garden I glimpsed as we arrived,' she told him with a shy smile. 'Could you please direct me?'

'Of course, Miss Henderson. Follow me, I shall show you the best way to access the rose garden.'

He preceded her to the back of the hall and then opened the door into a very pretty parlour, which had all the sun in the afternoons and was very warm, despite the open French windows.

'The garden is just out there, miss,' he said, 'and refreshments will be served in the front parlour on the first floor.'

'Thank you…Rawlings…' She smiled, pleased that she had remembered his name. 'You have been very helpful.'

'It is our pleasure to serve you, miss.'

Helene nodded and walked across the parlour to the open window. She went out into the garden, thinking how peaceful and pleasant it was. She could smell the heavy perfume of musk roses and hear the sound of birds twittering in some graceful trees at the far end of a smooth lawn. She was so lucky that this was to be her home.

She walked towards the rose arbour, inhaling the lovely scents and bending to sniff one particularly beautiful red rose.

'Hello…' a voice said behind her. 'I think you must be Miss Henderson—Max's fiancée?'

Helene turned and saw a man of perhaps two and twenty years. Of medium stature, he had a pale complexion and his hair was black, his eyes grey. She thought that perhaps he might have been ill at some time recently, for his pallor was not quite healthy.

'Hello,' Helene said and smiled; he was not unattractive and seemed friendly. 'I am sorry, but I do not know who you are.'

'No, I suppose Max did not think to mention me. I am Robert Heronsdale—his cousin.'

'Oh, yes, I remember something. I believe Max told us that you and your mama live at the dower house?'

'Max was good enough to give us a home after my father lost all his money and then suffered a fall from his horse,' Robert told her with a strange smile. 'He was ill for some months before he died and then we discovered that he had gambled away almost everything he owned. We were forced to leave our home. When Max heard of our misfortune, he generously asked us to come here.'

'Yes, that is so like him,' Helene said. 'I hope you will visit us sometimes? I have not met Mrs Heronsdale as yet, but I look forward to it.'

'Mama will call on you later,' Robert told her. 'I am sure she would have come this afternoon, but she is a little unwell. I hope you did not mind that I came at once? I must admit to being curious about the lady Max is to marry. I must congratulate him on his choice. You are very pretty, Miss Henderson.'

'Oh…' Helene was not quite sure how to answer. His eyes were bright as he gave her an intent look. 'Thank you.' She did not know what she would have found to say next, but she was saved by the arrival of Max. He came striding towards them, a smile on his lips.

'Helene, my love. Rawlings said I would find you here.' His gaze moved to Robert and his expression became thoughtful. 'Robert. It is good to see you up and about at last, my dear fellow. I trust that you are quite well now?'

'Yes, thank you, cousin,' Robert said. 'I should like to speak to you in private when you have time—but I am happy to report that my health has improved since *your visit.*' He seemed to give significance to the last two words. 'You understand me, sir?'

'Yes, I believe I do,' Max said and smiled at him. 'I am happy to hear that things have improved. I see that you have met Helene.'

'I envy you your good fortune,' Robert said and offered his hand. 'You have found yourself a lovely bride and I wish you both all the happiness in the world.'

'Thank you, Robert,' Max said and took his hand in a firm clasp. 'We are about to have some refreshment. I do hope you will join us?'

'I should get back, for Mama is unwell. I dare say she will be better in the morning. Her little turns only last a few hours. Perhaps you will invite us to dine one day?'

'Of course. You may call whenever you wish,' Max said. 'Send my good wishes to Mrs Heronsdale.'

'I shall do so, of course,' Robert said and inclined his head. 'Until we meet again, cousin—perhaps tomorrow morning.'

Max stood watching as he walked into the rose arbour and disappeared from sight through a tunnel of white, climbing roses.

'Is something the matter?' Helene asked, as he remained silent.

'I am not sure,' Max told her, his expression serious, and looked at her. 'Do not be alarmed, Helene. I believe you may trust my servants implicitly—but take care when speaking with anyone from the dower house.'

'You cannot think…' Helene was shocked. 'Surely not?'

'I do not think it,' Max replied. 'But Robert is the

only one who would benefit from my death until we marry—at least, that is what he or others may believe.'

'Yes, of course I shall be careful of him—and of anyone else I do not know well,' Helene said. She was thoughtful as they walked back to the house together. She had not disliked Robert Heronsdale on sight; he had seemed pleasant enough, but Max's warning was clear. He must be in a position to know more than she, of course.

It was very worrying—until the person or persons who had attacked Max were discovered and caught, his life would continue to be in danger. She had come to love him so much and she could not bear it if anything happened to him. Max seemed in command of the situation, but it could not hurt if Helene kept a watchful eye. She would listen and observe, as she always did, and perhaps she might discover something of interest.

Max smiled at her, taking her hand to kiss the palm. The touch of his lips made the heat flood through her, making her aware of all the reasons she wanted to be his wife. 'You must not worry too much, my dearest one. I warned you only so that you should not be fooled by a false message, but I promise you that I have everything under control.'

'I know that you will have taken every precaution, as much for my sake as your own,' Helene told him, her eyes warm with love. 'But you must take care, too—and perhaps the obvious is not always as it seems.'

'What do you mean by that, my wise little love?'

'I just think that sometimes we are misled by the things others say,' Helene replied thoughtfully. 'I have nothing in particular in mind.'

'No, how could you?' Max said, an odd look in his eyes. 'However, I think you may be right.'

Helene had no chance to ask him what he meant, for they saw Toby Sinclair walking across the lawns towards them. They greeted each other with pleasure and then went on up to the house.

Chapter Eleven

The Earl of Ravenshead was the next guest to arrive. He joined them in the drawing room for sherry before dinner that evening. Helene knew now that the three men were close friends and were meeting for a purpose. She caught snatches of their conversation, hearing the words Harry, and Northaven, a couple of times.

The earl seemed to be of the opinion that Northaven was up to his tricks again, whatever that might mean, but Max was clearly doubtful. However, they soon changed the conversation when the butler came to announce that dinner was served.

Max took Helene in to dinner; the earl offered his arm to her mama, who seemed pleased with the attention. The company consisted of three gentlemen and two ladies that evening—most of the guests were not expected until the next day.

'I have requested the pleasure of my aunt and cousin's company tomorrow,' Max told Helene. 'I dare say Dr Clarke may accompany them; he is a physician—or so I am led to believe—and I can hardly exclude him altogether. We shall have several guests by then, I hope, so you will hardly notice him.'

'If he is a pleasant gentleman, I shall be happy to meet him,' Helene said. 'Remember, I am a tanner's granddaughter.' Her eyes twinkled with amusement. 'I am hardly in a position to snub a physician.'

'Perhaps I deserved that,' Max retorted. 'However, it was not meant in that way—merely that I think we should reserve judgement for the time being. Besides, you are also the granddaughter of a duke.'

'Do not remind me,' Helene said, her smile fading.

'Annesdale has written to me,' Max said. 'He asks if I will add his name to mine in return for his fortune for our sons.'

'What did you answer?' Helene looked at him hard.

'I have not done so as yet,' Max told her. 'I know you are very angry with him, Helene. I thought you should have time to consider our reply.'

'You are consulting my wishes?'

'Of course. Would you expect me to do otherwise?'

'I know that matters of property are generally dealt with by gentlemen and their wives are seldom consulted.'

'I would never bother you with mundane details of business. However, this concerns you closely, Helene. You must certainly decide in this matter. I would not dream of accepting something that might distress you.'

'Thank you,' she said and sent him a look of gratitude. 'May I have some time to think about this, please?'

'Naturally you will wish to consider your answer. I should be sad if you were to reply without giving this thought. Annesdale is a proud man, but he is also an old man and perhaps he regrets things he has done in the past—as many of us do.'

'Yes, perhaps,' Helene replied.

The subject was dropped, as the conversation became general. They were dining in the small parlour that evening because there were only five of them. Toby entertained them all with the latest gossip from town. Helene laughed at his audacious description of something the Regent was reported as saying, thinking that it boded well for the future. They had good friends and it would be a happy life here at Coleridge.

The gentlemen did not linger over their port and soon joined the ladies in the drawing room. Helene played the pianoforte for a while to entertain them, but at ten o'clock her mama said she was tired and they left the gentlemen to their own amusements.

'The Earl of Ravenshead is a pleasant gentleman,' Mrs Henderson remarked as they went upstairs. 'He was telling me that he has joined his friend Lord Pendleton in a venture to import French wines into this country. Apparently Lord Pendleton suggested it to him as a way of repairing his family fortunes and it has been successful.'

'I believe Amelia likes the earl very well,' Helene said. 'Do you think she may marry him, Mama?'

'I should not think so for a moment,' Mrs Henderson said. 'She seemed very wrapped up with her plans to travel. I believe she means to take Emily and travel to Italy this winter.'

'Oh…' Helene did not continue the conversation—after all, it was not their affair—but she could not help wondering if Amelia's plans had come about because she was unhappy.

However, she did not dwell on the thought long for she had other things to consider. She was certain that even now the three gentlemen downstairs were plotting something. She had noticed significant glances between them at dinner and she imagined they were thinking of a way to draw out the rogue who had twice tried to murder Max.

Several ladies were amongst the guests that arrived the next day. Helene helped Max to receive them, feeling a tingle of excitement as the house began to fill up. She knew most of them, for they had been Max's friends in town, but one or two neighbours also came to call during the morning. Helene paid particular attention to learning their names for they would be her friends when she lived here. Max received an urgent message just after nuncheon and made his excuses.

'I must attend to some urgent business. You will excuse me, Helene. I shall not be away long. Perhaps you will make my excuses and see that our guests are received. You know everyone and most of those still to come are your own particular friends.'

'Of course,' Helene said. 'I shall be pleased to welcome them in your absence, and to explain.'

Amongst the flurry of arrivals, she almost missed the brief visit from Mrs Heronsdale. However, when Helene returned from greeting Captain Paul Marshall and his sister, she discovered Max's aunt sitting with her mama.

'Miss Henderson. I am Coleridge's aunt,' the lady said, rising as Helene entered. 'I believe you may have met my son yesterday? He told you I was indisposed. I had a slight headache. I was sorry not to have been here when you arrived. Please forgive me.'

'Robert made your apologies, ma'am,' Helene replied and offered her hand. She was drawn into an embrace, inhaling the almost overwhelming perfume of rose water and lavender. 'I am very pleased to meet Max's aunt.'

'Coleridge sent word that he wished to see me,' she said. 'However, he was out when I arrived, I believe on estate matters.'

'He will be sorry to have missed you,' Helene told her. 'However, I know that he invited you all to dine this evening. I am sure you will be able to speak privately then if you wish.'

'Yes, I dare say.' Mrs Heronsdale looked at her intently for a moment. 'My son was very taken with you, Helene— I may call you that, I hope?' She looked pleased as Helene inclined her head. 'I have seldom known him take to anyone so quickly. Robert is inclined to keep his own company, but he told me he was keen to know you better.'

'Oh…' Helene recalled the rather intense look in the young man's eyes and her cheeks felt warm. 'That is kind of him.'

Well, I must go,' Mrs Heronsdale said and stood up again. 'Will you walk with me to the door, Helene?'

'Yes, of course—but will you not stay for tea? Some of my friends have just arrived. I am sure they would like to meet you.'

'This evening,' Mrs Heronsdale said. She was silent until they left the parlour, then she placed a hand on Helene's arm. 'I had to speak to you alone. Please, Helene, take this as a friendly warning—do not trust Robert too much. I say this for your own sake. If he asks you to walk with him anywhere…be careful…'

Helene felt an icy trickle down her spine. Mrs Heronsdale's grip on her arm was almost painful and the look in her eyes was frightening.

'I am not sure I understand you, ma'am?'

'Robert is…excitable at times. Oh, he means no harm, and he truly likes you—but be careful of being alone with him.'

'I should not walk alone with any gentleman but Max,' Helene assured her. 'But surely you cannot think…?'

Mrs Heronsdale looked as if she might burst into tears. 'I do not wish you to think the less of him. It distresses me to say these things…but Doctor Clarke says that Robert becomes a little odd at times. It is the reason he has to—' She gasped and looked anxious. 'Please, say nothing of this to my nephew. If he knew, he might…' She shook her head. 'I have said too much…excuse me, I must go.' She walked quickly to the door and then glanced back. 'Do not forget my warning.'

Helene puzzled over her words. She wished that she could speak to Max concerning his aunt's warning. Mrs Heronsdale had begged her not to tell Max, but Helene knew that she must talk to him, and as soon as possible.

However, they now had ten extra guests. Max had invited three ladies he knew to be Helene's particular friends. They were all delighted with the news of her wedding and she found herself caught up in the chatter and excitement. Even when Max joined them for tea a little later she had no chance to speak with him alone.

It was the same for most of the evening. She saw Max talking earnestly to his aunt at one point, though neither the physician or Robert were present, which was rather strange. When she tried to catch Max's eye, he just smiled at her.

Helene did not have a chance to speak to Max alone until much later that evening. The hour was late and most of the ladies had decided to go up. Helene went to say goodnight to the gentlemen and Max drew her aside for a moment.

'I am sorry we have had no time to ourselves today,' he said. 'Perhaps I may take you for a little drive in the morning?'

'Yes, please,' she told him. 'I have something I wish to say to you.'

'Is it urgent, Helene?'

'Yes, it is—or it may be.'

'Then you must tell me now.' His gaze narrowed. 'I can see that you are distressed.'

'I hardly know how to say this, but it concerns something your aunt told me about Robert.'

Max frowned. 'Yes, this is important. Tell me exactly what she said to you, Helene.'

Helene repeated the warning almost word for word and Max was silent for a moment. 'It seemed strange for I cannot think that the young man I met yesterday would do anything to harm me.'

'No, he would not,' Max replied. 'But there may be more to this than we yet know.'

'Surely she would not lie about her own son and yet…' Helene shook her head. 'It is puzzling.'

'I believe I may begin to see what is happening here,' Max told her. 'However, it may be as well to heed her warning, my love.'

'Max, you do not think…?' Helene was shocked. 'He would not…'

'I warned you that there might be danger. Would you wish to leave?'

'Certainly not! I shall do whatever you tell me, Max—but I shall not leave you.'

'You are quite certain?'

'Yes, quite certain.'

'Very well.' His eyes seemed to burn into her. 'I cannot wait for the morning. I want you to myself so that I can kiss you, my darling—but it would have been rude to leave our guests on the very day they arrived. By the morning they will have found their own amusements, and many will not rise before noon. If we leave at nine thirty, we shall be back before anyone knows we have gone.'

'Yes, we shall,' Helene said. 'I shall look forward to it.' She took a reluctant leave of him.

Helene was thoughtful, a little restless as she undressed, for the mystery had deepened. Why should Robert's mother warn her to be careful of her son? Was she trying to point the finger of blame? Oh, it was all so disturbing and strange! It was difficult to know who could be trusted.

After she had dismissed her maid, she blew out her candle, drew back the curtains and sat by the window looking out. At first there was little she could see, for the moon was shadowed, but as the clouds moved away she saw its silvery light touch bushes, trees and statutes. She was gazing at what she thought might be the statue of a man when it moved. Helene was at first startled, then her interest was caught as the man came towards the house. Now she could see that he was wearing breeches, but no shirt, which was why he had appeared to be a statue in the moonlight. She leaned forward and her movement seemed to attract his attention. He peered up at her window, clearly straining to see her.

'Helene...' he called softly. 'Miss Henderson...come down, please. I must warn you.'

Helene shivered, for she was certain that the pale torso she could see must belong to Robert Heronsdale. His face had seemed very pale when they met in the gardens and instinct told her that it was he. She did not answer him, for his mother's warning was echoing in her mind. Besides, it was most improper of him to be wandering about the countryside without his shirt—especially outside the bedroom window of his cousin's fiancée!

'It is a matter of life and death,' Robert called. 'I am trying to help you...'

Helene stood up, still hesitating. As she wondered whether to open the window wider and call down to him, another man came from the shadows suddenly and grabbed Robert from behind. There was a short tussle and then Robert seemed to collapse into his arms. The newcomer hoisted Robert over his shoulder and retreated into the bushes.

Helene shivered. If she had not witnessed the whole with her own eyes, she would not have believed it. How could anyone overpower a young man so easily? And why would they do such a thing?

She frowned as she retreated to her bed and sat down. Her thoughts were confused as she tried to work out what she had just seen. She was uncertain of what she ought to do, because she could not be sure what had happened. It was such a shocking thing to happen! Either Robert had been kidnapped or...he had been controlled by the physician.

Helene's mind was beginning to work out a theory based on the warning that Mrs Heronsdale had given her earlier that day. She had told her that Robert had taken a liking to her and that she was to be careful because Robert sometimes became excitable. What was that supposed to mean...unless...but that was too horrid!

Helene's mind veered away from what she had just pieced together. It would fit in with what Max had told her about his cousin being ill at times...and his absence that evening. If perhaps he were not quite as he ought to be...and that when one of his... mad fits was upon him, he attacked young ladies.

No, it was too awful! Helene did not wish to believe such a thing. She admitted that the young man had been a little intense when they met in the gardens, but insane... No! She could not think it. His manner when he called to her outside her window had certainly been urgent, but she would not have said he was in a mad fit. Yet his mother's words had been intended to make her wary of him.

Oh, how horrible it all was! She would not have taken so much notice had not Robert cried out that it was a matter of life and death. Someone had tried to kill Max twice, and his cousin was his heir. The finger of blame pointed in Robert's direction, so why did Helene feel that something terrible had just happened?

She could not simply retire to bed and let this thing go unnoticed. She must speak to Max immediately.

Putting on a thick wrapping gown and a pair of slippers, Helene took her candle and went downstairs in search of Max. She did not know if he would have retired yet. If he had done so, she would have to ask the hall porter to fetch him, because he ought to know what was going on.

'Mrs Heronsdale informed me this evening that Robert has gone missing,' Max told his friends as they sat together in the library drinking a last nightcap. 'She says that it has happened half a dozen times in the last six months. He is—she says—of a nervous disposition. When he returns from these mysterious disappearances he is sometimes very ill and takes to his bed for weeks at a time.'

'Do you believe her?' Toby asked. 'You spoke to him yesterday. How was he then?'

'He seemed fine, if a little nervous,' Max replied. 'I told you that fellow Clarke had been keeping him drugged... If what my aunt says is true, it would appear that they do it for his own good.'

'What of these village girls who have been attacked? You said that they had arrested some yokel,' Gerard said and frowned.

'Yes, they did, but it seems that he is foolish, but harmless. At the time the attacks in our village took place, he was with his mother—or so she swears. The magistrate sent him to a place for idiots. My neighbour visited him and is of the opinion that he did not attack the girls in our village.'

'You are thinking that it was your cousin?' Gerard asked.

'I am not certain—' Max broke off as someone knocked at the door and then Helene walked in, wearing a heavy silk robe over her nightgown. 'Helene—is something wrong? You are not ill?'

'Forgive me for disturbing you,' she said, a faint colour in her cheeks. 'I know I am dressed improperly, gentlemen—but I have seen something disturbing and I believe you should know about it, Max. It concerns your cousin.'

'Good grief!' Gerard said. 'It was very sensible of you to come, Miss Henderson—please tell us.'

'I was restless because of something Mrs Heronsdale said to me earlier,' Helene told them. 'I blew out my candle and sat by the open window, looking out. At first I thought him a statue because he was so pale…he wore only his breeches—no shirt, coat or shoes on his feet, I think…' She saw that she had their attention. 'He called to me. He said that it was urgent that he speak to me because it was a matter of life and death…and then someone came up behind him. He struggled, but he was overpowered very quickly and went limp, as if he had suddenly been drugged.'

'Good grief! Was it Robert?' Max asked her.

'I believe so.'

'Thank God you did not go down to him!'

'I believe I have too much good sense,' Helene said. 'And yet I think he may truly have been trying to warn me of something.'

'Why is that?' Max asked, his gaze narrowed. 'I have been told that he disappears sometimes for days and when he returns he is ill. Apparently, he remembers nothing.'

'Did Mrs Heronsdale tell you that this evening?' Helene asked. 'You did not tell me.'

'She returned to the house and spoke to me privately after you retired, Helene. Besides…I am not certain I believe her,' Max said. 'She said she thought it her duty to warn me, but there is something not right. I cannot put my finger on it just yet.'

'Do you think that…?' Helene shook her head. 'No, I am being foolish.'

'You suspect her of something? What?' Gerard asked, giving her an intent look. 'Why would she concoct such a story about her own son?'

'There have been two attempts on your life,' Helene replied. 'I suppose she could not inherit if her son were dead—or convicted of murder?'

'Actually, she might,' Max said. 'My estate is not entailed to a male heir. It would go to Robert first if I died before we marry, Helene—but after that it would go to her, for she is my father's sister. At least it would have done had I not made certain changes.'

'Have you made Mrs Heronsdale and Robert aware of those changes?' Gerard asked, his eyes narrowed and thoughtful.

'No, I have not.' Max frowned. 'I could do so, of course, but then I might never discover what has been going on.'

'You are taking a huge risk,' Gerard said.

'Yes, I know. That is why I asked you to take certain precautions.'

Max threw a look of apology at Helene. 'Forgive me for bringing you to a situation like this, my love. It is more involved and dangerous than I imagined.'

'The situation is not of your making,' Helene replied.

'Besides, I want to be here. If you are planning anything—and I am certain you are—I should like to help.'

'You have already helped us,' Max told her with a smile. 'We do have a plan, but there is nothing you can do, dearest. Just be careful.'

'What of Robert? Will you send men to search for him?'

'I think we shall wait until tomorrow. I shall call on my aunt first thing in the morning and hear what she has to say.'

'You do not think he is in danger?'

'No…' Max shook his head. 'If what I think is going on is right, Robert is perfectly safe until I am dead.'

'Oh…' Helene wrinkled her brow in thought. 'Yes, I see…of course.'

'Forgive me if I tell you nothing more,' Max said. 'Go to bed and try to sleep, my love. I promise you I shall take great care. Gerard and Toby will help me—and once it is all over I shall explain everything.'

Helene hesitated. She would have liked to be included in their plans, but she knew it was unlikely Max would allow it. Whatever they had in mind carried a certain amount of danger and he would not wish her to be involved.

'I shall go up,' she told him. 'I felt that I should tell you what I had witnessed, Max.'

'I am grateful you did—you have confirmed something I was not sure of,' Max told her. 'I may have to postpone our drive until tomorrow afternoon, Helene.'

Helene nodded. She wished the other gentlemen good night and left them alone to talk. She did not think she would find it easy to sleep, because Max and his friends were clearly involved in some plot to make the murderer show his hand. The thought that he was in danger was disturbing, but she knew that she must do everything he asked of her and be as patient as she could.

Helene was up early in the hope that Max might still have time to take her for the drive he had promised, but when she went downstairs Mrs Hale told her that his lordship had gone out riding with two of his friends. Helene knew who the friends were and sighed inwardly. She would have liked to know exactly what was going on. The fear that Max might be in imminent danger made her restless.

She decided that she would take a little walk in the gardens, though she would not go out of sight of the house. The sun was shining and it was such a lovely morning that she had no desire to sit alone in the house, and most of the guests would not rise before noon.

Helene found a sunny spot on the lawns and sat down on a wooden bench. The warmth on her face and head was so pleasant that she was lulled into a sense of peace and well being.

'Miss Henderson?'

Helene looked up. She had never to her knowledge seen the man addressing her before. He was a thin faced, dark-haired man, his eyes deep set and his nose a little crooked.

'Excuse me?' she said, standing up a little warily. 'I do not think we are acquainted?'

'You are Miss Helene Henderson?'

'Yes, I am Miss Henderson,' Helene replied. 'And you are, sir…?'

'I am Dr Clarke. You may have heard that I look after Robert? I need your help because Lord Coleridge is in grave danger.'

'Max is in danger?' Helene was immediately alert, her nerves jangling. 'Tell me at once. What is going on?'

'Robert has lost his mind,' Dr Clarke said. 'It pains me to say this, for I have looked after him for years. I love Robert as my own son, but he is not always as he should be. He has an illness that manifests itself at certain times.'

'You are saying that he has bouts of insanity?' Helene felt cold shivers down her spine. Looking at him closely, she was suddenly certain, 'You are the one who grabbed him last night as he called to me. I saw someone take him.'

'You were in danger,' the physician told her. 'Robert has been getting much worse of late, more cunning. He came to himself before I could administer sufficient quantities of the drug we use to control him during his mad periods. He knocked me on the head and then ran away. He will kill both you and his lordship if he can.'

'You should be telling Lord Coleridge this,' Helene said, feeling uneasy. 'I do not see what I can do to help you.'

'Robert has Lord Coleridge tied up. I searched for him all night and finally found him, but it was too late. Lord Coleridge is his prisoner. If you come with me now, we may still save him. Robert likes pretty girls and he wishes to speak with you. He will not speak to anyone else—if you bring another person, he may lose control completely. I beg you, Miss Henderson, if you care for Lord Coleridge, you must come with me now.'

Helene's unease was growing. She was not sure what

to do—ought she to return to the house and fetch help? Supposing Dr Clarke was telling her the truth? Any delay and it might be too late.

'Yes, I will come,' she said, making up her mind. 'Where are they? Please lead on, sir.'

'You must hurry,' the physician urged. 'When Robert is like this, he might do anything.'

Helene frowned, because something was making her more and more uneasy. Her instincts were warning her she ought not to trust this man, but what choice did she have? If Robert were really mad and would only speak to her, she must do what she could to save Max's life.

She set off in his wake through the shrubbery. Her mind worked quickly. She did not trust this man! She was almost certain he was lying and it was possible he was leading her into a trap. Glancing at a delicate lace kerchief in her hands, she noticed that she had torn the lace in her anxiety. She would use it to leave a trail for others to follow! She pulled a piece off and dropped it on to a bush, her fingers working at the fine material until she had another little shred that she could drop.

If someone came to look for her, she could only hope that they would understand what she had done.

'Robert is missing,' Mrs Heronsdale said when Max inquired after his cousin that morning. 'His bed has not been slept in. He claimed to be ill when he came back yesterday, but when Dr Clarke went to look for him he had gone. He has not returned and we do not know where he is.' She twisted her hands in distress. 'Forgive me, Coleridge. I should have told you long ago about his disappearances, but I was afraid that you would send us away. I have nowhere else to go and without Dr Clarke…my poor Robert would end in Bedlam, chained up for the rest of his life.'

'I am certain we can do better than that for him,' Max told her. 'He must obviously be confined for his own safety and that of others.'

'My poor, poor boy…' A tear ran from the corner of her eye and she dabbed it away with a lace kerchief. 'I do not know what I would have done without Dr Clarke.'

'You trust him?' Max's gaze narrowed.

'Completely! I know he has to drug Robert at times, but it is for his own good. When you forced us to leave it off…I cannot answer for what he might have done.'

'You will allow me to look in his room?'

'Of course—but he is not there. Doctor Clarke is out looking for him now. Do you wish to search the house? We have already done so, but I shall not deny you if you wish to do so yourself. Indeed, I should be happy for you to set your mind at rest.'

'Very well, I believe you,' Max told her. 'I think I shall not need to search his room after all. You should have told me from the beginning, but we shall discuss that at another time. I must organise a search for Robert.'

'I pray you find him before he does more harm,' Mrs Heronsdale said and gave a little sob of despair. 'My poor boy…'

Max inclined his head and went out. She was afraid of something and he suspected that she was lying to him! He was not sure why she would lie, but he was fairly certain he knew exactly what had been going on here. It was imperative that he should find Robert before Dr Clarke did, because his cousin's life was in danger!

* * *

Helene looked uncertainly at what was clearly a summerhouse. There was an unused air about it, as if no one ever came here. She felt very nervous, her stomach beginning to tie itself in knots. She was certain now that the physician had lied to her. This was a trap! Even as she hesitated, the physician stopped, turned back and looked at her. His gloating manner frightened her. She turned, prepared to flee back the way they had come, but he was on her at once. His powerful hands grasped her arm, his fingers digging into the flesh as he held on to her.

'Has the penny dropped at last, Miss Henderson?' he asked, and suddenly she knew him. She had heard that voice on the night of Amelia's costume ball. He was the man who had threatened her with dire happenings if she would not give up her engagement to Max. 'I thought you might know me, even though I disguised my voice that night at the ball. But of course all you thought of was your precious Lord Coleridge. How foolish a woman in love can be!'

'Let go of my arm,' Helene said. 'You are an impostor, aren't you? You never were a doctor at all.'

'Oh, yes, I do have a certificate and I have worked in Italy as a physician. I was forced to earn my living after my father cut me off without a penny for disgracing his name. It was not my fault that the stupid girl struggled so hard I broke her neck...' His lip curled in a sneer. 'Women are all fools. They will believe anything you say, providing that they believe you love them.'

'You made Mrs Heronsdale believe her son was mad.'

'Actually, it is Mrs Clarke. It suited our purposes to keep the marriage a secret.'

'Does she know that you have tried to kill Lord Coleridge twice?'

'You ask too many questions,' he said and his fingers tightened their hold, making Helene wince.

'You are hurting my arm,' she said as he took a key from his pocket with his free hand and unlocked the door of the summerhouse. He thrust her inside and followed, closing the door with a bang. Helene kicked out at his shins in a desperate attempt to free herself, and in subduing her once more he neglected to lock the door behind them.

'Behave and perhaps I shall let you live,' he said. 'You really should have listened to me, Miss Henderson. You are a stubborn wench. I should enjoy taming you—as I might have done had you done as your grandfather asked you. Why would you not give up Coleridge and live under Annesdale's roof? I could have disposed of those who stood in my way of a fortune— and then I might have come courting. I think I should have enjoyed that.'

'What are you talking about? If you imagine that I would ever have married you...' Helene began, but a look from him silenced her.

'You might have had no choice,' he said. 'When the grandson of his long-lost cousin turned up, Annesdale would have been glad to give you to me.'

'You are related to Annesdale...' Helene stared at him in disbelief. 'How could you know of his offer to me? I do not believe you are his cousin. Were you planning to dupe a lonely old man by impersonating a member of his family?'

'Do you imagine I would tell you?' He smiled. 'But

I shall tell you that a certain lady is my friend. She told me all about you, because she hates you.'

'If you are going to kill me, what difference does it make?' she asked, and then, hearing a strangled sound behind her, she turned and saw the figure of a man struggling against the bonds that bound his ankles and wrists. He was lying on the floor, with his back towards them, but she knew at once that it must be Robert. She ran to him, kneeling by his side and pulling the gag from his mouth. 'Has that devil hurt you?'

'I wanted to warn you,' Robert gasped. 'I didn't know what he planned for a long time, but of late he had grown careless and talked to me when he believed I was drugged. When Max insisted on bringing in his own physician, he stopped drugging me. I began to remember things…I wanted to warn you. He is going to kill Max, blame it on me and then Mama will inherit the money. Once he can persuade her to give it to him, he will marry her and then she too will die.'

'You are somewhat behind the times,' the physician's sneering voice told them from his position near the door. 'Your mama is my wife. You, my so-dear Robert, will be killed after Coleridge is dead—and then in a while I shall dispose of my sweet lady when we are abroad. I shall return, wealthy, the prodigal son as it were, to be welcomed with open arms…' He smiled oddly as they stared at him in horrified silence. 'I killed your father, Robert—did you know? He was ill and it was easy to poison his medicine so that he faded slowly. I was Harriet's lover. After your father's death, we married in secret, because she did not want you to know—she feared your disapproval. When we discovered that your father had been in debt and there was no money left, we came here. I realised it would be simple to kill Coleridge and later you, the plan to blame the murder on you came afterwards, when he began to take an interest in marriage.'

'You devil!' Robert said and struggled furiously with his bonds. 'Your plan will backfire—no one will believe that I killed my cousin.'

'Poor Robert. You have been suffering from bouts of madness for a long time. Your dear mama believes me. She will swear to it, because she does what I tell her. When Max finds his beloved fiancée dead, he will blame you. I shall kill you both and put the pistol in your hand. You raped and killed the delightful Helene and then you killed Max in a fit of madness. Realising what you had done, you killed yourself in remorse.'

'Damn you!' Robert said and renewed his struggles. 'You are a cold devil! I will kill you for what you've done.'

'Unfortunately for you, you will never have a chance,' the physician sneered. His gaze moved to Helene. 'It would be a pity to kill you too soon, Miss Henderson. I enjoy pretty women, especially when they fight. I believe we have time to get better acquainted before Coleridge comes looking for you…'

'Stay away from me!' Helene screamed. 'I would rather die than let you touch me.'

She looked for a weapon, but could find none. Robert was still struggling to free himself, but the knots were too tight.

'Scream louder,' the physician said. 'I love it when you scream.'

He advanced towards her, but even as he did so the door crashed open and Gerard Ravenshead entered, closely followed by Toby Sinclair. Both of them were carrying pistols, which they had firmly trained on the physician.

'Lay one finger on Miss Henderson and you die instantly,' Gerard told him. 'Max thought if we gave you enough rope you would hang yourself.' He looked at Helene. 'I am sorry it took us a while to follow you inside, Helene, but we needed to hear his confession. It was the only way we could prove that he made those attempts on Max. We couldn't be sure it would work, but Max said he was an arrogant fool and would fall for it.'

'Damn you!' the physician said and lunged at Helene. He grabbed her and held her in front of him. He took a knife from somewhere about him and held it to her throat. 'Stand aside or I shall kill her.'

Even as Gerard hesitated, Robert threw off the bonds that secured his hands and, though his ankles were still bound, lunged at the physician, clinging to his leg and biting at his ankle. The sharp pain made the man grunt and for a second he released his hold on Helene. She brought her arm back sharply in his face and then ran towards the door. Toby pushed her outside. She heard a sharp scream of pain from inside and then a shot. Shocked and distraught, she hesitated, and then, seeing Max striding towards her, she ran to him.

'Max,' she cried, flinging herself at him. The words came out in a passionate torrent, 'He tricked me into coming here—and he was going to kill both Robert and me and you too when you came looking. The earl and Toby listened to his bragging confession and then came inside. He grabbed me and held a knife to my throat, but then Robert bit his ankle and he let go of me.'

'Helene, my love.' Max put his arms about her, holding her as she trembled. 'I am so sorry. I followed your trail. I was afraid something might happen and Gerard would be too late.' How pale her cheeks were! 'Forgive me, Helene. You were the bait. After what happened at the ball, I suspected that it must be Clarke. When his attempt to frighten you into crying off failed, he became desperate. I thought he might try to use you to trap Robert and me. He had to get us both together— somewhere he could be private. We knew it was a terrible risk, but Gerard and Toby promised they would not let me down. Can you forgive me? Had they not followed you closely, he might have harmed you and then I should not have forgiven myself.'

'I would have gladly taken the risk for your sake had you told me,' Helene said. 'He was the pirate at the ball, as you guessed. He claims to be Annesdale's distant cousin but I am not sure if he lies.'

'I care not who he is, providing you are unharmed— and will forgive me. I have been shockingly careless of your safety, my love.'

'I do not think it,' Helene told him with a smile. 'I was watched over the whole time. I was told that you had gone out with your friends, but I see now what you were planning last night.'

'We wanted people to think we had gone riding, but then we split up. We knew that if I was right, both Robert and I were safe until he could get us together. Gerard and Toby watched for you while I went to my aunt. I was sure that she was hiding something. I am not certain that she knew what Clarke was up to, but I believe she suspected something. I came to look for you immediately.

I found the shreds of lace you had cleverly left for me and followed the trail.'

'I think someone has been shot...' Helene began and then stopped as the door to the summerhouse opened and three men came out. Robert was limping. He had blood dripping from a wound to his hand, but otherwise seemed unhurt. Gerard and Toby had put away their pistols.

'The rogue is dead,' Gerard said. 'He would have killed Robert so I had no choice but to shoot him. It is best for everyone that he is out of the way, because he was a dangerous man. Had he succeeded in his plans, there is no telling what he would have done next.'

'We heard his confession,' Toby said. 'Robert can tell you more.'

Max looked at his cousin. 'What did your mama know of his plans?'

'I think she had begun to suspect him of something, for I heard them quarrelling,' Robert told him. 'She asked him where he had been one night when she found blood on his shirt. He told her that he had cut himself on a nail, but she did not believe him. After you insisted that I should not be drugged, Mama forced him to stop. He told her that I could be dangerous, but she wept over my bed when he was away for a few days. I believe she may have been afraid of him, because perhaps she had begun to realise that he was the one to be wary of, not me—and yet she did not challenge him. Indeed, she gave me the medicine he prescribed.'

'I dare say he may have exerted a great deal of influence over her. She married him and felt herself trapped,' Max agreed. 'I knew she was hiding something from me, but I was not sure how much she knew of the attempts on my life.'

Robert looked angry. 'He had bragged to me of his plans as I lay drugged, but I knew nothing of his attempts against your life until he brought me here. You must believe me, cousin!'

'I have acquitted you of any involvement since I found you lying in a drugged state. Before that I admit that you seemed the most likely person to want me dead. Although I disliked and distrusted Clarke from the first—if, indeed, that is his name, which I doubt—I could not see what he hoped to gain from my death. Had I known he was your stepfather, I should have understood much sooner.'

'Mama kept it from me,' Robert said. 'It seems he killed my father—but she is not blameless, for she was his lover while my father lived. She must have told him about her wealthy nephew, for it was his idea that we should come here—and it was only after we moved into the dower house that he began his evil work.'

'I do not understand why your mama allowed him to drug you,' Helene said. 'I had met you but once and you did not seem mad to me.'

'Thank you,' Robert said and smiled. 'You must understand that I was always prone to chills and ill health. Clarke came to look after me and at first he was considerate, even kind, but after my father died and he realised there was no money he changed. I did not realise that he had married Mama. He began to give me drugs, which made me sick and ill. I had black holes in my memory. He told me that when I was ill I did bad things, and, because I could not remember, I believed him. After a while I accepted whatever he told me.'

Max nodded. 'I distrusted the man from the start. I shall contact the magistrate and tell him that his mystery has been cleared up. I think we can be sure that our Dr Clarke was the rogue who attacked the village women.'

'What village women?' Helene asked in disbelief. 'You did not tell me your suspicions!'

'I wasn't sure,' Max said, looking at her white face. 'I assure you, you were always watched. You have been for a while, even in London—not by my friends, but by others.'

'Excuse me…' Helene said, feeling distressed. 'I think I should go home before Mama realises I have gone out and starts to worry.'

She started walking very fast. Max's revelation about the village women had come as an unpleasant shock to her. She was prepared to face danger, but that he should know what kind of a rogue the physician was and not tell her had upset her.

'Helene!' Max's voice called to her. Angry and upset, she started to run. Max ran after her, catching her at last. He took hold of her arm and swung her round to face him. 'Forgive me. I was not sure of anything until my aunt told me that her son was dangerous when he had one of his fits. It was then that I began to understand what was going on—and I realised that it must be Clarke or whatever his name may be. I am not sure whether he was trying to blacken my cousin's character in order to establish the myth of Robert's madness—or drew pleasure from the attacks.'

'He would have abused me had Robert not managed to free himself. Your friends could do nothing—he had a knife to my throat and he would have taken me with him.' Helene suddenly burst into tears. Max took her into his arms holding her close. 'He was horrible…'

'Yes, my darling, he was,' Max said and stroked her hair as he held her close. 'Evil is the right word in his case, I believe. He treated Robert abominably and my aunt allowed him to do it, for like you I believe she must have known her son was not mad. However, I acquit her of complicity in the attempts on my life.' Max's arms tightened about Helene as she looked up at him. 'I had to catch him out. Believe me, neither of us was safe while he continued to stay in the shadows. Can you ever forgive me?'

Helene glanced up at him. Her heart slammed against her ribs, her breath catching in her throat. She inclined her head slightly and he lowered his head to kiss her. The kiss was long and sweet, making her feel as if she were melting into him, becoming a part of him, never to be parted. She knew that she wanted to be his completely, wanted to know him in every way, and whatever happened to them she would always be his. He was the man she loved and would love until she died.

'I have to forgive you,' she whispered, her lips parting on a sigh, 'because I should only be half-alive without you.'

'I love you more than my life,' Max said. 'You are all that I have ever wanted in my life. I knew our plan was a risk, and at first I resisted—but I trusted Gerard and Toby. If we had simply waited for that devil to make his move, he would have had the advantage. I was afraid that you would be his next target and the only way to keep you safe was to give him his opportunity. Besides, you are so brave that I was certain you would know just what to do—and you did.'

'Brave or reckless?'

'That, too,' he agreed, a faint smile on his lips.

'I wish you had told me,' Helene said. 'I almost didn't go with him. Supposing I had refused? Supposing I hadn't gone outside alone?'

'Then we should have had to think of something else,' Max told her. 'But Toby said he was sure that if Clarke approached you, you would take a risk—and, knowing how impetuous you can be, I thought he was right. I knew that you would be restless and I was sure the garden would tempt you outside on such a lovely day. It was a perfect opportunity and Clarke could not resist the bait.'

'You know me too well,' Helene said ruefully. 'I understood it must be a risk when I went with him, for he told me that I must speak to Robert if I wished to save your life. I suspected he was lying, for I saw him capture your cousin last night. How did he do that so easily? Robert is a strong man.'

'I believe he must have learned how to control a violent patient by placing his finger on a pressure point,' Max replied. 'These things are known to certain medical practitioners; the Chinese have long known the secret and I dare say others, too. Clarke, as he called himself, may well have studied medicine. He certainly had access to powerful drugs—some of them unknown in our culture, I imagine.'

'How evil he must have been!' Helene looked at him. 'Your aunt—she was not a party to the scheme to kill you, but she did allow him to mistreat Robert. What will happen to her?'

'I shall consult with Robert. I do not know if he can forgive her. I am convinced she knew her husband was lying about Robert's madness, yet she tried to convince me of it. Perhaps she was afraid of what her husband would do if she defied him. Robert must decide her fate himself.'

'And your cousin?'

'If Robert will let me, I shall set him up with a residence, either in the country or in town. My fortune is sufficient to give him a decent allowance. I believe he deserves a chance to prove himself, Helene. He has had a wretched life and I should like to see him happy.'

'Yes, he does deserve his chance,' Helene agreed and looked thoughtful. 'You are generous and forgiving, Max. I think that makes me love you even more.'

'Then you have truly forgiven me?'

'Yes,' Helene replied and reached up to kiss him softly on the mouth. 'Providing you do not tell Mama what has been happening here.'

Max laughed huskily. 'You are so brave, my darling—and yet you fear your mama's displeasure?'

'I do not fear it,' Helene told him. 'It is just that she would make such a fuss and probably want to cancel the wedding.'

'Then you may be sure that I shall make every effort to make certain that she does not discover what happened this morning.'

'You may think me a fool, Helene, but I am not,' Mrs Henderson said and frowned at her daughter. 'I know something has been going on these past few days. You have tried to keep it a secret from me, but I have seen the glances between you all. Why has Mrs Heronsdale gone off so suddenly—and why has Lord Coleridge's cousin come to live in this house?'

'Mrs Heronsdale has been called to the bedside of a sick relative.' Helene could not look at her mama as she told the lie. Robert had banished his mother to stay with friends abroad until he could bring himself to forgive her, which might not be for some time. She was to have a small pension while she remained there. Helene did not know exactly what had taken place when the two met in Max's presence, but she understood that Mrs Heronsdale was much chastened and had confessed that her husband had threatened her when she began to question him about the precise nature of her son's illness. At first she had loved him blindly, but at the last she had begun to fear him.

'I still do not see why Robert should come to live here.'

'It is only until after the wedding,' Helene replied. 'Robert is to have a house in Bath. Max has an interest in a wine-importing business, as I told you before, and Robert will be in charge of outlets both in Bath and in London. He has no need to work, for Max has made him a generous allowance, but he wishes to do something in return. It is just so that Max can have the house made ready for you, dearest.'

'Well, I must say I like Robert well enough, but I still do not know what is going on,' Mrs Henderson grumbled. She looked at her daughter awkwardly, then, 'I have had a letter of apology from Annesdale. He says that he will provide me with a residence in Bath and an allowance. I am not sure how to answer him…'

'Max wrote to him and invited him to the wedding,' Helene replied. 'I have decided to forgive and to accept him in my life. Perhaps you should do the same, Mama?'

'He has written me a very decent letter, apologising

for what happened years ago. It is not easy for me to forgive him, Helene. However, I quite see that it would be awkward to be on bad terms with him once you are married, for we may meet in company, therefore I must try to come to terms with him. Coleridge is having the dower house refurbished for me, and he has also made me an allowance—but I do not see why I should not take what is rightfully mine, for I can divide my time between Coleridge House and Bath. I am not sure what your father would have thought.'

'If Papa knew that his father had apologised, I believe he would tell you to accept, Mama,' Helene said. 'You may be easy in your mind on that score. I am sure he would say we should not continue to hold a grudge, but let the past go and enjoy the future.'

'Very well, since you are so well settled and happy, I dare say I may accept Annesdale's offer.' She smiled at her daughter. 'So it is your wedding day tomorrow, my love—and you are truly happy?'

'Happier than I ever expected,' Helene told her. 'I cannot wait to be Max's wife.'

'You look beautiful,' Amelia said and kissed Helene's cheek. 'I am so happy for you, my dearest. I know you will be loved and spoiled by your husband—and I am glad that you have mended fences with Annesdale.'

'Max showed me by example that it was best to be generous and to forgive others,' Helene told her. 'I could not do less, Amelia. I want Max to be proud of me.'

'I am certain he already is,' Amelia replied. 'You are a beautiful bride, my love, but you are also brave and wise. Max told me what happened here and it seems that you behaved very creditably. I am sure that you will make him an excellent wife.'

'I shall try,' Helene said. She glanced at the diamond-and-sapphire bracelet on her arm. 'You have spoiled me once more, Amelia. After all you had already done, this bracelet is almost too much.'

'I wanted you to have it. Aunt Agatha had it as a girl and I know she would have been happy to see you wearing it at your wedding.'

'Thank you so much,' Helene said and kissed her cheek. 'Annesdale sent me a magnificent sapphire-and-diamond necklace and tiara set. He has also settled ten thousand pounds on me—and the remainder of his fortune will go to our sons.' Helene blushed. 'I hope we shall have at least three sons and two daughters. I was an only child and I would like a large family.'

'Does Max feel the same?'

'Yes, he does. He had a brother once, but Tom died when he was seven. Max says that he would like a house filled with children. You haven't seen him with his orphan boys, of course—they adore him! We are going to set up another home in one of the houses he owns locally so that I may take an interest in the children. And we are to set up a campaign to make it unlawful to force boys up chimneys, besides other projects I have brought to Max's attention.'

'Well, it seems that you will share your interests and that must bode well for the future,' Amelia said and a little sigh escaped her. She turned as the door opened behind her. 'Here is your mama, which means that you must go down if you are ready, Helene.'

'Yes, I must not keep Max waiting,' Helene said and smiled. 'I am perfectly ready, Mama…'

* * *

Helene turned her head as the vicar pronounced them man and wife, her heart beating fast as Max lifted her wedding veil to kiss her softly on the mouth. She seemed to be walking in a dream of happiness as they signed the register in the vestry and then went out into the sunshine to be met by the sound of church bells and a little storm of rose petals.

Max's eyes were warm with love as he turned to her. 'You are so lovely, my darling,' he said in a husky voice. 'I cannot wait to have you to myself. I am tempted to sweep you up now and run off with you.'

Helene laughed, because she too was impatient for the moment when she became truly his, but she knew that he was teasing her. Max was a gentleman. He would never desert his guests or behave in a manner that would cause hurt or offence to others—and perhaps that was why she loved him so very much.

'Be patient, my love,' she whispered back. 'We have the rest of our lives.'

'I like the sound of that,' he replied. 'If you will not run away with me, I dare say we should go back to the house and entertain our guests.'

'Well, Lady Annesdale-Coleridge, I must congratulate you on your choice of a husband,' the Duke of Annesdale told Helene a little later that day. 'Coleridge is a fine man. He has told me about his home for orphan boys. I hear that you intend to open one for girls? Coleridge asked me if I would associate myself with the project. I shall be happy to do so, for I like children—perhaps there is yet time for me to see my great-grandchildren before I die?'

'I hope that we shall oblige you, sir,' Helene said, a faint blush in her cheeks. 'I think I ought to apologise for the way I spoke to you before.'

'No! I deserved it,' the duke told her and there was a twinkle in his eye. 'You were the first person to stand up to me since your father. I have been fawned over too much, Helene. I was proud and cold and I have been much at fault. It was time someone refused me. Your comments shocked and hurt me, but they also made me realise that my unhappiness was my own fault. I am grateful that you forgave me and allowed me hope for the future.'

'Max is so generous and forgiving,' Helene said and her mouth curved into a tender smile. 'As his wife I could do no less. I am pleased to have a grandfather and I sincerely hope that you will have many more years left to you.' She leaned up and kissed his cheek. He patted her arm awkwardly, clearly unused to such displays of affection.

'Your husband has come to claim you, girl. I dare say he wants to be off.'

Helene turned as Max came up to her. 'Is it time for me to change, Max?'

'Yes, I think so,' he told her. 'Your mama was looking for you a moment ago.'

Helene knew that her mama would not approach her while she was with Annesdale. They had acknowledged each other at the wedding, but it would be a long time before they truly forgave each other.

'I shall go up,' Helene said, gazing up into her husband's eyes.

'At last,' Max said and drew her closer, his eyes burning her with the heat of his passion. She felt desire pool low in her abdomen as she lifted her face for his kiss. 'Have I told you how much I love you?'

'Only six times since we got here.' Helene laughed.

They were in the bedroom of a house loaned to them by one of Max's many friends. Their intention was to stop here one night and a day and then travel on to the coast where they would take ship for France.

'Not nearly enough,' Max said hoarsely. He swept her up in his arms and carried her to the bed, depositing her gently amongst scented sheets. Max lifted her nightgown, pulling it over her head so that he could feast his eyes on her lovely body. 'You are so lovely. I want you so very much, my darling.'

Helene shivered with pleasure as he removed his robe and then gathered her close, the touch of his flesh searing her with the heat of desire. His kisses thrilled her, making her body arch with pleasure as he explored her with lips and tongue, his hands stroking the satin smoothness of her skin.

'I love you…' she whispered, feeling as if she were being carried away on a wave of love and need.

Helene responded to his seeking heat, as the hard urgency of his manhood penetrated her, giving one little cry of pain as he broke through her maidenhead. Then, as the pain was forgotten in surging joy, she clung to him, her body moving with his in the sweet dance of love. She whimpered and moaned as the pleasure mounted unbearably and then cascaded through her in wavelets of pleasure that made her writhe and call out his name.

'I adore you, my sweet Helene,' Max murmured against her ear. 'You are all that I want and more.'

'I was so fortunate that you came to my rescue that

day when we stopped that awful man beating poor Jezra,' Helene said and smiled as he looked down at her. 'If you had not seen me, we might never have met or fallen in love.'

'I think we were destined to meet,' Max told her as he kissed her softly once more. 'You are my soulmate, Helene. We were meant to be together for always.'

'Yes,' she said. 'I think we are.'

MILLS & BOON

Historical

On sale 2nd October 2009

Regency

THE WICKED BARON
by Sarah Mallory

Luke Ainslowe's reputation as an expert seducer precedes him,
and innocent Carlotta refuses to become the Baron's next
conquest – she has lost her heart to Luke before. However,
the Wicked Baron *never* takes no for an answer!

HIS RUNAWAY MAIDEN
by June Francis

Rosamund Appleby is disguised as a youth and fleeing to London
when she meets Baron Alex Nilsson. Intrigued and suspicious of
this "boy", Alex seeks to protect her. But now hastily married to
Rosamund, Alex wonders which is more dangerous: his persistent
enemies – or the seductive lure of the woman in his bed…

ROCKY MOUNTAIN WIDOW
by Jillian Hart

The end of Claire Hamilton's marriage left her alone amidst a
lizzard of murder accusations and the cold, bitter winter – until
Joshua Gable saves her life. Josh's strength and closeness
ignite the flames of passion, and Claire wonders if it's
possible to love again…

millsandboon.co.uk Community

Join Us!

The Community is the perfect place to meet and chat to kindred spirits who love books and reading as much as you do, but it's also the place to:

- ■ **Get the inside scoop from authors about their latest books**
- ■ **Learn how to write a romance book with advice from our editor**
- ■ **Help us to continue publishing the best in women's fiction**
- ■ **Share your thoughts on the books we publish**
- ■ **Befriend other users**

Forums: Interact with each other as well as authors, editors and a whole host of other users worldwide.

Blogs: Every registered community member has their own blog to tell the world what they're up to and what's on their mind.

Book Challenge: We're aiming to read 5,000 books and have joined forces with The Reading Agency in our inaugural Book Challenge.

Profile Page: Showcase yourself and keep a record of your recent community activity.

Social Networking: We've added buttons at the end of every post to share via digg, Facebook, Google, Yahoo, technorati and de.licio.us.

www.millsandboon.co.uk

2 FREE BOOKS
AND A SURPRISE GIFT

We would like to take this opportunity to thank you for reading this Mills & Boon® book by offering you the chance to take TWO more specially selected books from the Historical series absolutely FREE! We're also making this offer to introduce you to the benefits of the Mills & Boon® Book Club™—

- **FREE home delivery**
- **FREE gifts and competitions**
- **FREE monthly Newsletter**
- **Exclusive Mills & Boon Book Club offers**
- **Books available before they're in the shops**

Accepting these FREE books and gift places you under no obligation to buy, you may cancel at any time, even after receiving your free books. Simply complete your details below and return the entire page to the address below. You don't even need a stamp!

YES Please send me 2 free Historical books and a surprise gift. I understand that unless you hear from me, I will receive 4 superb new books every month for just £3.79 each, postage and packing free. I am under no obligation to purchase any books and may cancel my subscription at any time. The free books and gift will be mine to keep in any case.

Ms/Mrs/Miss/Mr_____ Initials _____

Surname _____
Address _____

_____

_____ Postcode _____

Send this whole page to: Mills & Boon Book Club, Free Book Offer, FREEPOST NAT 10298, Richmond, TW9 1BR